D1591226

Ohio
Moravian Music

Ohio
Moravian Music

Lawrence W. Hartzell

The Moravian Music Foundation Press
Winston-Salem, North Carolina
London and Toronto: Associated University Presses

Associated University Presses
440 Forsgate Drive
Cranbury, NJ 08512

Associated University Presses
25 Sicilian Avenue
London WC1A 2QH, England

Associated University Presses
P.O. Box 488, Port Credit
Mississauga, Ontario
Canada L5G 4M2

The paper used in this publication meets the requirements
of the American National Standard for Permanence of Paper
for Printed Library Materials Z39.48-1984.

Library of Congress Cataloging-in-Publication data

Hartzell, Lawrence W.
Ohio Moravian music.

Bibliography: p.
Includes index.
1. Moravians—Ohio—Music—History and criticism.
2. Church music—Moravian Church.   3. Church music—
Ohio.   4. Church musicians—Moravian Church.   5. Church
musicians—Ohio.   I. Title.
ML3172.H37   1988   783′.02′646771   87-71082
ISBN 0–941642–02–X (alk. paper)

Printed in the United States of America

CONTENTS

TABLES

PREFACE

It has been thirty years since the establishment of the Moravian Music Foundation. During this time the foundation has promoted a steady stream of valuable research projects, each of which has demonstrated the importance of the Moravian contribution to American music. Consequently the student of American music now has access to solidly documented information concerning the eighteenth- and early nineteenth-century lifestyle of the eastern Moravian communities and the importance of music in that lifestyle.

The current volume represents an extension of the above work. The first move west attempted by the Moravian Church was to the Tuscarawas Valley of Ohio. Here were established Indian missions and, after the Revolutionary War, white settlements. The questions addressed by the current study include, What types of music could one hear in the Ohio Indian Missions and later white settlements? To what extent did Ohio Moravian musical life reflect that of the eastern settlements? and, finally, In what ways has the musical life of Ohio Moravians been of significance in the local culture?

I have been greatly assisted by so many people that it is impossible to mention them all. However, a few must be identified because of their total commitment to the project and my personal well being. First must come Mr. Robert Mills. As a Development Officer at Baldwin-Wallace College it was he who made the initial foundation contacts and carefully shepherded the subsequent grant requests that led to the successful conclusion of this research project.

The Reeves Foundation of Dover, Ohio provided the financial support through the conferring of two grants, the second of which made the publication of this text possible. The Chairman of the Reeves Foundation, Mr. Walter Zimmerman, was particularly kind in his assistance and support of the project.

Dr. Richard Little, Professor of Mathematics at B-W, having been raised in Tuscarawas, Ohio was able to lend much assistance. Particularly helpful was his kind offering of his parents' home in Newcomerstown. This served as a base of operations for my many research trips to the County.

During the course of my research activity I had the pleasure of working with two Moravian Music Foundation Directors. Dr. James Boeringer and

Dr. Károly Köpe offered every kindness in addition to placing all of the resources of the foundation at my disposal.

The Archives of the Moravian Church are wonderful repositories of material dealing with the Moravian Church. The Reverend Vernon Nelson, Archivist at Bethlehem, Pennsylvania, Miss Mary Creech (now retired) and Dr. Thomas Haupert, Archivists at Winston-Salem, North Carolina have been quite supportive of my work. Since the majority of my efforts were spent at Bethlehem, Mr. Nelson must be thanked for his tireless assistance both during the research phase and as a reader of the final manuscript.

Thanks must be given to my other readers, the Reverend Dennis Rohn and his wife Kay, Dr. John Robinson, Dr. Albert Frank and the editors at Associated University Press, principally Ms. Beth Gianfagna and Ms. Sandra Cookson.

Three Ohio institutions need to be mentioned here because their collections proved useful to my work. The Cleveland Public Library has a fine general collection of Moravian materials in its history department. The holdings of the Ohio Historical Society are quite valuable to the student of Moravian Indian missions with the Mahr Collection being of considerable importance. The Youngstown State University Library is extremely valuable to researchers of Indian culture because it holds microfilms of *all* diaries of eighteenth- and early nineteenth-century Moravian Indian missions.

One cannot be involved in an extensive on site research project without the assistance of many individuals. Particularly helpful in the area of local Indian lore and history were Ross Virtue of Gnadenhutten and Harold Everett of Fry's Valley. Roy and Helen Demuth must also be mentioned. These dear people were a constant source of information and support. Their knowledge of the church and community at Gnadenhutten provided me with valuable insights into the facts I was discovering in the church archives. Mrs. Demuth's uncle, the Reverend Allen Zimmerman, though deceased, was of important assistance. Mr. Zimmerman had begun a project of translating the Gnadenhutten diaries, which until 1850 are in German. At his death three years were left untranslated. These translations significantly reduced the amount of time necessary to read the early diaries. Since they are quite accurate I have included them when direct quotation was necessary.

Several Moravians in Tuscarawas County have become close personal and family friends because of their loving concern and interest in myself and my family as well as the project. Of these I should like to mention Herb and Margaret Ricksecker Zollar. These wonderful people were most caring in their assistance and their support of my work. I consider it unfortunate that both were called home to their Lord before the completion of this book.

I must make a special comment concerning the assistance provided by the pastors and their families during my research work. Paul and Miriam Couch (then of Sharon), David and Kim Smith (Fry's Valley), Dean and Elizabeth

Jurgen (then of Dover South), Jerry and Janice Witbro and especially their successors Al and Judith Frank (Dover First), Bill and Penny Surber (Uhrichsville), and Terry and Lynn Folk (formerly of Schoenbrunn Community). Without their interest in my work many valuable facts would never have come my way.

Finally there are no words that can describe the care, concern, and affection showered on my family and me by Kay and Denny Rohn and their children, Ginnie, Karen, Beth, and Susie. From a pleasant dinner offered on the first day of my research efforts at Gnadenhutten developed a deep friendship that will last the rest of my life. To the Rohn family belongs the thanks of those readers who find the material of this book valuable.

To my family, Vickie, Bill, and Adam belongs the gratitude of everyone connected with this book. It was their willingness to accept no husband and father for many weekends that made it all possible. To them I wish to dedicate this book which would never have been begun, let alone completed, without their love.

Ohio
Moravian Music

PART ONE
Introduction

1

MUSIC, OHIO, AND THE MORAVIANS

For years the musical accomplishments of the Moravian Church in America were relatively unknown. Standard texts on American music either did not mention them at all, or mentioned them only in a cursory way. Within the past forty years, however, the situation has changed. As each scrap of new information is unearthed, respect for the musical contributions of this small, energetic denomination increases dramatically.

In his book *Protestant Church Music in America*, Robert Stevenson touches on the church's most important gift to the field of American music.

> . . . [their] compositions . . .
> entitle the Moravian school of sacred
> composers centered in Bethlehem in the
> latter part of the eighteenth century to
> first-class honors in any history of
> protestant music. [1]

Stevenson lists seven additional points which highlight the value of Moravian music. Among these are included: (1) a school of organ builders whose most significant member, David Tannenberg, is recognized as the finest builder of Baroque organs in America; (2) the use of orchestrally accompanied vocal and choral music as part of regular worship services; (3) transfer of the *Collegium Musicum* to America.

To the above points the author would like to add: (1) the establishment of America's oldest continuing instrumental ensemble, the Bethlehem trombone choir; (2) a strong, healthy wind band tradition; (3) the creation of significant archival collections of musical manuscripts some of which preserve the only extant copies of works by important European composers;[2] (4) establishment of America's first civic orchestra, that is, the Bethlehem Philharmonic; (5) maintaining a musical culture that was able to provide the earliest American performances of Johann Sebastian Bach's major choral works, ultimately leading to the creation of the Bethlehem Bach Festival.

Research into the Moravian contribution to American music has necessarily concentrated on the records and music collections of the major eastern

17

settlements. These include Bethlehem, Nazareth, and Lititz in Pennsylvania, and Bethabara, Bethania, and Salem in North Carolina. Now that a basic knowledge of the musical life of these communities has been established it is possible to study other Moravian centers such as Ohio's Tuscarawas County.

Situated in the east central portion of Ohio, Tuscarawas County is 105 miles west of Pittsburgh, Pennsylvania. During the late eighteenth century it was the center of Delaware Indian activity. Originally an eastern tribe, the Delaware had moved west to the Tuscarawas River Valley, and established their capitol at Gekelemukpechünk, that is, present day Newcomerstown.

The initial Moravian contact with Ohio occurred when the Reverend Christian Frederick Post entered the Tuscarawas Valley in 1761. Post, the first Protestant missionary to work in the valley, was given permission to build a cabin and teach the local Delaware Indians. The next year he received an assistant, John Heckewelder, and the two attempted to bring the Gospel to the Delawares. Their work did not succeed and they left. Shortly afterward, in 1763, Pontiac's rebellion broke out and nine years would pass before Moravian work resumed.

By the year 1770 David Zeisberger had become the Moravian's primary missionary among the Delaware. His knowledge of their life style, habits, and languages was excellent, but most importantly, he had earned their abiding respect.[3] While maintaining a mission in western Pennsylvania at Langundo Utenünk (Friedenstadt),[4] Zeisberger received a message from the Ohio Delawares inviting him to establish a mission in the Tuscarawas Valley. While considering this request Zeisberger visited Gekelemukpechünk and preached the first Protestant sermon in Ohio.[5] Soon afterward a major smallpox epidemic that had been ravaging the Delaware ceased. The Indians took this as a prophetic sign and eagerly sought Moravian settlement on their land.

The Moravians were particularly careful with the Ohio question, sensing that deliberation on the issue was going to affect their entire North American Indian program. The final decision was indeed momentous, for the move to Ohio would be coupled with the cessation of all eastern missions.

The plan was to populate Ohio's first mission with Christian Indians from the eastern missions. This required an arduous journey across the length of Pennsylvania. Zeisberger's Friedenstadt mission was a valuable link in this chain of events, for it provided both land and river access to the Tuscarawas Valley. Thus, it would serve as a resting place and supply post.

After Chief Netawatwes gave the Moravians the final go-ahead, David Zeisberger led an advance party to the Tuscarawas Valley and established Ohio's first Moravian mission. It was located on a spot close to the Tuscarawas River near present day New Philadelphia. Because a large, beautiful spring was nearby the mission was called Beautiful Spring, Welhik Thuppeek in Delaware, and Schönbrunn in German.[6]

Once Schönbrunn was laid out the western migration began. By 20 June 1772 over 200 Indians had arrived at Friedenstadt, having been led by Bishop John Ettwein and the Reverend John Roth.[7] The latter missionary was probably second only to Zeisberger in his expertise with Delaware dialects. Roth's connection with the Ohio work was considerable for he would serve at various missions.

A missionary conference was held at Friedenstadt in August. At this conference many decisions relative to Ohio operations were considered.[8] With the completion of this conference, the Indians began the move to their new home. Friedenstadt would be completely abandoned on 13 April 1773 when the final contingent of Indians left by river under the leadership of John Heckewelder.[9]

NOTES

1. Robert Stevenson, *Protestant Church Music in America* (New York: W. W. Norton, 1966), p. 38.

2. Donald M. McCorkle, "The Moravian Contribution to American Music," *Moravian Music Foundation Publication, no. 1* (Winston-Salem, N.C.: The Moravian Music Foundation, 1956), pp. 9–10.

3. While still serving in Pennsylvania, Zeisberger had been made an honorary member of the Monsey Tribe.

4. This mission was located on the Beaver River, on Route 88, south of Wampum and north of the Pennsylvania Turnpike; between Shenango River and Slippery Rock Creek.

5. A monument to this event has been placed on the city's west side.

6. There are various spellings of this Indian name. The one used here comes from John Heckewelder. See August C. Mahr, trans. ed., "A Canoe Journey from the Big Beaver to the Tuscarawas in 1773: A Travel Diary of John Heckewelder," *Ohio State Archaeological and Historical Quarterly* 61 (July 1952): 287. However, Heckewelder has also been known to spell the name "Weelhick Thuppek" in his *Narrative of the Mission of the United Brethren among the Delaware and Mohegan Indians* (Philadelphia: J. B. Lippincott, 1859), p. 118.

7. August C. Mahr, "Diary of a Moravian Indian Mission Migration across Pennsylvania in 1772," *Ohio State Archaeological and Historical Quarterly* 62 (July 1953): 247–70.

8. Those that concern our study will be discussed in the appropriate chapters.

9. Mahr, "A Canoe Journey," pp. 283–98.

2

OHIO MISSION STATIONS
AND CONGREGATIONS

On 3 May 1772 the Moravian missionary David Zeisberger arrived in Ohio with five Delaware Indian families numbering twenty-eight people. In his diary he noted, "Here we encamped and even on this day reared huts for ourselves and looked over the grounds again for the most suitable place for our town. . . ."[1]

The town was called Schönbrunn and it has the distinction of being the first Christian town in Ohio, as well as the first Ohio settlement to contain white inhabitants. Ohio's first church and schoolhouse were also located at Schönbrunn, which would serve the area for five months until a second mission, Gnadenhütten (Tents of Grace), was erected a few miles to the southwest.

Because Tuscarawas County was in the direct path of the American frontier and Indians loyal to the British, the missions were considered with suspicion by both sides. In an attempt to protect the Christian Indians the Delaware nation permitted a new mission, Lichtenau, to be built near their second capitol at Coshocton. Lichtenau was begun 12 April 1778 and Schönbrunn abandoned eight days later. For various reasons two other missions would be established in Tuscarawas County: New Schönbrunn (across the river from the original town) and Salem (near Port Washington).

The unstable conditions became so intense that on 11 September 1782 all mission personnel were forcibly removed from the Valley. The "prisoners" were taken to a spot on the Sandusky River about eleven miles south of Sandusky, Ohio.[2] Although it never received an official name, historians call the place "Captive's Town."[3] From here the missionaries continued on to Detroit in order to answer charges of treason before the British Commandant.[4]

The winter of 1783 was particularly harsh and since the captives had no provisions they requested permission to send a group to Salem and Gnadenhütten to gather crops. Permission was granted, but protection was not provided. While the crop parties were completing their work, the group at Gnadenhütten was arrested by Pennsylvania militiamen under Colonel David Williamson. In a kangaroo court Williamson's party falsely charged the Moravian Indians with murdering white settlers and put them to death in the infamous "Gnadenhütten Massacre."[5]

Cleared of the spying charges the Moravian missionaries were allowed to return to their Christian Indians at Captive's Town. Ohio was becoming unsafe, however, so they accepted British protection and established a mission called New Gnadenhütten on the Detroit River.[6]

An unsuccessful attempt was made to return to Tuscarawas County in 1785. During this time the Moravians camped at a location close to Valley View, Ohio, in Cuyahoga County. The mission, which lasted from 1786 to 1787, was called Pilgerruh (Pilgrim's Rest) since it was never intended as a permanent town.[7]

From Pilgerruh they moved west and established a mission on the Huron River near the site of Milan, Ohio. This mission, called New Salem, would prosper until 1793 when Wyandot Indian ill will toward the Moravians became so intense they decided to settle among the Chippewa Indians in Canada. The Canadian mission was called Fairfield and would be their home until conditions were favorable for a return to Tuscarawas County.[8]

As early as 1783 the Moravian organization, *The Society of the United Brethren for Propagating the Gospel among the Heathen,*[9] had requested of Congress a land grant in Tuscarawas County for the use of the Christian Indians. Although the grant was approved 1 March 1784 hostile Indians made the area unsafe, and it was not until the spring of 1797 that John Heckewelder, William Henry, and three assistants could begin surveying operations. Once this was completed the Indians at Fairfield were able to return.[10] A new mission was built on the west side of the river, about two miles south of Schönbrunn. It was named Goshen, and would last until 1823 when Ohio Indian work ceased forever.

The land grant was in the form of three tracts (one each for Schönbrunn, Gnadenhütten, and Salem) totalling 12,000 acres. This was too much land for the Indians. In order to ease the financial burden, the Moravians extended settlement invitations to members and friends of the church. The project was under the guardianship of the SPG which selected Gnadenhütten as its Ohio headquarters and John Heckewelder as its agent.

Settlement families began to arrive in May 1799. Most of these people had been living at the Pennsylvania settlement, Gnadenhütten on the Mahoning.[11] They would settle opposite Gnadenhütten on the west bank of the Tuscarawas River. The two communities were divided by language as well as by the river since the westside settlement, soon to be called Beersheba, contained English-speaking Moravians, while Gnadenhütten contained German-speaking Moravians.

As more German-speaking settlers began to arrive it became necessary to open the Schönbrunn tract. This land included an area on the west side of the river about five miles north of Beersheba and one mile south of the Goshen Indian Mission. Beginning in 1810, the Beersheba pastor instituted services in the area, and this activity led to the establishment of the Sharon Moravian congregation in 1815.

These three congregations, Gnadenhütten, Beersheba, and Sharon, represent the earliest Moravian congregations in Ohio. Of these three only two remain today, Gnadenhütten and Sharon. Because of Methodist encroachments Beersheba's congregation, begun in 1805, diminished in numbers until it was combined with the Gnadenhütten congregation in 1828.

Even with the above settlement, the land grants were an impossible drain on the Moravian Church's finances. Thus, the church sold much of the land back to the American Government, causing non-Moravian settlement to increase rapidly. At first this settlement centered in the towns of Dover, New Philadelphia, and Uhrichsville, but later it moved to the rural areas. With the completion of the Ohio Canal in 1830, Dover, Trenton (later Tuscarawas), and Port Washington became centers of trade.[12] The Moravian church considered these towns part of its activity and established preaching stations in them. From these came the congregations of Dover First (1842), Uhrichsville (1874), and Port Washington (1881).

Originally begun as a Reformed church by Swiss emigrants, Fry's Valley's rural location made it difficult to attract and maintain ministers. For some time it was served by the Moravian minister at Gnadenhütten. After construction of the present church building the congregation joined with the Moravians in 1857.

Begun in 1807 Dover's growth was quite slow until the construction of the Ohio Canal from 1826 to 1830. With this the town was opened to commercial trade and it increased in size rather steadily. By the time of Dover's incorporation as a village in 1840 several Moravian families had settled there. While these families attended services at Sharon transportation often proved problematic. Consequently, as early as 1836, they began holding meetings in Dover homes.

The meetings were served by the Moravian ministers at Gnadenhütten until the pastorate of Sylvester Wolle (1841–49). He found that serving three pastorates more than fifteen miles apart was too difficult. Thus, he was provided with an assistant, the Reverend Louis Kampmann, who arrived in December 1842. Within days of Kampmann's arrival the Dover Moravians petitioned to be a separate congregation. The petition was granted and Kampmann found himself the pastor of a new congregation.

As the Reeves steel industry began to grow many people of Welsh descent moved to Dover as steel workers. In 1888 these "south side" people organized a Welsh congregational church and erected a small building that is still used today. By 1922 this congregation found it difficult to support a full-time pastor. As a result Joseph Weinland, pastor at Dover First, offered to conduct Sunday School sessions. These were continued until 11 April 1925 when the property was transferred to the Moravian Church. Thus, Dover South became a home mission congregation partially supported by Dover First. This arrangement lasted until 1958, when Dover South was yoked to Schoenbrunn Community Moravian Church.

As the twentieth century progressed two other churches found it necessary to employ combined pastorates. Port Washington and Fry's Valley were yoked together in the 1930s with Reuben Gross becoming the first man to serve under the new arrangement.

When the town of New Philadelphia was first laid out in 1804 the Moravian Society received a grant of four lots. Since no congregation developed the lots were eventually sold. In the early twentieth century C. A. Weber, pastor at Dover First, began to hold Moravian services in the town hall. Even though these were successful, they were suddenly stopped, and the county seat saw no further Moravian work until the 1940s.

When a congregation was finally established in 1947 it held services in Trinity Episcopal Church for several years. Under the guidance of its first pastor, Bishop W. Vivian Moses, a strong congregation was created. This group consecrated its own church building one mile east of the old Schönbrunn Indian village in 1955. Taking this into account, the church was named Schoenbrunn Community Moravian Church.

The above missions and churches have provided the material for this book. From the pages of their church records the author has gleaned the existence of a typically strong Moravian musical culture. This book details the establishment and growth of that culture. While some of its facts have been known for years, much that it contains will be new.

NOTES

1. Schönbrunn Diary, 3 May 1772, Moravian Archives, Bethlehem, Pa., Box 141.
2. This mission was located south of Bucyrus, Ohio at Routes 4 and 23.
3. Edmund de Schweinitz, *The Life and Times of David Zeisberger* (Philadelphia: J. B. Lippincott, 1870; reprint, N. Y.: Arno Press, 1971), p. 517.
4. The trip to Detroit, the sessions before the commandant and his acquittal are well documented in John Heckewelder, *A Narrative of the Mission of the United Brethren among the Delaware and Mohegan Indians* (Philadelphia, Pa.,: 1820), pp. 287–95.
5. Ibid., pp. 310–26.
6. The mission was located on the south side of the Clinton River at Moxon Drive.
7. The mission was located on the east side of the Cuyahoga River near Route 631.
8. The Fairfield experience can be gleaned from the translation of Zeisberger's Diary as found in Paul E. Mueller, trans., "David Zeisberger's Official Diary, Fairfield, 1791–1795," *Transactions of the Moravian Historical Society* 19 (1963): 5ff.
9. From this point on *The Society for the Propagation of the Gospel among the Heathen* will be identified with its accepted abbreviation, i.e., SPG.
10. Leslie Gray, ed., *From Fairfield to Schönbrunn 1798* (London, Ont., Canada: By the Author, 20 Renwick Ave., n.d.), [p. 3].

11. The Moravians used the name Gnadenhütten to designate no less than five towns. Three of these will be discussed in this book. Gnadenhütten on the Mahoney will refer to the first town to bear the name. It was located in Pennsylvania on the Mahoney River near present day Leighton. After the Indians left Pennsylvania it was reinstituted as a white settlement. The Ohio Gnadenhütten will be referred to by the single name. New Gnadenhütten will be used to indicate a Moravian mission established near Detroit, Mich. after the Moravians left Ohio.

Ohio actually had two towns with this name. The first was the Indian mission, while the second was a while settlement begun in 1791 just to the north of the mission. Throughout this text these two settlements will be differentiated by the use of the German umlaut. Thus, the Indian mission will be identified as Gnadenhütten, while the white settlement will be identified as Gnadenhutten.

12. Occasionally one encounters the name Canal Dover. This was the community's official name during the period of canal activity. After the canal ceased to be used the original name (Dover) was reintroduced. In order to avoid confusion this community will always be referred to as Dover, Ohio.

PART TWO

Music in the Ohio
Indian Missions
(1772–1823)

3

THE USE OF HYMNS IN MISSION LIFE

To the Moravian, hymns are the cornerstone of Christian wisdom. In them one can find words of understanding, confession, pardon, comfort, solace, guidance, hope, faith, love, inspiration, joy, and praise. From them one can gain the spiritual strength necessary to achieve insights into the great Christian truths. Through them unbelievers can approach an understanding of God, and thus achieve salvation.

Such a view of hymns naturally leads to a desire to employ them as often as possible in church services, and to expect the congregation to learn a wide variety of hymn texts. Consequently, Moravian litanies and liturgies include many hymns artfully woven into their rituals, where they represent congregational responses to statements of faith made by the liturgist.

As might be expected Moravian missionaries carried their church's love of hymns into the field with them. Because of this hymn singing became a vital ingredient in all Moravian Indian missions. Hymn texts were translated into native languages and taught in singing schools. Originally Indians of all ages attended these schools, however, by the time Ohio's missions were established most adults knew the hymn literature. Consequently, Ohio's Moravian singing schools were intended for children. The first of these of which we have records was held at Schönbrunn 2 September 1774.[1] Since the children were taught the rudiments of singing as well as memorization of hymn texts and melodies, this school represents the first instance of western European music instruction conducted in Ohio.

Worship at the missions included daily morning and evening meetings in addition to the usual Sunday services and festivals. Evening meetings were usually a uniquely Moravian service called a *Singstunde*, or singing hour.[2]

The *Singstunde*, which grew out of the Moravian's love of hymn singing, did not have a set order of worship. Normally the leader selected a theme, concept, or principle that would be exposed to the congregation through the singing of hymn verses. This was accomplished by the careful selection of hymn texts to underline the chosen topic. Since no one hymn could fulfill the job by itself verses were chosen from a variety of hymns.

Singstunden were ordinarily conducted extemporaneously. The leader began the first line of each hymn, to be joined by musicians and congregation as soon as they recognized the tune and text. A certain amount of tension grew in the congregation as it tried to identify the hymns as quickly as possible. This tension created a vivid awareness of the text. Through this awareness the *Singstunde* topic was revealed. Within the Indian missions such tension created heightened emotional situations which often spilled over into private *Singstunden* held in the cabins of individual Indians after the evening service. The diaries of the missionaries indicate that they were particularly pleased when, in the evening hours, they could hear parents singing hymns to, or with, their children before they retired for the night.

Obviously such hymn singing could be very meaningful. Two excellent examples, causing opposite emotions, can be cited from mission diaries. The first comes from Benjamin Mortimer's travel diary.[3] After many years in Canadian exile the missionaries and Indians could not contain their joy at returning to their beloved Tuscarawas Valley:

> We went up the [Cuyahoga] river several miles today. In the evening meeting Br. Zeisberger congratulated the brethren and sisters on their safe arrival thus far; after which in a cheerful singing-meeting, they made the woods to resound with hymns of thanks and praises.[4]

It was common practice for missionaries to kneel by the bedside of a sick or dying member and sing hymns of comfort. Over the years David Zeisberger had employed this custom many times. Therefore, it was a source of great consolation to him when the Indians at Goshen reciprocated. During the missionary's final days they met in his cabin and sang hymns from the hymnal he had edited for their use. The diary entry for 17 November 1808 reveals this scene on the day of his death.

> Zeisberger lay calm, without pain and perfectly conscious. The converts sang hymns, treating of Jesus, the Prince of Life, of death swallowed up in victory, and of Jerusalem, the Church above. He occasionally responded by signs expressive of his joy and peace. Amid such strains, at half past three o'clock in the afternoon, he breathed his last, without a struggle and went to God. All present immediately fell on their knees.[5]

There is little direct evidence concerning how the singing of hymns was conducted in the Indian missions. What evidence does exist suggests two different performance practices. The first and probably most common of these was unaccompanied, unison singing. In the second, singing was accompanied by some musical instrument.

The latter practice originated from the fact that certain Moravian missions owned spinets, or had individuals who played melody instruments such as violins, clarinets or flutes. Spinets were small keyboard instruments on which the string was plucked, like the harpsichord, rather than struck, like the piano. The first such instrument to be used in Ohio was located at Gnadenhütten, and was the only spinet ever employed in Ohio's Moravian missions.[6]

Occasionally, the question of part-singing in the mission is raised. Since the Moravians have had a long history of part-singing it would seem logical that this practice took root in the missions. Although there is no direct evidence to support such a belief, some indirect evidence can be found.

Singing schools conducted among the white congregations definitely included instruction in part-singing, and one of the primary methods used was the part-singing of hymns.[7] Therefore, it would seem that such instruction could have been used in the missions. Perhaps it was used in one or more of the Pennsylvania missions, but its use in Ohio's missions is highly unlikely.

Several reasons can be put forward for the above belief. First, most of the good singers mentioned in Pennsylvania mission diaries had died by the time of Ohio's missions. Secondly, while the main purpose of the white congregation's singing schools was choir preparation, the main concern in the missions was using hymns to teach Christian beliefs. In the former, four-part singing was necessary while, in the latter, it was an unessential artistic nicety that would consume entirely too much valuable time.

Finally, the teachers of white congregation singing schools were usually well-trained, musically gifted ministers. Most of the Ohio missionaries, however, had a rudimentary knowledge of the art. Thus, the missionaries lacked the skills necessary to teach part-singing. Johann Jakob Schmick was the only Ohio missionary competent enough to teach part-singing, and even at his Gnadenhütten mission there is no evidence of such singing.

Now that the importance of hymn singing and its methods of performance in the Indian missions have been discussed, our attention turns to the hymns themselves.

NOTES

1. Schönbrunn Diary, 2 September 1774, Moravian Archives, Bethlehem, Pa., Box 141.

2. Another translation, popular among Ohio pastors of the nineteenth century, is "singing meeting."

3. Mortimer was Zeisberger's assistant and he kept the official diary encompassing the removal from Fairfield, Canada to Goshen, Ohio.

4. Goshen Diary, 11 September 1798, Moravian Archives, Bethlehem, Pa., Box 171. Trans. in Gray, *From Fairfield to Schönbrunn*, [p. 25].

5. Goshen Diary, 17 November 1808, Moravian Archives, Bethlehem, Pa., Box 173. Trans. in William N. Schwarze, "Characteristics and Achievements of David Zeisberger," *Ohio Archaeological and Historical Publications* 18 (1909): 195.

6. This spinet will be discussed in chap. 5.

7. ". . . the singing school was continued in the parsonage, in which we have already attempted in the last month to have our musical young people become accustomed to sing our chorales in four parts." Diary of the Congregations of Sharon and Gnadenhutten, 6 Jan. 1840, Allen P. Zimmerman, trans., John Heckewelder Memorial Moravian Church, Gnadenhutten, Ohio.

4

SOURCES OF MISSION HYMNS

The Moravians believed strongly that all hymn texts employed in missions should be translated into the native language. While various languages were used at first, *Lenape*, the language of the Delaware Indians, was eventually preferred because the majority of Christian Indians were Delawares.

The hymns sung in the missions were primarily drawn from contemporary Moravian sources that can be divided into two groups: those German and British hymnals published before 1763, and those published after 1772. The first date refers to the work of Bernhard Adam Grube, the second to the efforts of David Zeisberger.

From 1760 to 1763, Bernhard Adam Grube served as missionary at Wechquetank, Pennsylvania. While there he edited the Moravian's first hymnal in an American Indian language, *Dellawärishes Gesang-Büchlein*.[1] Printed in 1763, this hymnal is a valuable source for the study of Moravian Indian hymnody. It is one-sided, however, for it only contains hymns that were "favorites" of the Indians. Consequently, one cannot assume that the hymns printed in Grube's *Gesang-Büchlein* were the only ones sung at the missions. Even so, it is an important tool in identifying some of the earliest hymns sung in Ohio.

Grube undoubtedly used three important Moravian hymnals as sources for his text, *Das Gesang-Buch der Gemeine in Herrnhut*, *Das Londoner Gesangbuch*, and the *English-Hymn Book* of 1754. The Herrnhut text was the first hymnal of the Renewed Moravian Church. Primarily the work of Count Nicholas von Zinsendorf, it was published in 1735 and, together with its many supplements, provided congregations with over 2,300 hymn texts.[2]

Although printed in London, *Das Londoner Gesangbuch* contained a German text. It was more of a compendium than a hymnal, being the first chronological collection of German hymns to appear in print. Between its two volumes (1753, 1754) it contained 3,264 different hymn texts.[3]

The *English Hymn-Book* of 1754 represents the first authorized collection of English-language Moravian hymns. It was primarily the work of John Gambold and contained 1055 hymn texts.[4]

The Grube text served the missions for many years, yet by 1772 its hymn texts were found to need revision. With the transfer of its mission work to

Ohio, the Church believed the time had come to require a complete revision of Indian hymns and liturgies. Thus, on 17 August 1772, the missionary conference held at Friedenstadt, Pennsylvania, assigned the revision effort to David Zeisberger. He was to be assisted by the missionary John Roth and a committee of Indians.[5]

Zeisberger's work covered thirty-one years, from 1772 to 1803. During this time three significant Moravian hymnals appeared in print and, by his own statement, Zeisberger employed two of these in his work. The three hymnals were the *Gesangbuch* of 1778, the *English Hymn-Book* of 1789, and the latter's 1801 revision.

The Gesangbuch zum Gebrauch der Evangelischen Brüdergemeinen, published at Barby in 1778, was the work of Christian Gregor.[6] It was universal in scope and contained in its 1750 hymn texts most of the finest Christian hymns. It became the official hymnal for continental, German-speaking Moravians throughout the nineteenth century.

The 1789 English hymnal was edited by John Swertner and, like Gregor's book in Germany, became the normal English hymnal.[7] Its full title was *A Collection of Hymns for the use of the Protestant Church of the United Brethren,* and it contained 887 hymn texts. It was revised and enlarged to include 1,000 hymn texts in 1801.[8] This revision was used by the English-speaking Moravian congregation at Beersheba, Ohio. Since David Zeisberger often conducted services at Beersheba, it was the 1801 revision that he employed, together with the Gregor text, in creating his own *Delaware Hymnal.*

All of the hymnals mentioned above contain texts only. The chorales to which these hymns were sung were originally maintained in two manuscript collections. The first of these was apparently compiled for the 1735 *Gesang-Buch,*[9] while a manuscript collection organized by Johann Daniel Grimm contains chorales that correspond to *Das Londoner Gesangbuch.*[10] After completing his *Gesangbuch* of 1778, Christian Gregor was assigned the task of preparing a chorale book to accompany it, and this resulted in his *Choral-Buch* of 1784.[11]

Zeisberger's text revisions proceeded in logical steps. These steps represent a process rather than a chronological organization. Therefore, all four steps to be discussed could, and occasionally did, occur simultaneously.

First, a group of hymns and scriptural passages would be submitted for revision. The committee wasted no time as the Friedenstadt diary tells us that John Roth began revising hymn and scripture passages the evening the assignment was made.[12]

The second step required that all newly translated hymns be tested to check their acceptability. This required the establishment of singing schools where the newly translated material could be taught to the children. If problems occurred at this point hymn texts were withdrawn and revised further.

The third step involved the presentation of new translations to the entire congregation. This was usually accomplished by having the children, or a missionary, introduce the hymns during a service, normally a *Singstunde*. If all went well and no objections were voiced, the importance of memorizing the newly-translated hymns was impressed upon the congregation. Zeisberger's prefatory remarks in his hymnal indicate that the Indians enjoyed learning the new hymns. "All our converts find much pleasure in learning verses with their tunes by heart, and frequently sing and meditate on them at home and abroad."[13]

The fourth, and final, step was the revision of all litany and liturgy translations. To this can be added services that had not yet been translated. It might be interesting for the reader to observe the entire process in operation. Thus, a brief outline of the translation work will be given in the following paragraphs.

No worship service is more sacred to Moravians than their Easter Dawn Service. Zeisberger began work on this litany in early 1774 and completed it in time for Easter Day. The praying of the Easter Morning Litany 2 April 1774, in Schönbrunn's God's Acre, represents a milestone in the revision effort. It was apparently the first time the entire service was completely conducted in the Delaware language.[14]

The Fairfield diary frequently states that Zeisberger was working on hymn translations, although we are given little information on what hymns these were. Apparently some were Christmas hymns. These seem to have been completed by late 1786 as they were sung for the first time in Christmas Eve services held at Pilgerruh that year.[15]

Zeisberger appears to have been totally absorbed in text revision at New Salem. On 11 January 1789 he introduced many of the hymns that deal with the Holy Ghost. The diary tells us he even took the unprecedented step of carefully writing out his translations for the Indians. Although some of the Indians could not write, they all could read both printed and manuscript texts.[16]

Completion of a new translation of the Good Friday Liturgy also occurred in 1789,[17] while most of the hymns dealing with the Passion and Death of Jesus were completed one year later.[18] The year 1790 also saw the complete Pentecost Liturgy conducted in *Lenape* for the first time.[19]

We do not know that a hymnal was planned when the revision project began. At some point in his work, however, Zeisberger came to realize the need for such a text. ". . . it has been for many years my ardent wish, to furnish, for the use of the Christian Indians, a regular and suitable hymn book, . . ."[20]

The final editing of the *Delaware Hymnal* was completed by Zeisberger and the Mohican Indian, Joshua, Jr. Their collaboration probably took place at Goshen, and was virtually completed by late 1800. In November of that year the missionaries Br. and Sr. John Peter Kluge and Abraham Luckenbach arrived at Goshen. These people were to begin a Delaware mission at White River, Indiana, and they had stopped at Goshen for training. During their stay, Luckenbach studied the hymnal manuscript and copied as much material from it as time permitted.[21]

When the White River missionaries left, Joshua, Jr. and his son went with them.[22] This required that Zeisberger complete the remaining text revision himself. All work was concluded in August 1802, and the final draft was sent to Pennsylvania 20 September 1802.[23]

The Hymnal was published through the assistance of Bishop George Henry Loskiel.[24] Bishop Loskiel brought copies of the newly printed Hymnal with him when he came to Ohio to lead a missionary conference at Goshen from 10 to 21 October 1803. The conference included the Goshen missionaries, their wives, John Heckewelder, the Fairfield missionary, and several other interested parties. Zeisberger had the great pleasure of distributing his Hymnal to the Indians and participating in its initial employment at a conference *Singstunde* held 9 October 1803.[25]

The Hymnal was a major accomplishment. Within two years it was employed at all Moravian mission stations in the Northern Province. Diaries of these missions indicate that singing was greatly improved through its use. These entries also give heartfelt thanks to David Zeisberger for his tireless efforts.

NOTES

1. John W. Jordan, "Biographical sketch of Rev. Bernhard Adam Grube," *The Pennsylvania Magazine of History and Biography* 25 (1901): 14–19.

2. Henry L. Williams, "The Development of the Moravian Hymnal," *Transactions of the Moravian Historical Society* 18 (1961): 243.

3. Ibid.

4. Ibid., pp. 251–54.

5. Langundo Utenünk, Minutes of Mission Conference, August 1772, Moravian Archives, Bethlehem, Pa., Box 137. See text, chapter 1, p. 5.

6. John Johansen, *"Moravian Hymnody," Moravian Music Foundation Publications, No. 9* (Winston-Salem, N.C.: The Moravian Music Foundation, 1980), pp. 16–18.

7. Williams "Development of the Moravian Hymnal," pp. 255–56.

8. Williams, "Development of the Moravian Hymnal,: p. 256.

9. Walter Blankenberg, "Die Musik der Brüdergemeine in Europa," in *Unitas Fratrum*, ed. Van Bruijtenen et al., (Utrecht: Rijksarclief, 1975), p. 368.

10. Ibid.

11. Christian Gregor, *Choral-Buch* (Leipzig, 1784); reprint, James Boeringer, ed. (Winston-Salem, N.C.: The Moravian Music Foundation Press, 1984).

12. Langundo Utenünk Diary, 17 August 1772, Moravian Archives, Bethlehem, Pa., Box 137.

13. David Zeisberger, *A Collection of Hymns, for the Use of the Christian Indians, of the Missions of the United Brethren, in North America,* (Philadelphia, Pa., Henry Sweitzer, 1803).

14. Edmund de Schweinitz, *The Life and Times of David Zeisberger,* (Philadelphia, Pa., J. B. Lippincott, 1870), pp. 394–98.

15. Pilgerruh Diary, 24 December 1786, Moravian Archives, Bethlehem, Pa., Box 153.

16. Petquottink Diary, 11 January 1789, Moravian Archives, Bethlehem, Pa., Box 155.

17. Ibid., 10 April 1789.

18. Ibid., 2 April 1790.

19. Ibid., 23 May 1790.

20. Zeisberger, *A Collection of Hymns*, v.

21. H. E. Stocker, trans., "The Biography of Brother Abraham Luckenbach," *Transactions of the Moravian Historical Society* 10 (1917): 372.

22. White River Diary, 24 March 1801, Moravian Archives, Bethlehem, Pa., Box 177.

23. Goshen Diary, 30 September 1802, Moravian Archives, Bethlehem, Pa., Box 171.

24. George Loskiel, *History of the Mission of the United Brethren among the Indians in North America*, I. C. LaTrobe [sic], trans. (London: The Brethren's Society for the Furtherance of the Gospel, 1794).

25. Goshen Diary, 9 October 1803, Moravian Archives, Bethlehem, Pa., Box 171.

5
MUSIC AT THE GNADENHÜTTEN MISSION

Ohio's second mission was begun at the request of the influential Mohican Elder, Joshua, Sr. His petition, which resulted from intertribal rivalries between Delaware and Mohican Christians,[1] was submitted to the Friedenstadt missionary conference.[2] Over the years the missionaries had tried to subdue these problems, but they were unsuccessful. Thus, with some reluctance, the conference agreed to Joshua's request.

Gnadenhütten was begun in October 1772 and was maintained without a permanent missionary until early in 1773, when John Roth and his wife were stationed there. The Roths were under temporary assignment, however, and returned to other work when the permanent missionaries, Johann Jakob and Johanna Schmick, arrived in August 1773.

Johann Jakob Schmick was the most musically gifted of all the Ohio missionaries being proficient on the spinet, zither (cithara), guitar, and violin, as well as possessing a fine voice.[3] He and his wife had served the Mohicans as missionaries at Gnadenhütten on the Mahoning, and Friedenshütten in Pennsylvania. Consequently, virtually all of the Indians living at Gnadenhütten, Ohio had received their initial instruction in religion, German, and music from the Schmicks.

Among those who arrived with the Schmick party was the Indian Joshua, Jr., son of Joshua, Sr. Schmick had taught Joshua, Jr. to play the spinet when he was a young boy and, next to the missionary, he was probably the most proficiently trained performer of European music in Ohio.[4] Joshua, Jr. performed as chapel musician, playing on the spinet for mission services. That a spinet could be found at Gnadenhütten is confirmed by two sources.

The first source is the Gnadenhütten Diary. During the summer of 1775 Joshua, Sr., was found to be dying. Word was sent to neighboring villages and many close friends, both Christian and non-Christian Indians, came to pay their last respects. On one such occasion a Shawnee chief from Meemkekak was entertained by Joshua, Jr. The diary states that Joshua played the spinet for the chief on 3 July 1775.[5] This represents the first documented keyboard performance in Ohio.

The second observation comes from the travel diary of James Woods, a deputy of the Virginia House of Burgesses. Woods attended Sunday services on 6 August 1775 and observed that the chapel had ". . . a very indifferent spinet on which an Indian [Joshua, Jr.] played."[6] This is the earliest record of service playing in the state.

How this spinet came to be in Ohio is unknown. One possibility, however, can be deduced from mission diaries. Joshua had built a spinet, with Schmick's assistance, at Friedenshütten, Pennsylvania in 1767.[7] He performed on that spinet as chapel musician for many years until the mission was disbanded in preparation for the move to Ohio. Since there is no evidence of a spinet being at Gnadenhütten prior to Joshua, Jr.'s arrival in 1773, it would appear that the Friedenshütten spinet was brought overland to Gnadenhütten when the Schmicks moved to Ohio.

Although neither of the above diary entries tell us what music Joshua, Jr., played, we can make some accurate assumptions. After his initial keyboard lessons with Schmick, he moved to Bethlehem where he received his education. While there he seems to have received the same training given Bethlehem organists. These musicians were expected to commit to memory a group of four hundred hymn tunes and be able to perform them in any key.[8] Additionally, they had to perform keyboard reductions of concerted anthems and sacred songs.[9] Joshua, Jr., would have been able to do these things, yet mission requirements were not that stringent. For instance, a mission service would require little beyond hymn accompaniment and, possibly, simple improvisation.

Moravian organists performed secular music also. Early in his career Joshua, Jr., could do the same, although the need for such music hardly existed at Gnadenhütten. Most likely any secular music he might have played in Ohio would consist of simple keyboard pieces played from memory.

The final musical observation is of particular interest to the Moravian Church. The Moravian liturgy for Advent I and Palm Sunday contains a choral setting called the "Hosanna Anthem." This music was composed by Christian Gregor in 1765 and has become a significant part of the liturgy. Although the piece is performed in many ways today, it was originally intended to be performed antiphonally by the congregation and children.[10]

The very first evidence of this music being performed in Ohio comes from the Gnadenhütten diary of 27 November 1774. Under that date Schmick states that the children sang "Hosanna."[11] There is no indication that the antiphonal performance was used, however, the congregation's participation can probably be taken for granted.

As the Revolutionary War drew closer, tensions became so extreme that many precautions were taken. One of these was the abandonment of Schönbrunn for Lichtenau, while another was the recall of Schmick and his wife from missionary service. After their departure the mission at

Gnadenhütten ceased to be a musical center. Never again would an Ohio mission enjoy the beauty of musical sound that existed at Gnadenhütten.

NOTES

1. Within the Moravian Indian literature one finds three spellings of this name, i.e., Mohican, Mahican, and Mohegan.

2. Lagundo Utenünk Diary, Minutes of the Missionary Conference, 12 August 1772, points 5 and 6, Moravian Archives, Bethlehem, Pa., Box 137.

3. Lawrence Hartzell, "Musical Moravian Missionaries: Part III: Johann Jacob Schmick," *Moravian Music Journal* 30 (Fall 1985): 36.

4. This is the same Joshua, Jr., who assisted Zeisberger in the preparation of the latter's *Delaware Hymnal*.

5. Gnadenhütten Diary, 3 July 1775, Moravian Archives, Bethlehem, Pa., Box 144.

6. R. G. Thwaites and L. P. Kellog, *The Revolution on the Upper Ohio, 1775–1777*, (1908; reprint, Port Washington, N.Y.: Kennikat Press, 1970), p. 64.

7. Friedenshütten Diary, 24 December 1767, Moravian Archives, Bethlehem, Pa., Box 131.

8. Rufus A. Grider, "Historical Notes on Music in Bethlehem, Pa.," *Moravian Music Foundation Publications, No. 4* (Winston-Salem, N.C.: The Moravian Music Foundation, 1957), p. 10.

9. Ibid.

10. Charles B. Adams, *Our Moravian Hymn Heritage*, (Bethlehem, Pa.: Department of Publications, Moravian Church in America, 1984), p. 61.

11. Gnadenhütten Diary, 27 November 1774, Moravian Archives, Bethlehem, Pa., Box 144.

PART THREE

Music in the Early
Congregations
(1799–1842)

6

IMPORTANT MUSICIANS

The white incursion into Tuscarawas County began with the arrival of the first settlement families in May 1799. It was inevitable that among these new arrivals would be musicians of more than passing talent. This chapter will introduce those individuals among the new settlers who are mentioned in church records as being the most important musicians. They are, therefore, the earliest Moravian musicians to work in Ohio after the SPG acquired the land grants.

DAVID PETER

From church records it appears that the first Moravian musician to settle in Ohio was David Peter. He and his wife came to Gnadenhutten in October 1799 to manage the Society store. Peter was a step-brother of Simon and John Frederick Peter.[1] Both of these men were fine composers, although John Frederick is generally considered to be the most gifted of all the American Moravian composers.[2]

David Peter was born 20 July 1766 in Nazareth, Pennsylvania. He received the typical Moravian education, probably at Nazareth Hall, where he later served as a teacher (1790–92). The first musical information we can connect with him comes from 25 November 1787.[3] On that day Peter, Georg Gottfried Müller, and Henry Müller provided instrumental music at the memorial service of the Lutheran patriarch, Henry Melchoir Muhlenberg. This service was held at St. John's Lutheran Church, Easton, Pennsylvania, and the Moravians participated at the invitation of Pastor Frederick Ernst. It is not known what instrument Peter played at the memorial service, but it is likely to have been the organ.[4] We know that he also played the guitar[5] and sang in a bass voice.[6]

Peter's first wife, Dorcas Chitty, died in 1806 leaving him with two daughters, Maria and Dorcas Elizabeth. One year later he traveled to Bethlehem, enrolled the girls in the Female Seminary and married Susanna

Leinbach. This marriage brought together two very musical families, the Leinbachs being particularly significant in the musical life of Salem, North Carolina.

Peter became very active in county government, serving as Tuscarawas County's first treasurer, in addition to many other such positions.[7] Often he served as liturgist for lovefeasts and frequently conducted *Singstunden* when the pastors were unable to do so.

At his death 22 November 1840 he left eight children.[8] Through these the Peter name and musical legacy would continue down to the present time.

HEINRICH KELLER

Unfortunately, we know very little about Heinrich Keller. Born in Arisdorf of Canton Basel, Switzerland, he arrived in America in 1802 with his brother Martin. They stayed at Lititz, Pennsylvania for a short time before moving to Ohio in 1803.

Keller was a charter member of the Sharon congregation and served it faithfully throughout his life. Although the church records do not mention him often in connection with music, one non-Moravian source refers to him as "a renowned bass singer."[9]

ABRAHAM LUCKENBACH

Abraham Luckenbach became the missionary at Goshen in November 1812. Born in Lehigh County, Pennsylvania in 1777, he had served in the missionary field for some time before the Ohio call. He was a good clarinetist, violinist, and vocalist, probably receiving training on the two instruments from David Moritz Michael, and definitely receiving training in singing from J. F. Frueauff when the three men were stationed at Nazareth.[10]

Luckenbach was one of the three missionaries who organized the ill-fated Delaware mission station at White River, Indiana during the early 1800s. After the mission was abandoned in 1806 he became Benjamin Mortimer's assistant at Goshen. Remaining in Ohio until 1809, Luckenbach was called to the mission station at Fairfield, Canada, where he served until reassigned to Goshen from 1812 until 1820.

While serving at White River, Luckenbach established the practice of accompanying hymn singing on either the clarinet or violin.[11] Apparently, he did not own a violin when he first served in Ohio, for Pastor Müller made a gift of his violin to Luckenbach 1 January 1814.[12] Immediately after receiving the instrument Luckenbach employed it for hymn accompaniment at Goshen.[13]

Generally speaking, the strongest music program to exist at an Ohio mission other than Gnadenhütten was at Goshen during Luckenbach's tenure. Because of its close proximity to Sharon, and because the missionary also held services at Sharon, many of the Sharon musicians were frequent visitors at Goshen. Undoubtedly, the Indians often heard these musicians performing music in Luckenbach's cabin.

Luckenbach's reputation as a teacher was quite good, thus children of Sharon members occasionally attended the mission school. Their presence was an aid to the Indian children in singing hymns, as was Luckenbach's reward system. On at least one occasion he is known to have given a copy of Zeisberger's *Delaware Hymnal* to a student for good scholastic achievement.[14]

Because of ill-health, Luckenbach was forced to retire from missionary work in 1843. He returned to Bethlehem where he prepared a new edition of Zeisberger's *Delaware Hymnal* before his death 8 March 1854.

JACOB BLICKENSDERFER

Blickensderfer was born at Lititz 26 December 1790. He arrived in Ohio in 1812 with a large contingent of Blickensderfer family members.[15] Settling first near Tuscarawas, Ohio he later moved to New Philadelphia and then to Dover.[16] In 1841 he built a new residence about four miles east of New Philadelphia called Benigna.

Being civic-minded he served as county commissioner, county auditor, and associate judge. Because of the latter position he is usually referred to as Judge Blickensderfer in county records. Being highly respected, he was elected to the state legislature for three separate terms and, while serving there, was influential in bringing the Ohio Canal through Dover.

As a musician Blickensderfer performed on the spinet and organ, and probably sang. It is highly likely that he served as organist at Sharon after its members purchased an instrument in 1828. He was the first organist of the Dover Moravian Church when that congregation was organized in 1842.[17]

His first wife, Regina Kreiter, died in 1831. Two years later he married Maria Peter, the eldest daughter of David Peter and Dorcas Chitty. Like her father and husband, she was a good musician. Having been trained at the Female Seminary in Bethlehem she was undoubtedly proficient on the spinet and a good vocalist. She died in 1840 after a serious illness.

ABRAHAM RICKSECKER

The first member of this family to reside in Ohio was born in Lititz 22 July 1788. He became associated with the Blickensderfer family when he married Maria Elizabeth Blickensderfer in Pennsylvania 24 February 1811. He and his new bride were among the large contingent of Blickensderfers who settled in Ohio during the summer of 1812.

Abraham was a surveyor by trade and laid out the present town of Tuscarawas. He also assisted in several other surveying projects in the county.

Ricksecker was a grandson of the Peter Ricksecker who brought the family name to America from Canton Berne, Switzerland. The family was very musical and Abraham appears to have followed in that tradition. He has the distinction of owning the first piano to be used in Tuscarawas County. The instrument was brought from Pennsylvania as part of his household goods, and was often employed in church musical performances.[18]

JOHNATHAN WINSCH

The first member of the Winsch family to reside in Gnadenhutten was Jacob Winsch, who arrived in 1805. He was a carpenter and cabinetmaker, and performed much of the work required to build the Beersheba church.

Although no evidence of musical interest has been found for Jacob, his son, Johnathan, was a good musician. Born at Graceham, Maryland 30 December 1804 Johnathan was a vocalist, singing in the Gnadenhutten choir for many years.

From the following diary entry it would appear that Winsch was a very active supporter of the church choir. "Our young musical brethren and sisters gave their first musical concert . . . in Bro. Johnathan Winsch's house."[19]

Johnathan married Caroline Juliana Peter, a daughter of David Peter and Susanna Leinbach 13 May 1832. Caroline was a good musician and sang in the choir with her husband. She also taught in the Sunday School program for nearly forty years. On 6 September 1835 a son was born to the Winschs. He was named Ludwig [Lewis] Simon, and his name will be mentioned often on future pages of this text.

NOTES

1. David E. Lewis, "Descendents of John Frederick Peter I," Moravian Music Foundation MS, Winston-Salem, N.C., n.d.

2. Albert G. Rau and Hans T. David, comps., *A Catalogue of Music by American Moravians, 1742–1842* (Bethlehem, Pa., 1938; reprint, New York: AMS Press, 1970), p. 18.

3. *Two Centuries of Nazareth, 1740–1940* (Nazareth, Pa.: Nazareth Pennsylvania Bi-Centennial, 1940), p. 67.

4. Grider, *Music in Bethlehem, Pa.*, p. 38.

5. One of the Ohio traditions concerning David Peter is that the guitar in the church archives belonged to Peter, and that he played the instrument.

6. Grider, *Music in Bethlehem, Pa.*, p. 38.

7. *The History of Tuscarawas County, Ohio* (Chicago: Warner, Beers and Co., 1884).

8. Unless otherwise indicated all vital statistics for Ohio persons are taken from local Church Books, Church Catalogs and/or Birth and Death Registers.

9. *Tuscarawas County, Ohio*, p. 674.

10. Stocker, "Abraham Luckenbach," p. 367.

11. White River Diary, Moravian Archives, Bethlehem, Pa., Box 177. The violin is first mentioned 7 September 1801, while the clarinet first appears 31 December 1802.

12. Goshen Diary, 29 January 1814, Moravian Archives, Bethlehem, Pa., Box 173.

13. Ibid.

14. Goshen Diary, 24 May 1818, Moravian Archives, Bethlehem, Pa., Box 175.

15. Diary of Gnadenhutten on the Muskingum, John Heckewelder Memorial Church, Gnadenhutten, Ohio. (Counting men, women, and children, this family group consisted of about 40 people).

16. Together with Christian Deardorff, Blickensderfer was one of the founders of Dover, Ohio. See Regina Lenz, "A History of the Moravian Church of Dover, Ohio [Dover First]," Dover, Ohio, MS, n.d.

17. Interview with Regina Lenz and Florence Gray, Dover, Ohio, 14 February 1983.

18. Deborah Rinderknecht, Ricksecker Family Genealogy, handwritten manuscript in the possession of the Margaret Ricksecker Zollar family, Dover, Ohio.

19. Allen P. Zimmerman, trans., Diaries of the Congregations of Sharon and Gnadenhutten, 20 May 1839, John Heckewelder Memorial Church, Gnadenhutten, Ohio.

7

THE MÜLLER ERA

Georg Gottfried Müller came to Ohio as pastor to the Beersheba congregation. A son of Bishop Burchard Müller, he was born at Gross Hennersdorf near Herrnhut, Saxony 22 May 1762. Being educated for the ministry, he graduated from Barby Seminary in 1782 and was sent to America in 1784. He was assigned to Nazareth Hall where he taught writing, arithmetic, and drawing in addition to music.

Müller was an excellent musician who sang in a bass voice, played the organ,[1] violin,[2] and double bass.[3] His singing skill was valuable, since his was the only bass voice at the Hall. Thus, when vocal part-music was performed, Müller would sing the bass and play the organ with the boys gathered around him singing the other parts.[4]

At present little is known concerning the origins of the Nazareth *Collegium Musicum*. It is assumed that the organization began during the 1780s and that it grew out of the musical activities at Nazareth Hall.[5] If so, it is highly likely that Müller was a major force behind the organization, if not its leader. Another reason for suspecting Müller of *Collegium* involvement is that when he was transferred to Lititz in 1788 he became the leader of that community's *Collegium Musicum* and raised it to a high performance level.[6]

Müller's Ohio responsibilities included the Beersheba and Gnadenhutten pastorates. Although he was called to Beersheba, the two congregations were yoked during his pastorate (1805–14). Additionally, Müller served as schoolmaster for the Moravian children.

Müller's contract with the SPG called for nine years of service. This was completed in the spring of 1814 and he left Ohio to serve First Moravian Church in Philadelphia, Pennsylvania.

After Philadelphia Müller served at Newport, Rhode Island, from 1817 to 1819. During this pastorate his health deteriorated to the point where he had to leave the active ministry. Thus, he and his wife retired to Lititz, where he became superintendent of the Married People. He died of consumption 19 March 1821 leaving behind a long and active career as pastor, musician, and composer.

Although Müller's diaries regularly inform us concerning liturgies and hymn-singing, they provide little real musical information. There is enough evidence, however, to indicate that his pastorate encompassed two distinct musical periods.

Between the period 1805 to June 1812 we are freely informed about which liturgies and hymns were employed at Sunday services, lovefeasts, and *Singstunden*. Although no details are given concerning performance practices, it is unlikely that monophonic singing was used with a musician of Müller's caliber as leader. What is likely is that singing was accompanied by Müller, and/or David Peter, on the violin or guitar. Since no other instruments were known to have been in Tuscarawas County at this time, except for Luckenbach's clarinet (1806–9, 1812–20), it is unlikely that other possibilities were available.

Regardless of what the musical situation in Tuscarawas County was during the early years of Müller's pastorate, its quality increased dramatically in the early summer of 1812. On 23 May 1812 several wagons carrying a large number of people connected with the Blickensderfer family arrived. These people had come from Lititz and included the Müller's daughter, Charlotte, the Jacob Blickensderfer family, the Abraham Ricksecker family and several other Blickensderfers.[7]

The arrival of this family group did much for the musical life of Ohio's Moravians, and the change appears to have been immediate. On 5 July 1812 a lovefeast was held at Gnadenhutten to celebrate the arrival of the new families. "In order to obtain more room, a wagon cover was spread before the church and seats were erected under it but there was still not room enough. The lovefeast was celebrated with suitable song and two musical selections: . . ."[8]

The last phrase, "two musical selections" is extremely important. Prior to this entry Müller describes musical performances as "singing," and the context of his comments always suggests nothing more involved than hymn singing. "Musical selections," however, certainly implies something more. There is every reason to believe that "musical selection" as used here, and in subsequent lovefeast entries, means solo song or anthem with instrumental accompaniment.

Since there were certainly enough vocalists to form a choir of eight people, and various instrumentalists, it is possible that Müller was now able to introduce the more extended forms of Moravian choral music. In any event, it was during the last two years of his pastorate that the Ohio Moravians laid the foundation for a "typical" Moravian musical culture.

NOTES

1. Grider, *Music in Bethlehem, Pa.*, p. 38.
2. "The Moravian Contribution to Pennsylvania Music," in *Church Music and Musical Life in*

Pennsylvania in the Eighteenth Century (Philadelphia, 1926–47; reprint, New York: AMS Press, 1972), 2:196.

3. Richard D. Claypool, "Johann Friedrich Frueauff," *Moravian Music Journal* 26 (Winter 1981): 79.

4. Ibid.

5. Barbara Strauss, "The Concert Life of the Collegium Musicum, Nazareth, 1796–1845," *Moravian Music Foundation Bulletin* 21 (Spring–Summer 1976): 3.

6. See n. 2.

7. See chap. 6, n. 5.

8. Allen P. Zimmerman, trans., Diary of Gnadenhutten on the Muskingum, 5 July 1812, John Heckewelder Memorial Moravian Church, Gnadenhutten, Ohio.

8

A PARADE OF FIRSTS

A "typical" Moravian musical culture requires certain specific, well-defined ingredients. The primary and most significant of these ingredients is hymn singing. Following closely in importance would be more extended vocal and choral music. Normally such music was in the form of concerted solo songs and anthems. These, in turn, created a need for church orchestras.[1]

To the above must be added a wind ensemble. During the eighteenth- and early nineteenth-century the usual Moravian wind ensemble was the trombone choir, although a wind band is now employed by many congregations.

Prior to, and for the majority of the Müller Era, hymn singing seems to have been the only ingredient available to Ohio's Moravians. As mentioned in the previous chapter, however, it is likely that some form of concerted music was introduced in July 1812. From this date a definite sequence of events can be observed which led to a strong, dynamic culture. The current chapter will contain only the most important of these events, namely, those that are unmistakably illustrative of the Ohioans' conscious attempts to create, in their own environment, a musical life similar to that enjoyed by Moravian communities in the East.

The first choral ensemble mentioned in church records performed at the dedication of the Sharon Church 24 December 1817.

> All the brethren and sisters of this section, together with a number from Gnadenhutten and Beersheba proceeded to assemble in the schoolhouse on Br. John Ulrich's land, and, after singing the verse "All we sinners are," and "Blot out our sins,"
> . . . .
> then went out of the schoolhouse, and went, in procession, toward the new church (1 mile to the South). After the people gathered there and placed themselves in rows both hall doors opened, and as the chorus began to sing: "Come, Holy Spirit Lord God," we entered the Church . . .[2]

Several services occurred that day and each included musical selections accompanied by a piano. Aside from the assumption that this was Abraham Ricksecker's piano, and that the musical selections were probably proper for church dedications and Christmas, little can be gleaned from existing records.

It is highly unlikely that this ensemble performed on a regular basis. Sharon's membership was too small to support a church choir and, in addition, Sharon records do not mention a choir again until 1840. Evidence points to this group being a *union* choir consisting of members from several churches organized specifically for these services.[3] Even so, it is the first documented Ohio Moravian choir, and very probably the first choir in Tuscarawas County.

When Gnadenhutten was reestablished in 1798 the congregation worshiped at the home of John Heckewelder. Later, in 1801, a parsonage was built and it was used as the meeting house. The first church building, a log cabin 20 feet square, was constructed on West Main Street in 1803. As the congregation grew a second building was constructed directly in front of the original church. Since the older church was to serve as a school building, a covered walkway connected the two buildings.[4] The dedication of the new church took place 13 August 1820.

> The congregation assembled first in the old church; after singing the verses "Countless proofs do we possess;" . . . and "Outwardly and inwardly he helped us," . . . Brother Rauschenberger [the pastor] . . . [read] . . . the proceedings of the solemn dedication of this building on July 10, 1803 . . . Then we went with the sound of trombones and the singing of the verse, "God bless our going out," . . . two by two through the courtyard, and formed a circle on the street, facing the new church. During the singing of, "Come Lord God, Holy" by the choir, the new church auditorium was solemnly entered;[5]

In addition to the hymns mentioned above the choir sang two anthems during the dedication service, *Sey Lob Ehr dem höchsten Gut* and *Preis und Dank und Ehre bringen*. At the afternoon lovefeast the choir also sang *Thee I'll Extol My God and King* and *Praise the Lord with Hymns of Joy*. Since the dedication was held on an important Moravian memorial day (the August Thirteenth Festival),[6] celebration of the festival was held the next day (14 August). At that service the choir sang yet another anthem. *Der Herr ist unser König der hilft uns*.

The diary was kept in German at this time, therefore, the diarist's use of English for some musical titles implies that these were sung in English. The German titles were very popular anthems by composers well known to American Moravians.[7] They are, therefore, the earliest examples of Moravian anthems sung in Ohio for which we have titles.

These anthems were originally written for orchestra and chorus, although keyboard reductions were available. Given the musicians living in Tuscarawas County in 1820, a small orchestra was possible. Perhaps for such a special day an orchestra was employed. If not, we must assume that Abraham Ricksecker's piano was pressed into service once again.

The lovefeast held on 14 August 1820 presents us with an important first of a non-musical nature. It was customary for lovefeasts to follow an order of worship. This order was called an ode, or psalm, and was usually published for the congregation's convenience. The diary states, "The festival lovefeast was held at two o'clock, in which a printed psalm was sung, which was the first one to be printed in this village."[8] Like the choir that sang for the Sharon dedication, the Gnadenhutten choir seems to have been a union choir organized specifically for the 1820 services.

The first church choir among Ohio's Moravians was located at Gnadenhutten. It was begun as a singing school under the directorship of Pastor Herman Julius Tietze on 19 November 1837. Their first public appearance was at Christmas Eve lovefeast of that year, where they sang three anthems. Apparently, the ensemble caused quite a sensation. "The report of our church music was widespread and being something never heard before, it had the effect of attracting the curious."[9]

This quote is valuable because it tells us much about the musical life of Tuscarawas County at the time. If the choir created such a stir one must assume that no other church choir existed in the county. Thus, Gnadenhutten's choir must have been the county's first church choir.

Before leaving the subject of Moravian choral music it is necessary to turn our attention to Cincinnati. Resting as it does at an important location on the Ohio River, Cincinnati quickly became Ohio's most important musical center. A singing school was in operation in 1800, and several were held over the next few years.[10] The Harmonical Society gave Cincinnati's first public concert in 1810[11] and, by 1813, music was being published in the town.[12]

In 1819 a dozen men formed the Haydn Society.[13] One of their stated goals was to aid the enjoyment of church music and on 25 May 1819 their orchestra, together with a union choir, performed a concert containing religious works by Clarke, Haydn, Holden, Arnold, Handel, and Gregor. The latter composer was Europe's most important Moravian composer, Christian Gregor. Gregor's "Hosanna Chorus" was performed that evening and it received a fine review. "[The piece . . . produced quite an exhilirating [sic] effect, and was well calculated to send the audience home satisfied with the divertisement [sic] and themselves."[14]

A search of names does not indicate any Moravians in the Haydn Society at the time of the concert. Several of the members, however, were Swedenborgians who had lived in New Jersey. It seems very probable that the Swedenborgian members had come in contact with Moravian music while living in the east and carried copies of Gregor's piece to Cincinnati. In any case this performance is the first presentation of Moravian music outside of Tuscarawas County.

The Moravians established their first church orchestra in 1838. Under the date 5 August 1838 the Sharon diary states, "For the first time in the preaching service some of the Sharon brethren accompanied the singing with clarinets, violins, and violoncello. The last of which had been bought for the church music by means of a subscription."[15]

Unfortunately, we never hear of the orchestra again. Although we have no way of identifying the orchestra members, the cello provides us with some interesting speculation. The Gnadenhutten instrument collection has a cello which created some interest in 1961 when Dr. Thor Johnson suggested that it might have been built by the Pennsylvania Moravian, John Antes.[16] Antes built the first violin to be made in America at Bethlehem in 1759.[17] Between this date and 1764, when he moved to Herrnhut, Germany, he made several other instruments, including a cello, which has disappeared. Unfortunately, someone has made an attempt at reconditioning the Gnadenhutten instrument, rendering it impossible to establish an accurate identification. The cello, however, certainly shares many characteristics with known Antes instruments.

Pastor Rauschenberg's diary entry for Gnadenhutten's 1820 church dedication contains the statement that "trombones" were used. Within the Moravian church that word usually means a trombone choir consisting of, at least, a soprano, alto, tenor, and bass.[18]

Research into the origins and development of the Gnadenhutten ensemble was reported in a recent article.[19] That research suggested 13 August 1820 as the earliest appearance of a trombone choir in Ohio. Since the writing of that article extensive research has been conducted in the diaries of Moravian Indian missions and, surprisingly, these records reveal an earlier date.

By 1818 the minister at Gnadenhutten was responsible for three congregations, namely, Gnadenhutten, Beersheba, and Sharon. It was impossible for one pastor to provide full care to three churches. Therefore, the missionaries at Goshen assisted by conducting preaching services at Sharon once a month and, when weather was bad, or the river too high to cross, any special services. Inclement weather was expected on New Year's Eve, 1818. Thus, Abraham Luckenbach was to conduct the Watchnight service at Sharon. The Goshen diary, however, relates that favorable weather conditions prevailed and, not only did Pastor Rauschenberg attend, he brought "the trombonists" with him.[20]

The obvious question is why does Rauschenberg never mention the trombones in the Gnadenhutten diaries? The answer, of course, is we do not know. We can only be thankful that the Goshen diary informs us of its existence at the earlier date.

Within the Moravian Church the trombone choir provides specific ecclesiastical functions. The most important of these are (1) announcing the New Year at Watchnight services; (2) playing for Easter services; (3) accompanying outdoor hymn-singing; (4) performing for special holidays and occasions; and (5) performing the traditional Moravian death announcement.

At Watchnight services the trombone choir announces the New Year by playing the German chorale *Nun Danket alle Gott* at midnight. Unless future research indicates otherwise, 1818 is the earliest appearance of a trombone choir at a Watchnight service held in Ohio.

By far the single, most important function of the trombone choir is connected with Easter. Following ancient practice the trombone choir assembles at the church between one and three A.M. It then moves through the town playing Easter chorales. Following this the congregation assembles at the church for the Easter Morning Litany. Usually starting at 5 A.M., this service begins in the church but, weather permitting, is completed in the cemetery. The trombonists lead the procession from the church to the cemetery, where they accompany the hymn singing.

Surprisingly, the earliest record of trombones being used at Easter is 15 April 1838, when they played at Gnadenhutten and Sharon.[21] The tone of the entry implies that the ensemble had performed for earlier Easters, yet 1838 is the first date that can be documented.

The death announcement is a uniquely Moravian function provided by the trombone choir. Although not widespread today, the announcement of a death within the community was usually made from the church steps or steeple. Three chorales were played. The first and last were settings of the well-known Passion Chorale, while the middle tune was related to the deceased's station in life.[22] At the funeral, the trombone choir accompanied hymn singing performed at the cemetery.

Extant Ohio church diaries never mention the trombone choir playing a death announcement. Many people living today, however, remember announcements being played during their childhood.[23] The earliest evidence of the trombone choir being used for a funeral comes from 2 October 1820 when it played for the funeral of Brother Barnabas Rhoads, who was buried in the Beersheba cemetery.[24]

The establishment of a trombone choir is one more indication of the musical growth of the Ohio Moravians, illustrating that they were intent upon developing a complete Moravian musical culture. That the group was a Gnadenhutten ensemble and not one consisting of members from other congregations is assumed because of the language used in the diaries. Over the next few years all references to the group indicate Gnadenhutten as its base of operations.

NOTES

1. Not all churches established orchestras. In such a case, a keyboard instrument was used to play a reduction of the orchestral parts.

2. Allen P. Zimmerman, trans., Diary of Gnadenhutten, Beersheba and Sharon, 24 December 1817, John Heckewelder Memorial Moravian Church, Gnadenhutten, Ohio.

3. The difference between a union choir and a church choir is one of purpose and membership. A union choir, as the term is employed in Ohio diaries, is organized for a specific event and draws its membership from several churches. A church choir, on the other hand, performs on a regular basis for the worship service of a particular congregation and draws the majority of its members from that congregation.

4. Ross M. Virtue, *A History of Gnadenhutten, 1772–1976* (Gnadenhutten, Ohio: By the Author, 1976), p. 10.

5. Allen P. Zimmerman, trans., Diary of Gnadenhutten, Beersheba and Sharon, 13 August 1820, John Heckewelder Memorial Moravian Church, Gnadenhutten, Ohio.

6. Ibid., 14 August 1820.

7. See chapter 13 for a discussion of these works and their composers.

8. See n. 6.

9. Allen P. Zimmerman, trans., Diaries of the congregations of Sharon and Gnadenhutten, 19 November 1837, John Heckewelder Memorial Moravian Church, Gnadenhutten, Ohio.

10. Leonie C. Frank, *Musical Life in Early Cincinnati and the Origin of the May Festival* (Cincinnati, Ohio: Privately printed, 1932), p. 4.

11. Harry R. Stevens, "Adventures in Refinement: Early Concert Life in Cincinnati; 1810–1826," *Bulletin of the Historical and Philosophical Society of Ohio* 5 (September 1947): 8.

12. Charles Hamm, "Patent Notes in Cincinnati," *Bulletin of the Historical and Philosophical Society of Ohio* 16 (October 1958): 299.

13. Harry R. Stevens, "The Haydn Society of Cincinnati, 1819–1824," *Ohio State Archaeological and Historical Quarterly* 52 (1943): 104.

14. Ibid., p. 105.

15. See n. 9, 5 August 1838.

16. K. Marie Stolba, "Evidence for Quartets by John Antes, American-Born Moravian Composer," *Journal of the American Musicological Society* 33 (Fall 1980): 566–67.

17. Ibid., p. 566.

18. The word actually used in the diary is *Posaunen*, which is German for "Trombones." Although the term *Posaunenchor* (trombone choir) was used as early as 1768, the two terms seem to have been interchangeable, with *Posaunen* being the more commonly employed. See, Harry H. Hall, "The Moravian Trombone Choir: A Conspectus of its Early History and the Traditional Death Announcement," *Moravian Music Journal* 26 (Spring 1981): 5–8.

19. Lawrence W. Hartzell, "Trombones in Ohio," *Moravian Music Journal* 28 (Winter 1983): 72–73.

20. Goshen Diary, 31 December 1818, Moravian Archives, Bethlehem, Pa., Box 175.

21. See n. 9, 15 April 1838.

22. Grider, *Music in Bethlehem, Pa.*, pp. 16–17.

23. Interview with Roy and Helen Demuth, Gnadenhutten, Ohio, 3 February 1983.

24. See n. 5, 2 October 1820.

9

THE TIETZE ERA

Herman Julius Tietze was born in Gnadenfrei, Silesia, and was proficient in six languages when he came to the United States. From 1832 to 1837 he taught at Nazareth Hall. While serving at Nazareth, Tietze made the acquaintance of several young Bethlehem musicians. Among these were flutist Israel Ricksecker and soprano soloists Lizette Bleck and Susan Stotz. The latter young lady soon became Tietze's wife.

Susanna Elisabeth Stotz was the daughter of the Reverend Samuel and Susanna Fetter Stotz. She was born in Salem, North Carolina 5 April 1807 where her father was the overseer of the Salem congregation. Susan attended Salem Academy from 1812 to 1820 and, with her younger sister, moved to Bethlehem in 1821. At Bethlehem she served as a resident teacher on the music staff of the Female Seminary from 1824 to 1832.

While at the Seminary she made the acquaintance of Lizette Bleck. Together they were soloists in the Bethlehem Philharmonic's 1832 performance of Andreas Romberg's *Song of the Bell*, and the 1837 performance of Karl Loewe's *The Seven Sleepers*. Her abilities were such that Bethlehem historian, Rufus Grider, refers to her as "a famous singer of solos."[1]

After their marriage the Tietzes moved to Ohio where he began his pastoral career at Gnadenhutten, serving from 1837 to 1841. From Ohio the Tietzes moved to Hope, Indiana. Later they returned to Bethlehem, where Pastor Tietze served as principal of the Female Seminary.

Eventually the Tietzes moved to West Salem, Illinois, where he became the local high school teacher. Most West Salem Moravians came from North Carolina. However, in 1849 a large number of German Moravian emigrants arrived. A split developed over language and Tietze became pastor of the German-speaking congregation, serving for twelve years.[2]

At his death in 1886, he left a large collection of music containing items belonging both to himself and his wife. The bulk of this collection was deposited in the Moravian Archives at Bethlehem by Tietze's granddaughters.[3] Its importance to Ohio music research will be emphasized in a later section.

Next to Georg Gottfried Müller, Herman Julius Tietze was probably the most musical of the early Ohio Moravian pastors. Thus, it should come as no surprise that the final steps necessary for establishing a typical Moravian musical culture in Ohio were taken during his pastorate.

Within five months of his arrival he had instituted a singing school at Gnadenhutten. His purpose was to train the young people in the art of singing, the ability to read music, to sing the church chorales in four-part harmony, and to provide anthems on the festivals of the church year.[4]

This ensemble has the distinction of being the first Ohio Moravian church choir and is the group discussed in the previous chapter.[5] The choir was not large, consisting of four sisters and four brothers, but it was enthusiastic.

After successfully establishing a choir at Gnadenhutten, Tietze turned his attention to Sharon. Although his efforts were well rewarded, he faced a problem of an overly enthusiastic group as his diary of 3 December 1840 informs us. "In the evening Sr. Tietze is of great assistance to me in the singing school in the kitchen, where on account of the great addition of school children no good order can be kept. I hope the learning of notes will frighten most of them away."[6] He got his wish, for the diary entry of the next week indicates fewer children attended the session![7] The remaining vocalists were molded into Ohio's second Moravian church choir.

Although Tietze's efforts to build a music program were highly successful, and for that reason he is deserving of much praise, we must recognize that he was very fortunate in that his pastorate coincided with the influx of many fine musicians to Ohio. Particularly important was the arrival, in 1838, of Israel Ricksecker and his new bride, the former Lizette Bleck. Israel had established Tuscarawas County's first jewelry store a year earlier. When he and his wife moved to Dover, the city of Bethlehem suffered two important losses. "One of the most noted sopran's [sic] that the town had ever produced . . . [was taken away by] the [Bethlehem Philharmonic] Society's best flutist, . . ."[8]

The first musical comment concerning the Rickseckers comes from the Gnadenhutten diary of 3 November 1839. At the harvest home service some music was performed by the Rickseckers, Jacob Blickensderfer, and Andrew Vognitz from Newcomerstown.

The latter individual was a tailor from Bethlehem who apparently came to Ohio sometime after the birth of his son Israel in 1835.[9] Vognitz is listed in Bethlehem records as a bugler in Bethlehem's Columbian Band[10] and a violinist.[11] He and Israel Ricksecker were members of a Serenade Club that existed around 1835.[12] From the above information we can hypothesize that the pieces performed at the harvest home service were Moravian solo songs for soprano, flute, violin, and keyboard.

The Tietzes, Rickseckers, and Blickensderfers formed a musical, as well as social, group. While they performed music for their own pleasure, and for their church, their musical talent was occasionally enjoyed by others. On 15

June 1840 the three couples visited the German separatists at Zoar, Ohio. While there they gave a concert in the Zoarites meeting house. Later that night they performed a similar function for a friend of the Rickseckers, Mr. Slingluff.[13]

With the death of Maria Peter Blickensderfer in August 1840, Jacob needed to care for the education of their children. He turned to the Tietzes. "Bro. Jac. Blickensderfer of Dover visits us and brings his daughter Hannah to her Aunt Sally Blickensderfer in Gnadenhutten, but wishes that she might enjoy instruction from my wife in music and from me in other sciences."[14]

When Tietze left his Ohio pastorate in October 1841 he could be proud of the work he had accomplished, especially in the area of music. The roots he and his wife had laid would continue to bear fruit in the congregations. Most important of all, however, was his work in the Dover area. Having begun preaching services in Dover, he created a sense of unity among the Moravians living in and around the town that would ultimately lead to the creation of Ohio's fourth Moravian congregation.

NOTES

1. Grider, *Music in Bethlehem, Pa.*, p. 40
2. *Lebenslauf* of Herman Julius Tietze, Moravian Archives, Bethlehem, Pa., p. 6.
3. Robert Steelman, cataloger, *Tietze Music Collection*, Moravian Archives, Bethlehem, Pa.,
4. See chap. 3, n. 7.
5. See chap. 8, p. 51.
6. Allen P. Zimmerman, trans., Diaries of the congregations of Sharon and Gnadenhutten, 3 December 1840, John Heckewelder Memorial Moravian Church, Gnadenhutten Ohio.
7. Allen P. Zimmerman, trans., Diaries of the congregations of Sharon and Gnadenhutten, 17 December 1840, John Heckewelder Memorial Moravian Church, Gnadenhutten, Ohio.
8. Grider, *Music in Bethlehem, Pa.*, p. 29.
9. Census records place Vognitz in Newcomerstown in 1840.
10. Grider, *Music in Bethlehem, Pa.*, pp. 25 and 39.
11. Ibid., p. 23.
12. Ibid.
13. Allen P. Zimmerman, trans., Diaries of the congregations of Sharon and Gnadenhutten, 15 June 1837, John Heckewelder Memorial Moravian Church, Gnadenhutten, Ohio.
14. Allen P. Zimmerman, trans., Diaries of the congregations of Sharon and Gnadenhutten, 27 August 1837, John Heckewelder Memorial Moravian Church, Gnadenhutten, Ohio.

PART FOUR

*The Late
Nineteenth Century
(1842–1900)*

10

IMPORTANT MUSICIANS

THE ISRAEL RICKSECKER FAMILY

Born 18 March 1813 Israel Ricksecker was exposed to instrumental music early in his life since his father, Johann, was expert on the flute, oboe, clarinet, and bassoon.[1] Undoutedly Israel's first music lessons were given by his father, who was the town's shoemaker. The earliest record of Israel playing in public comes from Rufus Grider who indicates that he played in a Serenade Club around 1835.[2] It would seem likely, however, that he had appeared in public prior to this date.

Ricksecker came to Ohio in 1837 to find a good location for a jewelry store. At first he seriously considered settling in Cleveland, but under the influence of friends and relatives, he established Tuscarawas County's first jewelry store.

By the time he left Bethlehem in 1837 Ricksecker was highly esteemed as a flutist and member of America's first civic orchestra, the Bethlehem Philharmonic. Although we do not know exactly when he entered the orchestra's ranks, it was probably the early 1830s. If so he would have played the flute part for Haydn's *The Creation* and *The Seasons*.

After establishing his store in Dover, Ricksecker returned to Bethlehem and married Lizette Bleck 20 June 1839. Miss Bleck was born at Graceham, Maryland 11 June 1816. The daughter of Pastor and Mrs. Charles G. Bleck, she enrolled at the Bethlehem Female Seminary in 1834. Once her studies were completed she accepted a position as teacher on the seminary's music staff.

During her Female Seminary years she participated in concerts given by the Bethlehem Philharmonic Society. These efforts caused Rufus Grider to refer to her as "an extra fine soprano soloist."[3] Her final Bethlehem performance was the soprano part of Haydn's *Creation*, which was given shortly before her marriage.[4]

As mentioned in the last chapter, the Rickseckers often performed with the Tietzes and Jacob Blickensderfers. From an entry in the Gnadenhutten diary of 5 August 1841 it is obvious that this group, plus several other

Moravians in Dover, had already formed a nucleus that would strongly influence the musical culture of the Dover-New Philadelphia area. ". . . an exceptionally beautiful hymn [was performed], accompanied by Bro. Israel Rixecker's [sic] flute playing, and by the singing of other Dover brethren and sisters."[5]

The Rickseckers became the center of musical activity, not only of Dover, but of the entire area. The piano in their home seems to have been one of the first in the town. Thus, it was a curiosity. One story handed down within the community tells that "many a time did she [Lizette] quit work to satisfy the curiosity of the people who came many miles to see the instrument and hear her play."[6]

Lizette Ricksecker died of a serious illness 19 April 1855. Her value to the community as well as the church can be gleaned from comments made by Pastor H. G. Clauder in the church's Memorabilia for 1855.

> Soon after the celebration of the Easter festival it pleased the Lord to call away out of our midst our sister Lizette Ricksecker who from the commencement of this congregation had served the same with her musical talents. While she is gone to join the choirs before the throne of God, her memory is cherished here, not only by the congregation where of she was so zealous and exemplary a member but by the community in general.[7]

Israel and Lizette had five children, three of whom became well-known musicians. Rufus, born 19 April 1842, had a splendid bass voice and became a fine violinist. He enrolled in the Union Army August 1862 becoming a sergeant, and later a lieutenant, in the 126th Regiment Ohio Volunteers Infantry. He kept a diary of his camp life and it frequently states that he led musical activities around evening campfires. Often he entertained the troops with his violin, which he always carried with him.

In the summer of 1864 General Grant ordered General Sheridan to undertake the devastation of the area around Winchester, Virginia. The fighting began on the morning of 19 September. Since half of Sheridan's men were not immediately available, his troops suffered many casualties. Rufus was one of these, falling at the battle of Opequon.

Shot in the wrist, abdomen, and neck he requested not to be moved by those who tried to save him. Because of this his final resting place is unknown, but assumed to be the Union Cemetery at Winchester. His violin and diary were sent home to the family. Eventually, Dover's Post No. 469 of the GAR was named for him.

Adelaide Ricksecker was born 21 April 1844 and attended the Female Seminary in Bethlehem for about a year in 1861. She married Charles Harger in 1875 by whom she had four children. Two daughters, Fanny and Lizette, became musicians and graduated from the Conservatory of Music at Oberlin, Ohio. In 1880 Adelaide became organist at Dover First and served until the early 1890s. Ultimately the entire Harger family moved to Seattle, Washington where Adelaide died in 1934.

Julius Ricksecker was born 11 July 1848. He stayed in Dover and took over his father's jewelry business at the latter's death. He became a valued member of the community serving, like his father before him, as School Director, and as a Dover Councilman. Yet his most important services were to his church, which he served faithfully as an officer and member of the choir.

From programs in the Dover First archives, it is obvious that Julius was active as a bass soloist and as a member of various vocal ensembles. His son Julius carried on the family musical tradition as a violinist.

Israel Ricksecker eventually married Mary J. Bleck, the widow of a Gnadenhutten pastor, but unfortunately she died in 1864. He lived another eight years, faithfully serving church and community until his own death 8 December 1872. His instruments, a metal fife and a beautiful ebony flute, are still preserved within the Ricksecker family.

JOSEPH JOHN RICKSECKER

Besides Israel, Johann Ricksecker had two other sons. Like their middle brother, Moses and Benjamin became musicians. Benjamin, in particular, developed into a very gifted musician, becoming proficient on the organ, piano, violin, viola, cello, and flute. He served as a missionary in the West Indies, and it was during this period that his son Joseph John was born at Basseterre, St. Kitts 6 April 1844.

Like his father before him, J. J. Ricksecker became proficient in music and served as a missionary in the Danish West Indies. Graduating from Nazareth Hall and Moravian Theological Seminary, Ricksecker taught at the Hall and served two congregations prior to Sharon.

The Ohio pastorate was his longest (1875–90) and by all accounts his happiest. He was the moving force behind Sharon's musical life during this period, and eventually guided the church through the purchase of a pipe organ. After retiring, Ricksecker moved to Glendale, California where he died in 1921.

J. J. Ricksecker was fondly remembered by the Sharon congregation and when they celebrated their Jubilee lovefeast in 1908, he was invited to participate. The diarist reports that the former pastor and organist was persuaded to perform at *his* instrument: "After much entreaty—he took his old place at the pipe organ. After improvising for a few moments, while apparently lightly feeling his way over the keys he began to play 'Home, Sweet Home, with variations.' "8

THE B. B. BRASHEAR FAMILY

B. B. Brashear was a medical doctor of considerable repute by the time he moved to Dover from Akron, Ohio. During the Civil War he served as surgeon in the 16th Ohio Volunteer Infantry. Following the war he settled in Pittsburgh, Pennsylvania for a time.

In 1866 he was in Dover, as reported in a newspaper article dated 22 June identifying him as a Director of the Dover Philharmonic Society that gave "an entertainment, in the opera style on Tuesday evening, at the M. E. church in Dover. The house was crowded, and the whole affair was highly creditable to Dover and the Society."[9]

The Brashear family joined Dover First in 1874 and shortly afterward Dr. Brashear became the choir director. Pastor C. C. Lanius proudly states in his diary that under Brashear's influence the choir "is considerably larger than it was."[10]

The Brashear family, which consisted of Mrs. Katherine Brashear and daughters Nina and Imogene, became important members of the Moravian and Dover musical circles. By 1875 both daughters were teaching music, Nina at the Bethlehem Female Seminary, and Imogene at the Episcopal Female Seminary in Pittsburgh, Pennsylvania. Nina married Charles Roepper of Bethlehem and eventually returned to Dover and spent her life participating in Dover First's music program.

Brashear and his wife moved to Akron, Ohio in 1878. He was fondly remembered, however, since various observations concerning his work and himself can be found in the Dover newspaper well into the year 1887.

THE SHEELERS

Al and Helen Sheeler were children of Christopher and Elizabeth (Kaldenbaugh) Sheeler. Their father had come to Dover in 1832, and had served the community as mayor for twenty years. Al and Helen were both vocalists and often performed as a duet, in addition to singing in various trios and quartets.

The quartet usually consisted of the Sheelers, Horace Deardorf and H. W. Thayer. On 21 October 1879 this group, called the Canal Dover Quartet, performed at a benefit concert for the Uhrichsville Moravian Church. The concert was intended to raise money to help retire the church debt. Unfortunately it did not secure enough funds, so the Quartet volunteered to present another concert.[11] The offer was accepted and the second concert took place 13 November. The program of this concert is found in the Uhrichsville diary and it indicates that Ohio's Moravians were right in step with programming practices of the period.[12]

Al Sheeler left Dover for Abilene, Kansas. However, Helen remained, serving as organist and choir member for many years. An interesting story concerning Miss Sheeler appeared in the local newspaper.

> The Methodist congregation sabbath evening was "in such a dilemma." The organist and nearly all the choir had gone off to Lakeside. The pulpit was filled by a strange preacher, who gave out the hymn, read it through, and sat down. Then a painful stillness reigned through the house. The organ was silent, and not a voice seemed willing to pitch in. In years gone by, some leather-lunged brother would have jerked the tune along without thinking of an accompaniment; or some pious old sister would have carried it without a break or discord. But here sat a whole housefull, and all were dumb. Finally Miss Helen Sheeler, organist of the Moravian choir, came to their relief.[13]

Ultimately, a serious throat problem forced her to give up singing as well as her organist position. She remained in the church, however, working in the Sunday School program, where she often organized musical performances. By 1895 she had married G. Cromwell and moved to Muncie, Indiana.

THE LEWIS WINSCH FAMILY

The son of Johnathan and Caroline Winsch, Ludwig (Lewis) Simon Winsch was born in Gnadenhutten 6 September 1835.[14] As a young man Lewis Winsch helped organize and serve in three different military units during the Civil War.[15] He then served all of them as band member or director.

Winsch's love of band music continued after the war and, in 1879, he organized the Gnadenhutten civic band. This ensemble, which appears to be the first in the town, would exist for many years with Winsch as its leader.

Winsch established a mercantile business in Gnadenhutten in 1877 and became the town's first mayor in 1884. He was also an Elder in the church and seems to have been well-liked by most of the church's ministers. Pastor Henry T. Bachman relates that Winsch was a willing participant when the pastor and his wife celebrated their twenty-fifth wedding anniversary. "We have a very pleasant evening, & close with singing, & prayer by bro. Lewis Winsch."[16]

Lewis Winsch was married three times. By his first wife, Anne C. Blickensderfer, whom he married 18 August 1859, he had two children, Charles Clement and Frank Cessna. Like their father, both boys were musically inclined. Frank, in particular, would become one of Gnadenhutten's most important musicians in the first half of the twentieth century and will be discussed in later chapters.

THE PETER-EGGENBERG-MCCONNELL FAMILIES

Peter

David Peter and Susanna Leinbach parented several children who became important musicians. The first of these was Edward (b. 1815). As Sunday School Superintendent at Gnadenhutten he often led the monthly Sunday School concerts. He also sang in the church choir for a number of years. One of his children, Oliver Louis (b. 1848), fathered a very important Uhrichsville Moravian musician, Miss Nellie Zoe Peter, of whom we shall speak in chapter fifteen.

Peter-Eggenberg

A second child Louisa Peter (b. 1819) married John Eggenberg. One of their children, Horace Eggenberg (b. 1856), became a very active musician. On Christmas Eve 1878 Horace and Mrs. E. G. Helwig of Gnadenhutten joined forces with Isaac Romig and Mrs. J. M. Levering of Uhrichsville to form the first Moravian choir to sing for the Uhrichsville congregation. They sang "Silent Night" and "Thou Child Divine," as well as leading the singing of "Morning Star."[17] Horace Eggenberg would become the Uhrichsville choir director in the early twentieth century.

Eggenberg-McConnell

The second child of Louisa Peter and John Eggenberg was Anna M. Eggenberg. She married William McConnell and parented two children who became valuable musicians. Horace McClellan McConnell was a vocalist of some note and a member of the Gnadenhutten trombone choir for many years. His sister Lucy McConnell (the future Mrs. Edwin Miller) would serve Gnadenhutten as organist for many years in the 1940s and will be discussed in chapter twenty.

Sarah Louisa Eggenberg was yet another musical child of Louisa Peter and John Eggenberg. She married a William McConnell and served as choir member and organist at Gnadenhutten for many years.

THE DEMUTH FAMILY

Another musical family among the Tuscarawas Moravians that came to prominence in the late nineteenth-century was the Demuth family. The Demuths are one of the few Ohio families that can trace their lineage to the ancient Unitas Fratrum. Christoph Demuth was a Magistrate in Karlsdorf, Moravia and one of the "Hidden Seed" of the Unitas Fratrum.[18] Three of his four sons fled to Herrnhut in 1726. Nine years later a grandson, Gottlieb, came to America with Bishop Spangenberg and the first Moravian settlers to arrive in Georgia.[19]

Ultimately two families of Demuths moved to Ohio and established the name in Tuscarawas County. The first of these to be mentioned in connection with music is Albert Demuth (b. 1854). The Ohio records do not mention Demuth often, however, they do identify him as a vocalist. The Sharon church records indicate that he served as vocalist in quartets sung in church.[20]

Demuth's daughter Edna (b. 1891) is often mentioned as a member of the Gnadenhutten choir and vocal soloist, but it is his son Wilbur who turned the family name into a musical one. Wilbur Demuth will be discussed in Part Four of this book.

THE FIDLER FAMILY

In 1843 George Fidler, Sr. moved to Tuscarawas County. Although neither this George nor his son George, Jr. were members of the Moravian church, the third and fourth generations represented by Erastus Smith Fidler (son of George, Jr.) and his children were staunch members of both the Uhrichsville and Port Washington Moravian churches.[21]

Erastus Fidler married Caroline Raenbaugh, although the exact date cannot be ascertained. They seem to have had at least three children, John H. (b. ?), Benjamin C. (b. 1873), and Edith N. (b. 1890). Like their father, who was a wind instrumentalist,[22] the children demonstrated various musical skills.

From entries in the Port Washington diary we know that John H. Fidler was a vocalist.[23] In fact, he is one of the earliest musicians to be identified as such in church records. He was active during the 1890s, singing in the choir(?) and in vocal quartets. He also served in the Sunday School for many years. Since his name is mentioned at an earlier date than Benjamin, it can be assumed that John was the oldest of the three children.

During the year 1912 Erastus Fidler moved his family to Ft. Lauderdale, Florida. It is not known whether John went with the family, although there are no twentieth-century references to him in church records. Of the remaining two children Benjamin stayed in Ohio, while Edith moved with her parents. Since Benjamin and Edith are important in the next generation of Moravian musicians they will be discussed in future chapters.

THE VAN VLECK FAMILY

Henry J. Van Vleck became a major influence in the Ohio Moravian churches during the last quarter of the nineteenth century. Born into one of the more important musical families of the Moravian Church, he was the son of Bishop William Henry Van Vleck and grandson of Jacob Van Vleck.[24]

A graduate of Nazareth Hall and Moravian Theological Seminary, he followed his father to Salem, where he became Director of the Boy's School. Returning to the Northern Province he served as Superintendent of the Nazareth Moravian Parochial School from 1850–1866.

Van Vleck married Augusta Bear of Bethlehem in 1850. Their five boys and two daughters were all born during the Nazareth years, which ended with a call to the South Bethlehem church. This pastorate, his first, lasted from 1866 to 1874, when the call to Gnadenhutten brought the family to Ohio.

HJVV, as he often signed his correspondence, served Gnadenhutten (1874–82), Fry's Valley (1882–90), and Port Washington as interim (1894–95). He was consecrated Bishop in 1881, and retired to Gnadenhutten in 1890 where he lived, with intervals of travel to various western churches, until his death in 1906.

Following in the Van Vleck tradition, the entire family became musicians. The Bishop was a pianist, organist, vocalist, and composer. As an organist he was apparently quite good, for when he performed during Dover First's fifteenth anniversary, the *Iron Valley Reporter* stated, "an inspiring Voluntary [was played] by the aged Bishop, who is a skilled musician."[25] He also served the area as organ tuner, tester, and mechanic. His three sons, Fred, Theodore, and Charles, were also trained in these categories, probably by their father.

Fred was organist and choir director at Gnadenhutten, taking over sometime after the family arrived in 1874 and continuing until he left for the East in December 1876. He is first identified as choir director in an 1875 diary entry when he led the choir at Br. and Sr. Simmer's home in Tuscarawas, Ohio.[26]

Like his father, Fred was quite skilled as an organ repairman. In this capacity he was contracted to repair the organ at Dover First. After tuning the organ in 1876 he was paid a fee of fifteen dollars.[27]

William Theodore was born 11 May 1851. He was quite proficient at the organ and became Gnadenhutten's church organist, probably in the early 1880s, and remained at that position until his death in 1919.

He is first mentioned as an organist in the Port Washington diary, which states that he played for Sunday service 2 August 1885.[28] Over the next twenty-four years he was in great demand as a performer for special services at the various Moravian churches.

Theodore married Catherine Demuth 30 October 1878 and, one month later was ordained a Deacon in the church. He had no ministerial aspirations, being a printer by trade, however, his father's work load was such that Theodore provided much needed assistance. Principally in administering the sacrament and conducting singing services he was a great help to the future Bishop.

When Theodore died in 1919, his daughter Mary Demuth Van Vleck succeeded him as church organist. She was the wife of Albert A. Wohlwend and would hold the organist position until 1929, when Mrs. Elizabeth Ebenhack succeeded her. This change marked the first time in approximately fifty-five years that a member of Bishop Van Vleck's family did not hold Gnadenhutten's organ post.

Charlie, the youngest son, ultimately moved to Uhrichsville where he served the church as choir member, Elder, and janitor for many years.

NOTES

1. A highly complimentary, yet amusing account of Johann's prowess on the clarinet can be found in Grider, *Music in Bethlehem, Pa.*, p. 6.
2. Grider, *Music in Bethlehem, Pa.*, p. 23.
3. Ibid., p. 41.
4. Ibid., pp. 29–30.
5. Allen P. Zimmerman, trans., Diaries of the congregations of Sharon and Gnadenhutten, 15 August 1841, John Heckewelder Memorial Moravian Church, Gnadenhutten, Ohio.
6. "Dover Enterprises, Jewelry: Israel Ricksecker," Dover, Ohio, *Daily Iron Valley Reporter*, 16 August 1888, p. 3.
7. Memorabilia for 1855 of the Moravian Congregation at Dover, Ohio, Moravian Archives, Bethlehem, Pa.,
8. Diary of the Sharon Moravian Church, 15 November 1908, Tuscarawas, Ohio.
9. "The Dover Philharmonic Society," New Philadelphia, *Ohio Democrat*, 22 June 1866, p. 3.
10. Diary of the Moravian Congregation at Dover, Ohio, 15 November 1874, Moravian Archives, Bethlehem, Pa.
11. Diary of the First Moravian Congregation of Uhrichsville, Ohio, 28 October 1879, Uhrichsville, Ohio.
12. Diary of the Moravian Congregation at Dover, Ohio, 13 November 1879, Moravian Archives, Bethlehem, Pa.
13. "The Methodist Congregation," Dover, Ohio, *Daily Iron Valley Reporter*, 23 August 1879, p. 3.
14. See chap. 6.
15. 51st Ohio Volunteer Infantry Brass Band (1861), 161st Regiment Infantry (1864), and 189th Ohio Volunteer Infantry (1865).
16. Diary of Gnadenhutten, Fry's Valley, and Ross Congregations, vol. 5, 28 October 1885, John Heckewelder Memorial Moravian Church, Gnadenhutten, Ohio.
17. Diary of the Moravian Congregation at Uhrichsville, Ohio, 24 December 1878, Uhrichsville, Ohio.
18. C. F. Battershell, *The Demuth Family and the Moravian Church* (Privately printed, 1938).
19. Ibid.
20. Diary of the Sharon Moravian Church, 15 April 1900, Tuscarawas, Ohio.
21. Church records concerning this family are often quite sketchy and accurate information is difficult to obtain, however, the material given in this text is solidly documented. Any assumptions on the writer's part are carefully indicated.
22. See chap. 12.
23. Diary of the First Moravian Congregation, Port Washington, 1 November 1891, Moravian Archives, Bethlehem, Pa.
24. Jacob Van Vleck was the first Moravian of American birth to engage in musical composi-

tion. He was a very respected individual, serving in many important positions. He was consecrated a Bishop in 1815.

25. "Dover First 50th Anniversary," Dover, Ohio, *The Daily Iron Valley Reporter,* 17 May 1894, p. 3.

26. Diaries of Gnadenhutten, Fry's Valley, and Ross, 18 November 1875, John Heckewelder Memorial Moravian Church, Gnadenhutten, Ohio.

27. Diary of the Dover Moravian Church, 4 March 1876, Moravian Archives, Bethlehem, Pa.

28. Diary of the First Moravian Congregation, Port Washington, 2 August 1885, Moravian Archives, Bethlehem, Pa.

11

ORGANS AND ORGANISTS

Although the use of organs in Moravian churches has a strong and significant history, their introduction into the Ohio congregations was quite slow. This was partly because economic conditions of the nineteenth-century Ohio congregations were quite different from those of the eighteenth-century eastern settlements. Also, while the eighteenth-century Moravians had access to Moravian organ builders such as John Klemm, David Tannenberg, Johann Bachman, and Joseph Bulitschek, there were no such builders working during the nineteenth century.[1] Finally, some of the Ohio congregations were naturally conservative and reserved such an expensive purchase until they were sure the congregation could afford it and that a regular organist could be secured.

The first congregation to purchase an organ was Sharon. We know nothing about the instrument except that it was purchased sometime in 1828 and was first employed at the Watchnight service of that year.

We can only speculate on the identity of the Sharon organists. There is every likelihood that Jacob Blickensderfer served at various times. He could not, however, have been a regular organist because his government positions often required long absences. During the Tietze era it could have been Susan Tietze. Sylvester Wolle mentions that his wife, the former Caroline Rice, occasionally played when another organist could not be found.[2]

The next intrument was a melodian purchased by Dover First. It served the congregation for nine years, from 1844 to 1853. The church's second instrument was a pipe organ. Again we know very little about this instrument, except that it is described in the Memorabilia of 1853 as "of suitable size & capacity"[3] to fill the church building. At the time of the above purchase, the Dover organist was Jacob Blickensderfer. In addition, Israel and Lizette Ricksecker seem to have served as assistant organists.

Gnadenhutten purchased the next instrument. This congregation had a checkered career with regard to organs. As early as 1854 one John Weber offered to sell his organ to the church, but the majority of the Board did not approve.[4] Nine years later a similar offer was made by a Mr. Rintz of New

Philadelphia. He wanted $175 for an organ harmonium. Again the committee in charge decided in the negative, "greatly doubting whether the cong. would at this time be willing to pay the $175."[5]

The committee had misjudged the congregation, for an organ was purchased the very next year (1864). The new instrument was a harmonium, which was purchased from a Philadelphia, Pennsylvania, firm for three hundred dollars. Unfortunately, there was much dissatisfaction with the instrument when it was put in place "because the instrument was not a 'cabinet organ.' "[6] Dissatisfaction or no, the instrument was dedicated 17 April 1864.

There is no information on who might have played this organ. We do know that Sarah Louisa McConnell, daughter of John and Louisa (Peter) Eggenberg, was organist for many years.[7] It cannot be ascertained, however, whether she was organist before or after the Van Vlecks moved to Gnadenhutten. If before, it is unlikely that she became organist prior to 1869. She turned sixteen in that year, and it seems to have been standard practice for churches not to employ organists younger than this. If after, she could have begun in 1876, when Fred Van Vleck left Ohio, thereby serving between Fred and Theodore Van Vleck.[8]

The above three organs seem to have been the only Moravian organs for the next fourteen years. Then, in 1878 we enter a twelve-year period in which organs were purchased for, or made available to, every Moravian church in the County.

Sharon purchased a new reed and pipe organ in 1878. This seems to have been an intermediary step, for two years later the same church purchased a new Hook and Hastings organ. That same year found the Uhrichsville church obtaining a "used" organ from Sharon. The records of neither church are clear on which organ this was. Very likely it was the 1828 organ, since the 1878 organ appears to have been used in Sharon's Sunday School.

Sharon's new Hook and Hastings organ was built to the specifications of its pastor J. J. Ricksecker. In addition to being the pastor, Ricksecker was also the church organist. Thus, the organ was built into a recess behind the pulpit. It was equipped with a swivel chair instead of an organ bench so that Ricksecker could turn toward the congregation immediately after playing.

When the Uhrichsville congregation began in 1874 they met in members' homes, local auditoria, and various church buildings until their own building was consecrated 10 November 1878. Although the dedication services do not mention an organ, the church must have had one because one month later, pastor Levering identifies the church's first organist as Miss Carrie Everett.[9]

Miss Everett was sixteen at the time. Apparently she was proficient enough to please Pastor Levering, but not his successor, John H. Clewell. She and Clewell had their differences and Carrie resigned after serving as organist for one year.

Gnadenhutten purchased a Durner organ in 1887. It was built in Quaker-town, Pennsylvania, and was set up in the church during the fall. Although pastor Bachman does not indicate any special dedication service, his diary states that it was first played at Sunday service 23 October 1887.[10] It remained in service for thirty-nine years, until it was replaced in 1926.

The organist during most of this time was Theodore Van Vleck. Although it is impossible to ascertain precisely when he began as organist, all evidence points to the early 1880s.

The *Iron Valley Reporter* of Dover reported in its issue of 7 November 1889: "The Moravian congregation held special services Sunday evening, in the interest of their new organ fund. Their present pipe organ has been in use 37 years and its voice has become somewhat huskey and its wind wheezy and broken."[11]

The church contracted with the Hook and Hastings Organ Company for an instrument that would cost $875. When the new instrument was dedi-cated 10 August 1890, the congregation had raised $880 so that no debt was assumed.[12]

The reviews and diary entries do not give us any information on Dover's organist. Mrs. Adelaide Ricksecker Harger served as organist from 1880 to some unspecified time. Her relative, Miss Emma Harger, was the regular organist, at least by 1892, if not earlier.[13] From this it is likely that the two ladies may have shared the position when the new organ was installed. Regardless, Theodore Van Vleck performed on the instrument at the eve-ning service commemorating the congregation's fiftith anniversary 17 May 1894.

An organ was also owned by the Fry's Valley congregation. Our earliest knowledge concerning this organ comes from an 1892 notation which men-tions an organist, but gives no name.[14] Unfortunately, we know nothing about the organ, nor can we speculate on the organist.

The earliest mention of keyboard performance at Port Washington comes from a 21 February 1884 diary entry which indicates that Miss Nannie Kilgore had agreed to play for services as Miss Hammersley had resigned. Nothing is said concerning the instrument on which the ladies played.

Pastor M. F. Oerter states that Sharon's old "log cabin" organ was sold to Mr. McClellan of New Philadelphia and he later resold it to a church in Port Washington.[15] Oerter does not mention his source, but it was probably one of the missing Sharon diaries. If he is correct the Sharon organ definitely moved to Port Washington.

The Port Washington Moravian Church was begun in 1882 with the help of Uhrichsville pastor John H. Clewell. It is possibile that Mr. McClellan, with Clewell acting as intermediary, sold the old Sharon organ to the Port Washington Church, and this was Port Washington's first organ.

The remaining pipe organs, Port Washington's 1905 Hook and Hastings,

Uhrichsville's 1909 Hinners, Gnadenhutten's 1926 Moller, and Dover First's 1915 Moller and 1950 Reuter, will be discussed in chapter nineteen.

NOTES

1. William H. Armstrong, *Organs for America: The Life and Work of David Tannenberg* (Philadelphia: University of Pennsylvania Press, 1967).

2. *Diarium von Gemeinen in Gnadenhutten und Sharon*, 21 March 1847, John Heckewelder Memorial Moravian Church, Gnadenhutten, Ohio.

3. Memorabilia for 1853 of the Moravian Congregation at Dover, Ohio, Moravian Archives, Bethlehem, Pa.

4. Diary of the Gnadenhutten Congregation for the year 1854, 12 March 1854, John Heckewelder Memorial Moravian Church, Gnadenhutten, Ohio.

5. Diary for 1863, Gnadenhutten and Fry's Valley, 9 November 1863, John Heckewelder Memorial Moravian Church, Gnadenhutten, Ohio.

6. Diary of the Congregations of Gnadenhutten and Fry's Valley for 1864, 6 April 1864, John Heckewelder Memorial Moravian Church, Gnadenhutten, Ohio.

7. Gnadenhutten Church Book, Death Register, 30 August 1890, John Heckewelder Memorial Moravian Church, Gnadenhutten, Ohio.

8. The church records are so incomplete on this point that it is impossible to decide which possibility is most likely. Regardless, the records strongly indicate that Sarah McConnell served the church as organist, assistant organist, or Sunday School organist for several years.

9. Diary of the First Moravian Congregation of Uhrichsville, Ohio, 17 November 1878, Uhrichsville, Ohio.

10. Diary of Gnadenhutten, Fry's Valley and Ross Congregations, vol. 5, 23 October 1887, John Heckewelder Memorial Moravian Church, Gnadenhutten, Ohio.

11. "The Moravian Congregation," Dover, Ohio, *Daily Iron Valley Reporter,* 7 November 1889, p. 3.

12. Diary of the Moravian Congregation at Dover, Ohio, 10 August 1890, Moravian Archives, Bethlehem, Pa.

13. "Dedication of Remodeled Moravian Church," Dover, Ohio, *Daily Iron Valley Reporter,* 27 October 1892, p. 3.

14. Minutes of the Annual Meeting of the Church Council for 1892, 13 January 1892, Fry's Valley, Ohio.

15. Rev. Maurice Frederick Oerter, *A Brief Historical Sketch of the Moravian Congregation at Sharon, Tuscarawas, Ohio*, (Canal Dover, Ohio: Seibert Printing, Co., n.d.), p. 31.

12

BANDS

During the late nineteenth century there was a band in virtually every American community. This was particularly true in the years immediately following the Civil War.[1]

As might be expected Tuscarawas County reflected the national trend. Also, as might be expected, the Tuscarawas bands were liberally sprinkled with Moravians. Because of this, bands were the chief medium through which Moravians influenced the secular musical life of their communities.

The earliest record of a band in Tuscarawas County thusfar discovered comes from the Dover First diary. On 18 June 1857 the various Dover Sunday Schools held a union festival. They marched from downtown Dover to the fairgrounds, led by a band, which Pastor Henry Clauder calls "an excellent brass band."[2] Unfortunately, no identification of band personnel is given.

A similar situation occurred at Gnadenhutten 31 January 1865. On this day the school children of Port Washington, their teachers and friends, took a sleigh ride to Gnadenhutten to share the afternoon. Pastor Clement Reincke states that the Port Washington band came along and that "the band played a national air (not without the Pastor's approval)."[3] Again, band members are not identified.

While the Port Washington band played with the pastor's approval, churches were not always pleased to see their members play in bands. Sharon church records indicate that the Board of Elders was quite unhappy with the participation of Bro. Cyrus Demuth in the Trenton (now Tuscarawas) band. The band held a Sunday practice session in preparation for a contest. The Sharon Elders considered this an unworthy way for a Christian to spend a Sunday afternoon. Thus, they requested that Pastor Henry T. Bachman speak to Bro. Demuth concerning the incident.[4] The records do not state what Demuth's response was, but the Gnadenhutten diaries of 1880–81 give a very detailed description of the animosity that could develop between bands and local denominations.

During this period Henry J. Van Vleck was pastor at Gnadenhutten. Sometime in late 1879 several individuals formed a town band which re-

75

hearsed in the store of its leader, Lewis Winsch.[5] Either by accident, or design, band practice coincided with evening prayer service. Since Winsch and several others in the band were officers in the Gnadenhutten church, the good pastor assumed that a conversation with the Moravian members would solve his problem. He talked, they listened, and band practices continued. With each practice session Pastor Van Vleck's anger rose, until it finally erupted on 12 December 1881.

> On returning home one of the two young sisters . . . appointed by the Band, to go about collecting in its behalf, solicited a contribution from me, which gave me occasion to address them & their companions visiting my two daughters on the subject of the Band, & the shameful indifference & contempt of all the Moravian members thereof, in regard to the duties which they owe the church,—Bro. J. Gutensohn being the only one who can be excepted.——The young sister, who succeeds in collecting the most *is to get a ring.* is [*sic*] it not outrageous?[6]

The primary objects of Van Vleck's rath were the band's leader, Lewis Winsch, and his wife Sarah. Van Vleck lamented that the two Winsch children, Charlie and "little Frank the drummer boy," were being ill-taught by their parents, who permitted them to play in the band, but were not very concerned with the boys' Christian education.

In defense of the band we must say that they performed many useful civic services, most of which were very dear to the local Moravian church. For instance, they were quite prominent at the Gnadenhutten Massacre ceremonies of May 1882.[7] Also, the band was a training group for trombone choir members.

In defense of Pastor Van Vleck it must be stated that he was not the only Moravian clergyman to be irritated by a band. His fellow pastor at Uhrichsville, John H. Clewell, faced a similar situation in February 1880. A service he was conducting had to be concluded early because "the band began to serenade the newly married couple over the way, & it was impossible to continue the service."[8]

The first town band for which we have a membership list is the Port Washington band. This group had performed for the 1877 senatorial convention and, according to the *Ohio Democrat*, it, "furnished good music and aided in preserving 'harmony' at [the convention]."[9]

The band consisted of thirteen men. Eight of these, Erastus Fidler, Robert Nelson, Adam Chappel, Benjamin Carr, Charles Lang, Charles Schug, Benjamin Ross, and George Fidler, would become members or friends of the Port Washington Moravian Church when it was organized four years later. George Fidler, owner of Port Washington's Carr & Fidler store, was a grocer and merchant. His son, Erastus Fidler, is identified as the band's leader. Erastus was twenty-seven in 1877 and was a leading musician in the community.[10]

Other Moravian names connected with county bands can be gleaned from local newspapers. In 1884 the Dover paper presented an article which states that the first brass band organized in Tuscarawas County was located at New Philadelphia. Among the band's personnel was a Moravian bass drummer, Jacob Knisely.[11] The Fry's Valley correspondent for the same paper reported that "Charles Tschudy, the leader of our band, is still in Wyandot County; therefore we have but little music."[12] Yet another band leader was Albert Demuth, who is described as a very capable leader.[13]

Moravian support for bands often went beyond membership. According to the local newpaper of 1886 the Dover band was the recipient of new instruments. "Mr. [Julius] Ricksecker made the purchase, and the style and make are to his credit."[14] This was a very generous gift; the article lists no less than nineteen instruments purchased for the Dover band by Mr. Ricksecker.

The final band to be mentioned was not a civic band, rather it was associated with the Gnadenhutten Sunday School. Known as the Juvenile Mission Band, it consisted of children and was begun 26 January 1890 under the careful management of the pastor's wife. Sister Mary Huebner Oerter must have done her task well since the band lasted for many years and was an important part of the Sunday School program.

NOTES

1. Richard Franko Goldman, "Band Music in America," in *One Hundred Years of Music in America,* ed. Paul Henry Lang (New York: G. Schirmer, 1961), p. 129.

2. Diary of the Dover Moravian Church, 18 June 1857, Moravian Archives, Bethlehem, Pa.

3. Diary for 1865, Gnadenhutten and Fry's Valley, 31 January 1865, John Heckewelder Memorial Moravian Church, Gnadenhutten, Ohio.

4. Minutes of the Board of Elders, Sharon Congregation, 8 September 1866, Sharon Moravian Church, Tuscarawas, Ohio.

5. Diaries of Gnadenhutten, Fry's Valley and Ross, vol. 3, 6 January 1880, John Heckeweler Memorial Moravian Church, Gnadenhutten, Ohio.

6. Diaries of Gnadenhutten, Fry's Valley and Ross Congregations, vol. 4, 12 December 1881, John Heckewelder Memorial Moravian Church, Gnadenhutten, Ohio.

7. Ibid., 24 May 1882.

8. Diary of the First Moravian Congregation of Uhrichsville, Ohio, 18 February 1880, Uhrichsville, Ohio.

9. "The Port Washington Band," Uhrichsville, Ohio, *Ohio Democrat,* 2 August 1877, p. 3.

10. See chap. 10.

11. "Pioneers of Tuscarawas County," Dover, Ohio, *Daily Iron Valley Reporter,* 15 August 1884, p. 3.

12. "Fry's Valley," Dover, Ohio, *Daily Iron Valley Reporter,* 2 February 1883, p. 3.

13. "New Philadelphia Band," New Philadelphia, Ohio, *Ohio Democrat,* 13 April 1866, p. 3.

14. "The Band Horns Arrive," Dover, Ohio, *Daily Iron Valley Reporter,* 19 February 1886, p. 3.

13

THE CRACKERBOX COLLECTION

Beginning in the eighteenth century Moravian congregations established collections of music manuscripts. These collections often became quite sizable and consisted of solo songs, anthems, and occasionally, instrumental music.[1] As printed music became less expensive the manuscript collections lost their importance, were placed in boxes, and stored in some convenient part of the church, usually the attic.

It was the attic at Dover First that yielded just such a collection during its last major remodeling program (1948–50). Amid a myriad of paraphernalia that had accumulated over the years an Akron Baking Company crackerbox was discovered. While preparing to burn the box a workman happened to comment to Pastor Roy Grams that it contained old music. Upon investigation the music proved to be a typical Moravian manuscript collection.

The box was saved and its contents were ultimately turned over to Dr. Donald McCorkle, the first director of the Moravian Music Foundation. Dr. McCorkle found the collection contained some fifty folios which included 140 pieces, complete, or in part. Among the more important items in the collection were two previously unknown compositions by Moravian composers, "How Beautiful Upon the Mountains" by John Antes, and "Lamb of God, Thou Shalt Remain Forever" by Georg Gottfried Müller.[2]

The importance of the above items was somewhat overshadowed by the discovery that a majority of the crackerbox collection had originally been part of the Bethlehem congregation collection. That a large body of manuscripts was missing from the Bethlehem collection had been known for years, however, its whereabouts remained a mystery. Documentation of the Bethlehem connection was made possible because the original call numbers had never been erased from the Dover music.

The most obvious question to arise from the above findings is, When was the Bethlehem music sent to Ohio? Two theories have been advanced in an effort to answer this question. The first theory claims that the music came to Ohio when Bishop Peter Wolle served Dover First.[3] Wolle was interim pastor at Dover from 1853 to 1855. Since he was one of the leading Moravian musicians of his day, and since he undoubtedly had access to the Bethlehem collection, he could easily have brought the music with him, or had it sent.[4]

The second theory is put forward by Dr. Robert Steelman, a Moravian Music Foundation researcher who is very familiar with the Bethlehem collection. Steelman observes that the Bethlehem collection underwent a major revision in 1849. This revision involved a new cataloging procedure which, in turn, required new accession numbers. Thus, all items that went through the revision process contain old numbers that have been crossed out and replaced with new ones. Since none of the items in the crackerbox have the new numbers, they must have been in Ohio prior to 1849.[5] Steelman's theory, of course, completely negates the Wolle theory.

Unfortunately, as he readily admits, Steelman's theory is problematic. Apparently, the new numbering system was not universally applied, that is, some older pieces remained in the Bethlehem collection but did not receive new numbers. Thus, even though it is unlikely that a group of manuscripts as large as the crackerbox collection could have entirely missed renumbering, the possibility does exist.

Fortunately, a third theory has emerged from the research conducted for this book. It results from two particularly important facts: (1) the collection itself implies that it may have been a repository for compositions that were assembled over a period of time and; (2) the diaries clearly indicate performance dates for some pieces found in the collection that are at variance with those suggested in the Wolle and Steelman theories. For the next several paragraphs we will consider evidence relating to point one.

The collection contains a group of compositions that must be called non-Bethlehem music. This name is used because these items were never in the Bethlehem collection.[6] Among these is a set of three sacred songs for vocal solo with keyboard accompaniment. They were written by Peter Ricksecker (1791–1873), a minor Moravian composer.[7]

Among other positions, Ricksecker held a teaching post at Nazareth Hall.[8] Two of his crackerbox compositions, "O could we but love that Savior" and "Out of Love and boundless grace," come from this period, while the third, "Holy Bible, Book Divine," was written in 1856, when he served at the Delaware Indian mission in Kansas.

Since nothing of this type is found in the Bethlehem collection, or any other Moravian collection, these pieces must have come to Ohio in some other way. While there are various possibilities the two most plausible are that Ricksecker left the music during one of his visits to Ohio, or the pieces were part of a Ricksecker family collection that was placed in the crackerbox collection.

A second group of non-Bethlehem items found in the crackerbox collection are a *Quartet for Male Voices*, a funeral anthem, and what appears to be a sacred solo for alto. The first of these items is entitled "Soft be the gently breathing notes" and comes from the songbook, *Pioneer* (1865–66). The funeral anthem, "I heard a voice from Heaven," is by John Callcott. The crackerbox version is found on page 181 of the tunebook, *Boston Sacred Harmony, No. 3*. The third item, "The Lord will comfort Zion," comes from page 308 of *United States Collection*, and is possibly by Carl Maria von Weber. All of these items come from materials that were readily available at music stores. They could have belonged to any of several Ohio Moravian ensembles mentioned earlier.

The presence of these items by themselves says very little about the collection, since they could have been odd pieces placed in the crackerbox at the time it was stored. It is at this point that performance dates become important. Evidence of widely differing performance dates for crackerbox items would be valuable because the more remote the performance dates the more likely it would be that the collection came to Ohio in parts rather than as a whole. This evidence, in conjunction with the non-Bethlehem music, would provide a strong argument for the repository theory.

The repository argument would also be strengthed if performances of crackerbox music occurred at churches other than Dover First. Although it has never been stated publicly, the crackerbox collection has encouraged the belief that, since it was located at Dover, it must have been intended for Dover. If, however, it can be proved that some of the crackerbox music was intended for other churches, this would provide a third piece of evidence supporting the repository theory. The accumulation of this much evidence would virtually assure the theory's validity.

The following table presents the earliest evidence in support of the repository theory. It lists the first references to compositions sung by choirs for which there are titles. They were all performed at Gnadenhutten festivities of August 1820.

The German titles found in table 1 pieces are anthems by prominent Moravian composers. Also, each of these German anthems is found in the crackerbox collection. Two copies of the first anthem are found there, one by John C. Bechler and one by John Gambold, while the second and final anthems exist in versions by Bechler and Johannes Herbst respectively.

Neither of the two English items is found in the crackerbox. This leads one to suspect that they were hymns sung in place of anthems, English anthems that never became part of the crackerbox collection, or German anthems given "homemade" English translations.

A check of early English Moravian hymnals produces no texts with these words. Again, a check of English-text anthems employed by Moravian congregations is fruitless. Neither of these texts is even remotely similar to those found in other congregation collections. The final option is to search the German-language anthems in the crackerbox music with the hope of finding a piece that was given an English translation. This is impossible since

Table 1

Choral Pieces
Sung by the Moravian Choir
at Dedication Services for Gnadenhutten's
Second Church Building and the August 13th
Festival
1820

Anthems sung at Dedication service, August 13th
Sey Lob Ehr dem höchsten Gut
Preis und Dank und Ehre bringen

Anthems sung at afternoon lovefeast, August 13th
Thee I'll Extol My God and King
O Praise the Lord with Hymns of Joy

Anthems sung at August 13th Festival, August 14th
Der Herr ist unser König der hilft uns

---

*At this time the Gnadenhütten diary was kept in German. However, some music titles are given in English. The language used for the above titles exactly corresponds with that used by Pastor Rauschenberg in his diary entries.

the diary gives only the first line of the text and nothing more. The only other possibility is that non-Moravian hymns were used. In any event no definite identification can be made.

From the above facts it becomes obvious that table 1 presents two valuable pieces of information: (1) at least three anthems from the crackerbox collection were in Ohio by 1820 and, (2) none of the collection's English anthems were yet in the state.

The next group of anthems for which titles exist were performed during the Tietze era and are listed in table 2.

Like the table 1 titles, table 2 items were performed at Gnadenhutten. Also, like the items listed in table 1, the pieces listed in table 2 include both German and English texts. Unlike those in table 1, however, the English items in table 2 are anthems found in the crackerbox collection.

The German anthem is a setting by Johann Soerensen. A medical doctor, Soerensen was a musician by avocation. Though he was not a Moravian,

Table 2
Anthems Sung during the Tietze Era

Anthem sung 7 April 1838.
O Bethanien,
du Friedenshütten

Anthem sung 29 March 1839.
He was despised
and rejected

Anthem sung 20 April 1840.
Holy Redeemer,
by thy rest
most glorious

Soerensen's composition was performed during Passion Week in many Moravian congregations.

The first English anthem is by the German composer Karl Graun. While not a Moravian, Graun was well liked by them and many of his compositions are found in Moravian collections. The final anthem was written by the most well known English Moravian composer Christian LaTrobe.

The crackerbox collection contains 133 anthems. Of these 108 are based on German texts, while 25 are based on English texts. Table 2 informs us that at least two of the English-language anthems were in Ohio by 1840. It is possible that some, or all, of the remaining twenty-three were also in Ohio by this time but documentation is lacking.

A third group of choral pieces for which titles exist, comes from the pastorates of Sylvester Wolle and Louis Kampmann, and are found in table 3.

Several pieces of information are contained in table 3. First, the items marked with a (D) were sung at Dover. Therefore, they represent the first compositions to be sung by a Dover choir for which titles exist. The remaining pieces were all performed at Gnadenhutten. Again one finds both German and English texts. All but one of the English texts present the same problems encountered with table 1 items. "Christians dismiss your fears" can be found in every English Moravian Hymnal since 1785.

The German titles are all anthems and are found in the crackerbox. "O Bethanien, du Friedenshütten" has already been discussed. "Dank, Anbetung, Lob und Ehre sey dir" is by John C. Bechler. "Lobsinget heut und bringet Dank und Rühm" is interesting in that it is by Joseph Haydn. The Moravians were particularly fond of Haydn's music and the crackerbox collection contains ten compositions by the Austrian master.

This survey provides important documentation. First, performances of pieces that can be found in the crackerbox may be traced over a twenty-seven year period from 1820 to 1847.[9] Second, it would appear that Steelman's cut-off date of 1849 may be correct. The diaries indicate performances of a large number of anthems at Gnadenhutten, Sharon, and particularly Dover from 1842 to 1847. Since most of these entries give no titles it is not certain that they were crackerbox items. It is logical, however, to assume that they were.

What the above information indicates is that performances of crackerbox items were indeed widely spaced, and that many anthems were intended for Gnadenhutten rather than Dover. These compositions were then employed at other churches when necessary.

Thus, a strong argument for the repository theory has developed. However, new questions arise. The most obvious of these are, How did the crackerbox compositions come to be in Dover, and why?

Unfortunately, there are no certain answers to these questions. Yet, the combined weight of knowledge at this time strongly suggests certain possibilities. These possibilities lead into areas covered in the next chapter.

Table 3

**Anthems Sung during the
Wolle-Kampmann
Pastorates**

Sung 28 March 1842
Hark Ten Thousand voices

Sung 25 December 1842
Lobsinget heut und bringet
Dank und Rühm

Sung 9 April 1843
O Bethanien, du Friedenshütten

Sung 1 August 1847
Be Joyful in God all ye lands (D)
Dank, Anbetung, Lob und
Ehre Sey dir (D)

Sung 23 April 1848
Christians dismiss your fears

NOTES

1. At present the contents of only two such congregation collections have been published: Frances Cumnock, ed., *Catalog of the Salem Congregation Collection* (Chapel Hill: University of North Carolina Press, 1980); and Robert Steelman, ed., *Catalog of the Lititz Congregation Collection* (Chapel Hill: University of North Carolina Press, 1981).

2. Donald M. McCorkle, "Church Attics and Crackerboxes," *Bulletin of the Moravian Music Foundation* 5 (Spring–Summer 1961): 2.

3. Lenz, p. 8. "Moravian Church of Dover, Ohio [Dover First]," MS, Dover Church.

4. Rau and David, *Music by American Moravians*, p. 112ff.

5. Interview with Dr. Robert Steelman, Moravian Archives, Bethlehem, Pa., 22 August 1982. (Notations to this effect in Steelman's hand can be found on a photocopy of a catalog of the Bethlehem collection located at the Moravian Music Foundation.)

6. This is so because the music never appears in any of the known catalogs of the Bethlehem Collection.

7. Rau and David, *Music by American Moravians*, p. 111.

8. H. H. Hacker, *Nazareth Hall* (Bethlehem, Pa., 1910).

9. It is possible that anthems sung at Sharon 24 December 1817 were crackerbox items. Unfortunately, the diary entries for these services give no titles.

14
THE CRACKERBOX AND OTHER OHIO COLLECTIONS

Information provided in chapter eight indicates that, while choral singing did occur prior to the arrival of Herman Julius Tietze, it was not until his pastorate that church choirs were established. Consequently, the need for large amounts of choral music would not exist until 1837. From this time on, however, much choral music was necessary.

As usual music was acquired through copying: "We apply this day to looking for musical pieces for passion week and Easter and to write them out for rehearsal with our music class, which brings us much pleasure."[1] Tietze's musical sources were three-fold. One was a new chorale-book: "The change of the year was observed in the manner which is customary with us, first Lord, Lord God, (from Peter Wolle's Choralbuch) was sung by the choir."[2] The Wolle text to which Tietze refers was published in 1836.[3] "Lord, Lord God" occurs on page 140 and is an anthem by Christian Gregor.

The Wolle book was a major contribution to nineteenth-century Moravian musical life and was constantly used in Ohio for many years.[4] It was an excellent source from which to select music, but it was quite limited. Fully two-thirds of the text consists of four-part chorale settings and service music. The remaining material includes anthems and duets for the major parts of the church year and festival pieces. While the last category contains four pieces, there is one anthem apiece for Passion Week, Easter and Christmas.

In addition to the Wolle text, Tietze had his own private music library. Following in the tradition of his eighteenth-century predecessors, Tietze maintained the Moravian ministerial tradition of copying, or otherwise securing, musical scores. When he married Susan Stotz, her musical library was combined with his to create a collection of nearly eight hundred separate items.[5]

While the Tietze Collection contains some anthems, the majority of its contents are keyboard compositions and vocal solos. Thus, the library would have been quite helpful when sacred solos were needed, but it did not appreciably help the need for choral literature. Another source was available for this, namely, the crackerbox collection.

We must assume that crackerbox items sung in 1820 were still at Gnadenhutten when Tietze arrived. These were probably placed in his care, but since they represented festival music they were not of immediate value. They may, however, have given Tietze the idea to request music from Bethlehem.

As mentioned in chapter nine, the Tietzes were heavily involved in the Bethlehem music program. Therefore, they were friends with musicians who had access to the Bethlehem Collection. Consequently, it would have been a simple matter for Tietze to request anthems from these people.[6]

Travel between Ohio and Bethlehem was active, and music requests could easily be filled within a month of their having been made. In fact, a well-known musician did a great deal of travelling during the period Tietze would be requesting anthems, that is, from 1837 to 1840. He would have been the most likely conduit through which requests could be made and filled. This individual was Israel Ricksecker!

Interestingly, the Ricksecker name keeps reappearing in connection with the crackerbox. The appearance of Peter Ricksecker compositions in the collection is suggestive. Also, Peter Ricksecker had access to the Bethlehem collection. Once it was reorganized by C. F. Seidel in 1849, Ricksecker was engaged to make a copy of the German titles,[7] Ricksecker's work provides the evidence Steelman employed in suggesting that the Dover material had gone to Ohio by 1849. This fact points to Ricksecker involvement.

The quartet materials mentioned in chapter thirteen were just the type of music sung by Israel Ricksecker's son, Julius, in the late nineteenth century. Typical was a Uhrichsville concert given by several Dover Moravians in 1879.[8] In this concert Julius not only sang a bass solo, but performed in two quartets (one SATB, the other TTBB). While these particular quartets are not found in the crackerbox collection, those that are, are exactly the same type.

The vast majority of crackerbox contents are sacred pieces. There are, however, eight secular compositions. These are soprano arias from Joseph Haydn's *The Seasons*.[9] Of these, six contain flute parts, or indications of "Flute tacet." This is just the type of literature one would expect to find in the home of Lizette and Israel Ricksecker, as both had figured prominently in Bethlehem performances of this work.

The scenario that presents itself is this. Israel Ricksecker probably carried Tietze's requests for anthems to Bethlehem. He may even have had a hand in the selection process. Upon Israel's return to Ohio the music was given to Tietze, who maintained the collection at Gnadenhutten. When the Tietzes left Ohio, Ricksecker was probably entrusted with the Bethlehem music. At some point in the late nineteenth century, after the music had ceased to be of value, the collection was stored in the crackerbox and placed in the church attic. At present the best guess on when this storage took place was some time between Israel Ricksecker's death in 1872 and the turn of the century.

There is in Gnadenhutten, a small group of manuscripts that appear to be the remnants of a congregation collection. The contents of this collection can be found in table 4.

Although these pieces have a similar appearance to the crackerbox collection, they are actually quite different. There are four anthems by typical Moravian composers, LaTrobe, Freydt, Gregor and Reichardt.[10] In addition, there are several manuscript copies of hymns, including the Hagen and Mason pieces, and those marked (?).

Francis Florentine Hagen was the best of the late nineteenth-century Moravian composers and the hymn found in table 4 is the most famous of his compositions in this genre. It is usually performed during the Christmas Eve lovefeast. The Gnadenhutten collection contains a rare 1857 organist copy, plus two hand copied choral parts, one for tenor and one for bass. These copies, plus the soprano part for "Thou Child Divine," are very helpful in dating the period during which the collection was employed.

Chapter ten states that Horace Eggenberg performed with three other individuals at the Uhrichsville Christmas Eve service in 1878.[11] Two of the works this quartet sang were "Thou Child Divine" and "Morning Star." It would appear that the copies of these pieces found in the Gnadenhutten

Table 4

The
Gnadenhutten
Collection

Johann Ludwig Freydt	Seh Ich in deinen Seelenschmerzen
Christian Gregor	Glory to God in the Highest
Christian I. LaTrobe	Glory to Him, who is the Resurrection
Johann Reichardt	Unto you is born a Savior
Francis F. Hagen	The Morning Star
Lowell Mason	From Greenland's Icy Mountains
?	Hark! What mean these Holy Voices?
?	Thou Child Divine

collection are the ones used at the Uhrichsville service. Obviously, Gnadenhutten was still maintaining a manuscript collection as late as 1878.

At present, citations for the other items in table 4 have not been located. It would seem safe to assume that the four anthems were "left overs" from the crackerbox collection that were somehow separated from the main collection when it moved to Dover. Yet, the 1849 catalogs of the Bethlehem collection do not support this belief. Copies of the Freydt and Gregor anthems currently exist in the Bethlehem collection. Therefore, if the Gnadenhutten items came from Bethlehem they were copied from the Bethlehem holdings. The LaTrobe and Reichardt compositions did not exist in the Bethlehem collection prior to 1849. However, the Reichardt piece contains a notation in C. F. Seidel's hand that is dated 1856. Seidel had access to the Bethlehem collection and his note indicates that he sent pieces that were copied from the collection well after 1849.

The above information indicates that after Tietze left Gnadenhutten in 1841 a congregation collection was maintained at Gnadenhutten and that this collection was probably preserved into the early twentieth century.

NOTES

1. Allen P. Zimmerman, trans., Diaries of the congregations of Sharon and Gnadenhutten, 8 February 1838, John Heckewelder Memorial Moravian Church, Gnadenhutten, Ohio.

2. Allen P. Zimmerman, trans., Diaries of the congregations of Sharon and Gnadenhutten, 31 December 1837, John Heckewelder Memorial Moravian Church, Gnadenhutten, Ohio.

3. Peter Wolle, *Hymn Tunes, Used in the Church of the United Brethren, Arranged for Four Voices and the Organ or Piano-forte* (Boston: Shepley and Wright, 1836).

4. Copies of this book can be found in the music holdings of several Ohio churches. Gnadenhutten has a well-used copy of the 1872 reprint.

5. See chap. 9, n. 3.

6. That the crackerbox collection was primarily intended to fill a need for anthems can be gleaned from its contents. Of the almost 189 items in the collection, fully 158 are anthems that would be appropriate for the major celebrations of the church year.

7. The English titles were copied by Daniel (?) Steinhauer.

8. Diary of the First Moravian Church of Uhrichsville, Ohio, 21 October 1879, Uhrichsville, Ohio.

9. See p. 00.

10. Christian Ignatious LaTrobe and Christian Gregor are both important Moravian composers who have been discussed elsewhere in this text. Johann Ludwig Freydt and Johann Friedrich Reichardt were not Moravians, but their music was well liked by Moravian musicians. Because of this one would expect to find music by Freydt and Reichardt in any typical Moravian music collection.

11. Diary of the First Congregation of Uhrichsville, Ohio, 24 December 1878, Uhrichsville, Ohio.

PART FIVE

*The Early
Twentieth Century
(1900–1944)*

15

IMPORTANT MUSICIANS

WILBUR O. DEMUTH

Born in 1879 Wilbur Oliver Demuth attended Oberlin Conservatory of Music and earned a Bachelor's degree. He did not wish to teach music, however, and returned to Tuscarawas County to work in his family's greenhouse business. The greenhouses were located near Seventeen, Ohio, so, like many of his neighbors, Demuth attended Sharon Moravian Church. In 1916 he and his wife (the former Alice McCreary) moved to Gnadenhutten where he served the church in many ways over the next fifty years.

Demuth devoted a large amount of time to civic activities, serving on the Gnadenhutten town council, as village mayor and schoolboard member. He was an organizer of Indian Village Federal Savings & Loan and the Bowerston Shale Company. He served the latter company as president, a position he held until retirement in 1946.

As a vocalist, Demuth sang with a tender, sweet tenor voice.[1] His repertory ran the gamut of musical types including Ira Sankey's, "The Ninety and Nine," the mandatory Mother's Day solo, "Mother, o'Mine," and the standard religious solos. A loyal choir member, he also served as choir director when needed. Although he seems not to have been a commanding director, his groups realized the love he had for his church, for the music they were performing, and for their individual efforts. Because of this his choirs were able to create some excellent performances.

Although Demuth was not trained as a wind instrumentalist, he could play all of the brass instruments. In 1932 the regular trombone choir director had failed to provide an ensemble for the Watchnight service. Because of this Pastor Robert Brennecke asked Demuth to conduct the instrumentalists on Easter. Working in his methodical way Demuth began rehearsals 19 February 1933 almost two months before Easter. His efforts bore fruit as the town was awakened Easter morning by a brass choir of twenty-five people![2]

Demuth's son Roy remembers that his father left nothing to chance. Roy, like a few other trombonists, did not read music very well. These musicians found position numbers penciled in their music. Thus, if they did not read music, they could still find the proper notes.[3]

Demuth was an accomplished violinist. Unfortunately, his wife did not like that instrument, at least not when he played alone in their home. Therefore, when he practiced he did so on the back porch, with the door closed, in order to respect her privacy. With the arrival of Pastor Frederick R. Nitzschke in 1922 Demuth gained a fellow instrumentalist. Nitzschke was a violinist also and throughout his pastorate he and Demuth regularly performed duets.[4]

When Wilbur Demuth died 8 June 1965 he left a rich musical legacy that is still remembered with great fondness.

FRANK C. WINSCH

Frank Cessna Winsch was the son of Lewis and Anne C. Blickensderfer Winsch.[5] Born in 1869 Frank Winsch was serving the Gnadenhutten church as choir director by 1897. Although this position was occasionally occupied by others Pastor James Gross could state that, at his death in 1956, Winsch was the primary director for over fifty years.[6]

Winsch has been praised by those who worked with him for his directing ability. He was apparently the type of director who could bring out the best in his ensembles regardless of the talent of its individual members.[7] Normally, Winsch's choirs performed the typical church music of the period, however, he would occasionally demand more extended compositions such as the "Gloria" from Mozart's *Twelfth Mass* and the Dubois *Seven Last Words*.

As part of the New Year's Eve festivities for 1897 the Gnadenhutten choir performed the cantata *Queen Esther* at the town hall. A local teacher, Mr. O. Luethi, conducted the performance since one of the major parts, that of Haman, was taken by Frank Winsch.[8]

Although Winsch did sing solos, he was more likely to be found performing in local groups. One such ensemble was a male quartet that sang for various occasions in the early twentieth century; it consisted of Winsch, R. L. Frazier (sometime Gnadenhutten choir director and school teacher), Wilbur Demuth, and [H. McCellen] McConnell.[9]

Frank Winsch served the church and community in various capacities that touched on music. At one time or other he was chorister, chairman of the music committee for the 125th anniversary, trombone choir member, trombone choir director, and president of the Ohio Moravian Historical Society.

His work with the trombone choir began by 1898 when he is listed as a participant in the Easter services. He performed with the ensemble from that point on, becoming director by 1928.

Frank's brother, Charles Clement also played in the trombone choir for many years. Charles Winsch died in 1941 at the age of eighty-one years. When his brother Frank departed this world in 1956, a name that stretched back to Gnadenhutten's first choir disappeared from the church's musical ranks.

THEO SCHUG

During the first forty years of the twentieth century the musical life of the Uhrichsville Moravian church became a significant part of twin-cities cultural life.[10] Throughout this period Theo Schug was a major participant in his church's music program.

Schug was born at Port Washington in 1880 and moved to Uhrichsville in 1908. His earliest documented participation in the Uhrichsville music program occurred 22 December 1909 when he is listed as the vice director of the choir, serving under Horace Eggenberg. After this Schug is frequently mentioned as vocal soloist, member of various vocal ensembles, and choir director. He may have assumed the directorship as early as 1919, when he led the choir in Ashford's cantata *Resurrection Light*. He was definitely the choir director by 1926 and seems to have maintained that position until the early 1940s.

Possessing a strong voice of good quality he continued to perform vocal solos at various churches up to a month before his death 25 November 1943.

THE FIDLER FAMILY

As mentioned in chapter ten various members of this family could be found in both the Uhrichsville and Port Washington Moravian churches. Of particular interest in the twentieth century are Benjamin and Edith, children of Erastus and Caroline Fidler.[11]

Benjamin Carlton Fidler was born at Port Washington 7 August 1873. At the age of sixteen he took a job as car wheel inspector in the railroad yards at Dennison and apparently moved to that town.[12] Sometime prior to 1897 he married Rose Becker of Fry's Valley. This union produced a daughter Kathleen Eva (b. 1897), and a son Carlton Benjamin (b. 1906). Sometime during 1906 the family moved to Port Washington where Fidler became choir director.[13]

Early in 1907 the family either returned to Dennison, or moved to Uhrichsville, for they transferred their membership to the Uhrichsville Moravian church. At Uhrichsville Fidler became active in the choral program, singing in the church choir, a male choir, and in vocal duets with Theo Schug.

The Uhrichsville diary of 7 June 1912 indicates that a "Fidler Family Band" provided music for an evening service. No names are mentioned, but it undoubtedly was the Benjamin Fidler family that is intended. The "band" was probably a trio consisting of Ben, his wife and their fifteen-year-old daughter, Kathleen Eva. At six years of age it is doubtful that son Carlton Benjamin played in the group.

Eventually, the family moved to Arizona, although the exact date is unknown. Benjamin died there 14 January 1917 and the family returned to Ohio. Mrs. Fidler joined the Uhrichsville church in 1917, but subsequently settled in Port Washington.

Edith Fidler was born at Port Washington 5 October 1890. A good musician, she became the Port Washington organist by 1905, when she was only fifteen. Nothing is known about the first organ on which she played. However, on 21 May 1905 the Port Washington Church dedicated a new pipe organ. It was a two-manual Hook and Hastings organ, with pedal board, and contained ten stops. The dedication of the instrument included the Gnadenhutten choir, which sang the anthem "I Waited on the Lord" under Frank Winsch's leadership, and several organists who presided at the new instrument.[14] Among these were Mrs. Mary Moore (wife of Pastor O. Eugene Moore), John Moore (the pastor's son), Mrs. Maud Gram, Miss Anna Gram, Theodore Van Vleck, and Edith Fidler.

No music titles are listed in a news article of the event printed in the *Democratic Times* but an interesting comment relating to Miss Fidler states that a relative of hers "gave largely to the purchase of the organ."[15] Edith Fidler's abilities as an organist can be gleaned from the following comment made by Pastor William H. Fluck, "Miss Edith is a very efficient organist and is deserving of more than the congregation can ever give. She is worth a good salary."[16]

The Fidler family, including Edith, moved to Ft. Lauderdale, Florida, in 1912, and she seems never to have returned to Ohio.

BEN AND GEORGIA HILL CUNNING

Ben Walton Cunning was born in 1886 at Tuscarawas, Ohio. His family had been active in the Sharon church for some years, and he attended Sunday School there. He went on the stage as a young man touring the country as an actor. Playing in various stock companies he eventually moved into Shakespearean parts. His parents transferred their membership from Sharon to Dover First in 1919, and when Ben returned to the Valley he followed them, being confirmed there in 1924.

Georgia Hill Cunning was the daughter of P. W. and Sarah (Winsch) Hill. She was an excellent organist and served Dover First for twenty-two years, beginning in 1910. While at Dover First she was the student of Dr. Albert Riemenschneider, Director of the Conservatory of Music at Baldwin-Wallace College.[17] From him she received a thorough grounding in the traditional organ literature, especially the music of Johann Sebastian Bach.

Georgia Hill and Ben Cunning were married 15 December 1926 and together they formed a musical team that was of importance to the Dover area. Mrs. Cunning left her Dover post in 1932 and moved to the First Presbyterian Church in New Philadelphia. Six years later she entered Lakewood Hospital in Lakewood, Ohio for a mastoid operation. Unfortunately, she contracted an infection and died 24 January 1938.

After his wife's death Ben moved to Sugarcreek, Ohio and remarried.

FREDERICK R. NITZSCHKE

Nitzschke graduated from Moravian Seminary in 1894. The same year witnessed the call to his first pastorate and his marriage to Grace M. Blickensderfer of Bethlehem. From 1913 to 1926 he was editor of a periodical that is now known as *The Moravian Missionary*.[18]

Together with his fellow Ohio pastor, M. F. Oerter of Sharon, Nitzschke served on the Hymnal Revision Committee of the Moravian Church. This committee eventually produced the 1923 *Hymnal*,[19] which served the church until it was replaced by the present 1969 *Hymnal*.[20]

As a composer Nitzschke wrote several hymn tunes. One of them, "Grace," appears in the current Hymnal. It was composed in 1908 while he was serving the Moravian church in Elizabeth, New Jersey. Although he is supposed to have written several hymn tunes, no others are known to the writer. Also, there is no evidence that any compositional activities took place in Ohio.

Nitzschke was a gifted musician whose violin performance is remembered by many people as having a sweet, lyrical quality.[21] The pastor would occasionally perform solos in church, but his most pleasant moments were spent performing violin duets with Wilbur Demuth.[22] The two regularly played for their own pleasure during church services and for the Sunday School.

At one point in his pastorate, Nitzschke served as choir director at Gnadenhutten High School.[23] This began in 1925, and by 1927 his work included the choral program in grades five through eight. Nitzschke did not have certification in music. According to Mrs. Helen Demuth this was not a problem until his high school choir won a district contest.[24] A fellow choir director took umbrage at being beaten by an uncertified colleague. A disagreement occurred and Nitzschke's choir was not permitted to receive its award.

It was Nitzschke who started the first junior choir to be mentioned in Gnadenhutten records. The group was quite active during his pastorate, singing often during church services, with a very promising young pianist, Ruth Peter, as its accompanist.[25]

EUGENE LIGHTELL

Eugene Lightell was the leader of the instrumental music program at Dover First throughout the early twentieth century. Born in Uhrichsville, he worked for the Reeves Steel and Manufacturing Company of Dover for over twenty years. Although a lifelong Methodist, he was director of the Sunday School orchestra and trombone choir at Dover First for twenty-five years.

The first mention of Lightell in the Dover First records is 4 March 1921 when he led the Sunday School orchestra in a concert. Two months later he performed as a member of the first trombone choir to serve at Dover in thirty years. It performed for the church's anniversary, which was celebrated 15 May 1921. The ensemble consisted of Charles Miksch and Frank Winsch of Gnadenhutten, Maud and Florence Gray of New Philadelphia, and Dover members Lightell, Alexander, Thomas, Kessler, and Smith.[26]

Lightell's position as leader of the trombone choir was a natural one since he was also a member of the Dover Cornet Band. Through his efforts the trombone choir became an active part of Dover First church life.

When Lightell died 5 July 1945 it was truly the end of an era in Dover First's musical life.

THE EVERETT FAMILY

Fry's Valley records identify no less than five musically active Everetts. Taken in roughly chronological order they were Florence, Harold, Annabelle, Isabelle, and Shelba. Florence, Harold, and Isabelle are all children of William and Elizabeth (Chappelear) Everett. Annabelle is the daughter of Floyd and Laura (Rank) Everett, while Shelba is the daughter of C. Eugene and Wilmer (Miller) Everett.

Florence was organist at Fry's Valley from the 1920s until 1933. In that year she married William T. Hannon of Pittsburgh, Pennsylvania and they left the valley. In addition to her expertise on the organ Florence was proficient on the violin, often playing in an instrumental ensemble that included Harold Everett, Pastor Robert E. Clewell, and the pastor's wife Mamie.

Isabelle and Annabelle rose through the ranks, as it were. Beginning in the Sunday School program they became Sunday School pianist and assistant Sunday School pianist, respectively. They performed piano duets in church and accompanied various vocal soloists. By 1934 Annabelle had become the assistant organist, but her activities ceased with her marriage to Edwin Stevenson in 1939.

After Annabelle's departure Isabelle Everett continued to rise in the church's musical program until she became church organist in 1941. She served in this capacity until 1950 when her husband, Fry's Valley Pastor Karl Bregenzer, accepted a call to the Moravian church in Berea, Minnesota.

Shelba also moved from Sunday School pianist to church organist. She served as an assistant organist until her marriage to Jack Lambert in 1960.

THE KAISER FAMILY

A second Fry's Valley musical family was the Kaiser family. Miss Naomi Kaiser appears to have been the church organist in 1896 and 1897. She married Ira Shull in 1898 and left the valley shortly thereafter. Church records say very little about her except that she was given a music book in appreciation of her services.[27]

The next individuals of this name to appear are Daniel L. Kaiser and his wife, the former Viola Cedella Fox. The Kaisers were married in 1891 and became active members of the Fry's Valley church. Mr. and Mrs. Kaiser served as vocal soloists and, when the occasion demanded, formed a quartet choir with Paster and Mrs. Clewell.

Mrs. Kaiser and her daughter Anne often sang duets for church services and socials. Anne married Charles Montague in 1927 and they remained members at Fry's Valley. During the 1930s Mrs. Montague served as Sunday School pianist, assistant organist and, from 1933 to 1941, as church organist.

Throughout this time she continued to do a great deal of vocal work, singing duets with her mother and Mrs. Dorothy Gross, wife of Pastor Reuben Gross. In 1947 the Montagues transferred to Gnadenhutten and she ceased to be as intensely involved in music, although she still sang occasionally.

NELLIE ZOE PETER

Oliver Louis Peter was a grandson of David Peter and Susanna Leinbach.[28] He married Sarah M. Crouch in 1870 and that union produced three children, one of whom was Nellie Zoe Peter. Zoe, as she was known, was born at Uhrichsville 23 May 1885, two years after her parents left Gnadenhutten.

Her name first appears in the Uhrichsville diary in connection with a 1896 concert given at the church.[29] A newsclipping that apparently reviews the concert states, "Miss Zoe Peter is beginning to handle the violin in a manner that bespeaks for her a future and exceptional degree mastery [sic]. Her solo was an interesting feature of the program."[30]

The eleven-year-old girl described in the above review rapidly developed into a serious musician. In addition to violin she studied piano and organ. Her progress on the organ was such that she was elected assistant organist in 1900, when she was only fifteen years old. By 1905 she is listed as the Uhrichsville Moravian Church organist. She was a vocalist as well, singing in duets, trios, and probably in the choir. Her work at Uhrichsville, however, was interrupted by studies at the Chicago Conservatory of Music.

After returning home she again assumed the organ bench and apparently the choir directorship also. During the 1910s Uhrichsville had a very strong Sunday School orchestra and Zoe Peter was a member of the group, if not the director. She frequently performed in public as soloist and in various string ensembles.

Zoe Peter served as organist and choir director until 1931, in which year she accepted the position of organist at the Dennison Presbyterian church. Unfortunately, she died on 3 January 1932, shortly after beginning her new position.

THE REUBEN GROSS FAMILY

When Reuben Gross and his bride Dorothy Smoyer Gross arrived in 1934 Fry's Valley was experiencing difficulty with its choral organizations. Taking matters in hand Gross established a singing school within five days of his arrival. The next month he was elected chorister in the Sunday School and, thus, found himself in charge of the total vocal music program of the church.

His choir was ready for public scrutiny by November 1934 when a group of thirteen people, including the pastor and the organist, Mrs. Anne Montague, sang at the Thanksgiving service that month. It was Gross's concern that the choir provide leadership in hymn-singing. Therefore, the "anthems" at the above service were two hymns taken from the Hymnal.[31]

Throughout his Ohio career, Gross often sang the typical religious solos of the period. In addition to these he frequently participated in duets with his wife. She, in turn, performed duets with others, especially Isabelle Everett.

The yoking of Fry's Valley and Port Washington in 1936 provided Gross with a congregation that had always had a wealth of organists, but an inconsistent choral program. When Gross became pastor three organists were serving: Leona Stocker,[32] who was the organist, and Sadie Cappel and Louise Weingarth, who were the assistants. Since Mrs. Stocker was the main organist she was also the choir director.[33] Even with her work the choir's performances were not always at the level Gross expected. Therefore, he began to help out. Success came within a year for he was able to conduct a cantata entitled *When Jesus Was Born* Christmas Eve 1937.

After Ohio, Gross settled in the Bethlehem area and became an active supporter of the Early American Moravian Music Festivals. He was the executive secretary for the 1950 Festival, and held the same post, plus dean of the seminar faculty, for the 1954 and 1957 Festivals. In addition he also sang in the festival choirs for many years.

NOTES

1. Interview with Ruth Peter Pfeiffer, Dover, Ohio, 2 July 1985.
2. Diary of the Gnadenhutten Moravian Church, 16 April 1933, John Heckewelder Memorial Moravian Church, Gnadenhutten, Ohio.
3. Interview with Roy and Helen Demuth, Gnadenhutten, Ohio, 3 February 1983.
4. Diary [of the Gnadenhutten Moravian Congregation], vol. 15, 10 October 1928, John Heckewelder Memorial Moravian Church, Gnadenhutten, Ohio.
5. See chap. 10.
6. Gnadenhutten Church Book, Death Register, 29 September 1956, John Heckewelder Memorial Moravian Church, Gnadenhutten, Ohio.
7. Interview with Ruth Peter Pfeiffer, Dover, Ohio, 2 July 1985.
8. The Gnadenhutten Church Diary, vol. 7, 31 December 1897, John Heckewelder Memorial Moravian Church, Gnadenhutten, Ohio.
9. Diary of the John Heckewelder Memorial Moravian Church, 13 May 1906, Gnadenhutten, Ohio. The first names of these individuals are not given in the diary entry. However, there are no other individuals who could have participated.
10. Because of their immediate proximity, Uhrichsville and Dennison are referred to as the twin cities.
11. See chap. 10.
12. "Dennison," Dover, Ohio, *Daily Iron Valley Reporter,* 3 October 1889, p. 3.
13. Diary of the First Moravian Congregation, 5 December 1906, Port Washington, Ohio.
14. Ibid., 21 May 1905.
15. Presently it is not possible to identify this relative.
16. Diary of the First Moravian Congregation, 25 December 1906, Port Washington, Ohio.
17. Interview with Regina Lenz and Florence Gray, Dover, Ohio, 19 February 1983.
18. "Obituary," *The Moravian,* 28 February 1944.
19. *Hymnal and Liturgies of the Moravian Church (Unitas Fratrum)* (Bethlehem, Pa.: Provincial Synod, 1920). Although the date 1920 appears on the title page, the hymnal was not actually printed until 1923. Thus, it is usually referred to as the 1923 *Hymnal.*
20. *Hymnal and Liturgies of the Moravian Church* (Chicago: Rayner Lithographing Co., 1969).
21. Interview with Ruth Peter Pfeiffer, Dover, Ohio, 2 July 1985.
22. Comments to this effect appear frequently in Nitzschke's diaries.
23. Later he also taught music in the Tuscarawas School system.
24. Interview with Roy and Helen Demuth, Gnadenhutten, Ohio, 17 February 1983.
25. Ruth Peter would become Mrs. Carl Pfeiffer and will be discussed in chap. 18.
26. Unfortunately, the Dover members are listed by last name only. It has not been possible to put first names with last. Some may not have been church members at all, but members of the Dover Cornet Band.
27. Pulpit Register and Diary of Fry's Valley Moravian Church, no. 1, 11 April 1897, Fry's Valley, Ohio.
28. See chap. 10, p. 26.
29. [Uhrichsville Church Diary], 30 September 1896, Uhrichsville, Ohio.

30. "Musical Entertainment," 1896 (?) (Unidentified newsclipping found in the Uhrichsville Church Diary.)

31. The hymns were No. 864, "O Praise Jehovah," and No. 861, "Come ye Thankful People Come," as found in the 1923 *Hymnal*.

32. Mrs. Stocker would become Mrs. Homer Arth and will be discussed in chap. 19.

33. Interview with Leona Arth, Port Washington, Ohio, 2 July 1985.

16

THE ANCIENT TRADITION

The *Collegium Musicum*, or music society, originated in German universities. *Collegia* were quite popular in the seventeenth and eighteenth centuries as they provided an opportunity for amateurs to perform instrumental music. The Moravian minister, Christopher Pyrlaeus, established the institution in America when he created a *Collegium Musicum* at Bethlehem in 1744.[1] It was so successful that *Collegia* were established at the Moravian centers of Lititz (1765), Nazareth (ca. 1780), and Salem (1786).[2]

The Moravian *Collegia* served several functions: accompanying sacred choral works and oratorios, playing symphonic and chamber music, as well as providing some musical instruction. Their usefulness decreased with the rise of civic orchestras and public concerts, and all *Collegia* ceased to exist by the middle of the nineteenth century.

Apparently there never was a *Collegium Musicum* in Ohio. No music is known to exist for such an ensemble and the term is never used in any church records. Yet, certain groups found in the twentieth century seem to have operated in the spirit, if not actual fact, of the ancient tradition.

By far the most active and public of these twentieth-century groups were the ensembles that centered around Gnadenhutten pastor, Frederick R. Nitzschke. At times these were only violin duos consisting of Nitzschke and Wilbur O. Demuth, but very often they were trios of two violins and a pianist, or organist. When he was in town, Olin Pfeiffer's cornet made a quartet.

In roughly chronological order, the pianists would have been Mrs. Mary Demuth Van Vleck Wohlwend, Mrs. Ruth Peter Pfeiffer, Nitzschke's daughter Eleanor, and Mrs. Elizabeth Ebenhack. The repertoire of the group consisted of standard literature by Pleyel, Mazas, Farmer, Dancla, Danaluis, Mozart, Brigo, Lerrare, and Maehlig.

Aside from performance for private pleasure the Nitzschke groups performed at high school graduation ceremonies, local Farmer's Institutes, PTA meetings, for other Moravian churches, and generally throughout the community. They also played regularly for the Gnadenhutten Sunday School, thereby influencing future generations of Moravian musicians.

Another such group existed at Fry's Valley and centered around Pastor Robert E. Clewell (1926–34). Generally, it included the pastor (violin), Mrs. Clewell (piano), Florence Everett (violin), and Harold Everett (cornet). In addition to these one could also find Annabelle Everett, Isabel Rank, Mrs. Anne Montague, or Mrs. Helen Everett. These ensembles seem to have been more freely organized than the Nitzschke groups, and more for private enjoyment than public notice.

A strictly parsonage family ensemble was maintained during the pastorates of Edwin Kortz (Sharon, 1936–41) and Robert Brennecke (Gnadenhutten, 1931–41). The members consisted of Margaret Schwarze Kortz (violin), Mrs. Fannie Brennecke (piano), and another family member who played the cello. Unfortunately, the latter individual cannot be identified. It does not appear that this was a regularly rehearsing group, but merely one that played when social visits occurred.

One family ensemble was of some importance in the Moravian confines of Tuscarawas County. The Horace Reed family moved to Dover from Cincinnati in 1929. Dr. Reed, his wife Frances, and their year-old daughter Frances Anne had been members of Immanuel Presbyterian Church in Cincinnati. They quickly joined Dover First and Dr. Reed became active in the choral program.

A second daughter, Sue, was born in Dover and both girls were participants in Dover First's music program from an early age. Eventually the girls and their mother began to perform as a trio. Anne played the violin, Sue the cello, and their mother the piano. The "Reed trio" as it was called by Pastor Roy Grams, did a great deal of playing for various church functions, vesper services, and other auxiliary programs.

While it is true that none of the ensembles mentioned in this chapter conform to the complete requirements of the eighteenth-century *Collegia*, they do indicate that, even in the twentieth century, the Moravian church's emphasis on music kept alive the spirit of instrumental performance. The most obvious example of the influence of the *Collegia* are the many church orchestras found among the ensembles that appear in the Ohio congregations. In 1909 the Gnadenhutten diary states that an orchestra assisted at Sunday School exercises. One year later it accompanied a choir of twenty-five voices in a performance of the Christmas cantata *Prophecy and Fulfillment*.[3]

Eventually each Ohio Moravian church established its own orchestra during the early twentieth century. Depending on the church these orchestras served various functions. For most, however, they were associated with the Sunday School program, performing during the Sunday School hour and accompanying pageants and programs given by various Sunday School groups.

During the period 1912–17 Uhrichsville had a particularly active orchestra. It participated in church concerts playing various types of secular music and arrangements of well-known hymns. Often it combined with the church choir to present concerted music. Following Moravian tradition it occasionally accompanied singing during Sunday services. Since Uhrichsville's congregation always had difficulty maintaining its own brass ensemble, the orchestra would take the place of trombones at Watchnight services. Sometime after 1917 the orchestra seems to have been disbanded as it is not mentioned again until 1925, when the diary refers to it as "our new orchestra."[4]

During the Nitzschke pastorate (1922–31) Gnadenhutten enjoyed many fine orchestral performances. Wasting no time Nitzschke had organized a church orchestra soon after his arrival in July 1922. The earliest group consisted of Nitzschke, Robert Petry, Olin Pfeiffer, and Carrie Seiss, and performed in October 1922. Since Seiss was a pianist, Pfeiffer a cornetist, and Nitzschke a violinist, Petry is the only person to whom we cannot attach an instrument.

By 1923 Nitzschke was conducting the orchestra for Gnadenhutten High School commencements. These orchestras were not very large ensembles, but virtually always consisted of Moravians. Thanks to a very complete program printed for the 1924 commencement we can indicate, in a general way, the type of literature performed at such gatherings. As the reader can observe in table 5 the music is typical of the period.

The diaries rarely give much information concerning church orchestra instrumentation. Thus, we are grateful to the Fry's Valley diarist who indicates that the church had an orchestra of six instrumentalists with piano in 1930.[5] Also, Pastor Nitzschke kindly informs us that he frequently worked with an orchestra of two violins, one cornet, and a piano. By 1928, however, his orchestra consisted of several brass, strings, and a saxophone.[6]

The two churches that seem to have maintained the most consistent

Table 5

Compositions Performed by the
Nitzschke Orchestra at the
1924 GHS Commencement

Determination Overture	Poet's Dream
Tuxedo March	Gibraltar Overture
Merry Makers	

orchestral programs were Gnadenhutten and Dover First. The former received excellent training during the 1920s at the hands of Olin Pfeiffer and
Pastor Nitzschke, while the latter was led by Eugene Lightell. When Lightell died in 1945 Ruth Pfohl Grams became the ensemble's director, and
continued the church's excellent instrumental tradition.

Port Washington appears to have maintained an orchestra in 1917–18. At
least, this seems to be the implication of diary entries for these years, which
state that an orchestra played for the Farmer's Institute.[7]

Sharon's orchestra existed primarily during the 1920s. The first mention of
the ensemble occurs 24 November 1921. The citizens of Tuscarawas, Ohio
held a Community Thanksgiving Day service at the town hall and Pastor
M. F. Oerter observes "our Sunday School orchestra furnished music."[8] The
last diary entry to mention a Sharon orchestra, called "Sharon's Jr. Orchestra," is found in the Gnadenhutten diary 29 April 1933.[9] It indicates that
the group performed at the Tuscarawas County Moravian C. E. Spring Rally
which was held at Gnadenhutten that year.

Dover South maintained a church orchestra between 1930 and 1932. The
Trustee's Minutes for 1 November 1930 indicate that the Sunday School
orchestra director should receive payment for services rendered. A similar
notation is found in the minutes of 4 April 1932. Unfortunately, no other
references to a director, or ensemble, have been located.

The only Ohio church which seems not to have ever had a church orchestra was Schoenbrunn Community Church. Undoubtedly, this is due to
the fact that the church was begun after the "heyday" of Moravian orchestras. In any event, such an ensemble is never mentioned in its records.

NOTES

1. Lawrence Hartzell, "Musical Moravian Missionaries: Part I: Johann Christopher Pyrlaeus," *Moravian Music Journal* 29 (Winter 1984): 91–92.
2. Donald M. McCorkle, "The Moravian Contribution to American Music," *Moravian Music Foundation Publication, No. 1* (Winston-Salem, N.C.: Moravian Music Foundation, 1956), pp. 3–4.
3. Diary of the Congregation, Gnadenhutten, Ohio, vol. 9, 25 January 1909, John Heckewelder Memorial Moravian Church, Gnadenhutten, Ohio.
4. Diary of the Uhrichsville Congregation of the Moravian Church, 27 September 1925, Uhrichsville, Ohio.
5. Diary [of the] Fry's Valley Moravian Congregation, 10 August 1930, Fry's Valley, Ohio.
6. Diary [of the Gnadenhutten Moravian Congregation], vol. 15, 10 October 1928, John Heckewelder Memorial Moravian Church, Gnadenhutten, Ohio.
7. Diary 1907–22, 7 and 8 February 1917, Port Washington, Ohio.
8. Diary of the Sharon Moravian Church, 24 November 1921, Tuscarawas, Ohio.
9. Diary of the Gnadenhutten Moravian Congregation, 29 April 1933, John Heckewelder Memorial Moravian Church, Gnadenhutten, Ohio.

PART SIX

The Mid-Twentieth Century
(1944–1960)

17

MUSIC AND THE PARSONAGE FAMILY

It is a denominational characteristic of the Renewed Moravian Church that musical leadership in a congregation often emanates from the parsonage. Either the pastor, the pastor's wife, or other family members serve as catalysts for the total musical program. Ohio's congregations have tended to follow this pattern. At no time, however, were the Ohio parsonages as influential as during the twenty-year period immediately preceding the Ohio Moravian Music Festival. From 1941 to 1961, no less than twelve very musical parsonage families could be found within Ohio's Moravian churches. By far the most productive years were 1952–54 when all eight churches were served by musical families.[1]

THE GRAMS FAMILY

Prior to his Ohio pastorate, Roy Grams served the Moravian Church as editor of *The Moravian*, the Northern Province's chief publication. He took over this position in 1938, and in 1940 became editor of *The Moravian Missionary* as well. He resigned both positions, along with his Bethlehem pastorate, when he moved to Ohio in 1944.

Always a strong believer in civic responsibilities, Grams became involved in many Dover area projects. He served on the Board of Directors for the Tuscarawas Philharmonic Orchestra, was instrumental in the construction of a new building for the Dover Public Library (1954), and worked on many other city projects. These activities led the Chamber of Commerce to present the Dover Civic Award to both Roy and Ruth Grams 24 April 1957.

Ruth Pfohl Grams came from Winston-Salem, North Carolina. Her father, Bishop J. Kenneth Pfohl, played the flute and clarinet, while her mother, the former Bessie Whittington, was organist at Home Moravian Church for a number of years. Their six children, of whom Ruth was the third, demonstrated a predilection for music, and were given piano lessons by their mother. Ruth was introduced to the harp by the head of the violin department at Salem College and was immediately drawn to the instrument.[2]

Graduating from Salem College in 1927 Ruth taught in the public schools for several years. Moving north she studied harp with Carlos Salzedo at the Curtis Institute in Philadelphia, attended the Female Seminary at Bethlehem, and taught in the seminary's music department. This was followed by work on a Master's degree at the University of Michigan, where she became Head of the Harp Department.

Shortly after arriving in Ohio Ruth Grams began to concertize, an activity that would be continued throughout her husband's pastorate. Eventually, she would play harp concerti with the Wooster Symphony, Kent State University Symphony, and Tuscarawas Philharmonic. She also presented recitals at such places as Canton, Newcomerstown, Cambridge, and Coshocton.

In 1946 she assumed directorhsip of both the junior and intermediate choirs at Dover First. She also established and directed the chapel choir which was begun in 1947 and served as the "feeder" group for the adult choir.

The year 1947 saw her assume the leadership of Dover First's trombone choir. Dover First diaries are quite specific about the demands this ensemble made on the parsonage. Easter day usually began at 1:00 A.M. The brass choir would form shortly thereafter and make a tour of Dover. It would return to the church for breakfast, and then go to Schoenbrunn Indian Village and play for the Moravian Easter Morning Litany.[3] The ensemble at the village was augmented with instrumentalists from other Moravian churches and had been rehearsed for several weeks before hand. Depending on the year they would play for approximately one thousand people.

The Dover First renovation project, which led to the Crackerbox discovery, was concluded with a week of services that lasted from 19 February to 26 February 1950. As part of these services Bishop J. Kenneth Pfohl preached the dedicatory sermon, while Mrs. Pfohl presided at the new organ. During the service the well-known "Hosanna" anthem by Edward W. Leinbach was performed.[4] This marks the earliest documented modern performance of early Moravian music in Ohio. Thus, it represents the first step in the gradual reintroduction of Moravian music to the state.

Eventually, Ruth Grams became the main spokesperson for Moravian music in Tuscarawas County. Giving many presentations on the subject at local churches she began to make Ohio Moravians aware of their rich musical heritage. In 1954 she became a member of the seminar faculty for the Moravian Music Festival, where she taught courses in hymnology. She also taught a course in Moravian music at Tar Hollow Moravian Youth Camp.[5] Through the latter course she influenced many of the people who would become church music leaders during the 1950s and 1960s.

A call came to Roy Grams in 1957 to serve as pastor of the Downey Moravian Church in Downey, California, and to head the Pacific Coast

Development Committee of the Moravian Church. Accepting the call, the Grams family moved to California in January 1958.

THE JAMES GROSS FAMILY

Like Ruth and Roy Grams, Emma and James Gross were of considerable influence in Moravian musical circles. A soprano and tenor, both were active vocalists. Throughout the fourteen years of their work at Gnadenhutten they performed as soloists and members of various vocal ensembles in their own church, as well as others.

Shortly after their arrival the church bulletin announced a "voice culture class" to be conducted by Mrs. Gross. She offered a service that was calculated to strengthen an already strong program. The announcement read, "Free instruction in proper breathing, posture, vocalizing, etc. will be offered to girls and boys of Junior and Senior age."[6]

The 500th Anniversary of the founding of the Unitas Fratrum took place in 1957. As part of the festivities surrounding this event, the choirs of Fry's Valley, Port Washington, and Gnadenhutten were combined for a union service. At this service, held 25 February 1957, Mrs. Gross directed the combined youth choirs, Mrs. Robert Baker the combined junior choirs, and Gnadenhutten's Mrs. Mabel Gallagher the senior choirs.[7] Apparently, the 500th Anniversary created enough interest in Moravian music that fourteen people from Gnadenhutten participated in the 1957 Moravian Music Festival.[8]

It was during the Gross pastorate that Gnadenhutten's trombone choir gained national attention. The ensemble was featured in the April 1955 issue of *Ford Times*. This article brought them to the attention of a U.S. Congressman who made it possible for the choir to tour Washington, D.C. playing in many churches, cathedrals, and synagogues.

When the Gross family left for Pennsylvania in 1958 they were replaced by John and Marie Morman.

THE MORMAN FAMILY

John Morman served both Uhrichsville and Gnadenhutten during his pastoral career. When he was installed at Uhrichsville 28 October 1945 he faced important vacancies in the music staff. Since Pastor Edward Fischer had been the chorister a new person was needed. Also the choir director had resigned. Harold Ginther and Bill Rennecker filled these positions respectively.

A major addition to Uhrichsville musical life occurred when John Morman married Marie Bittner in 1946. The new Mrs. Morman was an excellent musician who, at the time of her marriage, served as organist at Jordan Reformed Church in Allentown, Pennsylvania. In addition she also possessed a good soprano voice.

Mrs. Morman became church organist at Uhrichsville in the fall of 1946. From this point on the church's music program grew rapidly with the addition of several young people who would become the church's next generation of music leaders. The exposure these individuals received bore fruit quickly. A class entitled "Religion and Music" was taught in 1948 by Mary Lois Ginther, who would eventually become a Uhrichsville choir director. She and Mrs. Morman often performed piano-organ duets in church services.

By 1948 Bill Rennecker had left and Mrs. Morman became choir director. She would not hold this position long, however, for her husband was called to First Church in Bethlehem.

Upon returning to Ohio in 1958 the Mormans inherited the Gross's strong music program. Mrs. Morman became director of the primary choir and the girl's choir, and occasionally conducted Moravian union choir programs.

The strength of the Gnadenhutten program can be ascertained by the Advent I service of 1960. Five different choirs, numbering ninety-five vocalists, participated in the service.[9] Two Moravian pieces were sung at this service: "Glory Be to David's Son" by Jeremiah Dencke, and the traditional "Hosanna" by Christian Gregor.[10]

The year 1948 brought two musical families to Ohio parsonages. September saw the arrival of the Richard Michel family at Sharon, while the Clarence Riske family replaced the Mormans at Uhrichsville.

THE MICHEL FAMILY

With the arrival of the Richard Michel family in 1948 Moravian music in Ohio would benefit from three very strong musical parsonages. These were found at Dover First (Roy and Ruth Grams), Gnadenhutten (James and Emma Gross and John and Marie Morman), and Sharon (the Michels). From these parsonages would emanate the drive and leadership necessary to bring out the best in the other parsonages and the musical programs of their congregations. Pastor Michel was the son of missionaries, being born at Bluefield, Nicaragua, in 1919. Sr. Michel, the former Winifred Strahler, was born the same year in Bethlehem.

Pastor Michel was a frequent vocal soloist not only at Sharon, but at other churches as well. Mrs. Michel's musical participation was primarily as a member of vocal ensembles, singing duets with her husband, and trios and quartets with various individuals. One example comes from the late 1950s when the Michels combined with Schoenbrunn Community's parsonage family, Pastor and Mrs. Donald Kirts, to perform vocal quartets.

Beginning in October 1950 the local Dover radio station, WJER established a religious program in which area churches participated on a rotating basis. Generally, the Moravian presentations included a great deal of music in conjunction with a brief message. Sharon's offerings frequently included soprano and tenor duets by the Michels.

Eventually the entire Michel family became active in Sharon's musical life. Beginning in 1959 Richard, Jr., performed in services as a pianist, while daughter Sharon began to appear as a vocal soloist.

Once the decision to hold a Moravian Music Festival in Tuscarawas County was approved, Pastor Michel became a leading member of the Festival Committee. We shall discuss his role in more depth in chapter twenty-three.

THE RISKE FAMILY

When Clarence and Anne Riske arrived at Uhrichsville they faced a major overhaul of the music program. Since Mrs. Morman had been both organist and choir director, the two most important musical positions needed to be filled. Fortunately, the former organist Mrs. Alma Arthurs returned to the organ bench, a position she would now hold until 1971, while Anne Riske became the choir director.

Under Mrs. Riske the choir presented two choral cantatas, *King of Glory* (1949)[11] and *King Triumphant* (1950).[12] Early in 1951 she was forced to resign due to pregnancy, but she would return and serve again from 1953 to 1955, when her husband accepted a new call.

Mrs. Riske's work directly connects with the current Uhrichsville choral program. During her second term she was assisted by Mrs. Margie Craft, the present choir director.

KENNETH ROBINSON

The Rev. Kenneth Robinson took the reins of the Fry's Valley-Port Washington pastorate 26 August 1951 and immediately became engrossed in Moravian musical life. Playing E-flat alto horn, he made the Easter morning rounds with Dover First's trombone choir in 1952. Later that day he also performed with the combined wind ensemble for services at Schoenbrunn Indian Village.

As an oboist he played second oboe in the Tuscarawas Philharmonic, serving from 1952 until he left Ohio in 1954. Instrumental performance, however, was not the only way in which Robinson contributed to the county's musical life.

Robinson found many opportunities to perform in vocal groups. He could be found singing in the combined choir for the Port Washington High School Baccalaurate, singing solos at Youth Fellowship gatherings, and singing in a Moravian "pastoral quartet" consisting of himself, Roy Grams, W. J. Weinland, and Richard Jones.[13]

Undoubtedly the most unusual singing performance he ever gave was a special entertainment for a community social held at Fry's Valley 25 July 1952: "The [Community Social Committee] put on a musical fashion show entitled 'The Romance of a Hat.' The Pastor played and sang all the songs depicting the different women's hats. Whew!"[14]

THE WEINLAND FAMILY

William J. Weinland was installed as pastor of Schoenbrunn Community Church 27 January 1952. Like Bro. Robinson, Bro. Weinland immediately became involved in instrumental music. The Pastor and church members Russ Graham and Sarah Kilchenman toured with Dover First's trombone choir and performed at Schoenbrunn Indian Village 13 April 1952.

Like Robinson, Weinland also sang. He and his wife occasionally appeared in public singing duets, and he could be found singing solos from time to time. Of course, his participation in the Moravian ministerial quartet of Roy Grams, Kenneth Robinson and Richard Jones has already been mentioned.[15]

With Weinland's move to Ohio every Ohio Moravian church had a musical parsonage. This situation would exist for two years, until the Riskes left Uhrichsville. It should not be surprising that this was a very active period in Ohio Moravian musical life.

NOTES

1. Not all of the families will be discussed in this chapter. Only those that made a significant musical contribution during the period 1941–61.

2. "Mrs. Grams Had Early Training on Irish Harp," *Dover Daily Reporter,* 4 February 1955, p. 8.

3. During this period of time all of Ohio's Moravian churches, except Gnadenhutten, assisted in this service. Being the oldest of Ohio's Moravian churches, and because of the close proximity of their cemetery (making it possible to conduct the traditional service) Gnadenhutten has always felt the need to conduct its own Easter service.

4. Dedication Week: First Moravian Church, Dover, Ohio, Sunday, 19 February 1950.

5. Tar Hollow is the Moravian Youth Camp for the Western District of the Northern Province of the Moravian Church.

6. Sunday Bulletin, 29 July 1945, John Heckewelder Memorial Moravian Church, Gnadenhutten, Ohio.

7. Scrapbook Diary of the Rev. James Gross, 25 February 1957, John Heckewelder Memorial Moravian Church, Gnadenhutten, Ohio.

8. Sunday Bulletin, 30 June 1957, John Heckewelder Memorial Moravian Church, Gnadenhutten, Ohio.

9. These were the senior choir, girl's choir, primary choir, junior high girl's choir and the junior choir.

10. "Five Choirs will present Advent Service at Gnaden," *New Philadelphia* , Ohio, Daily Times, 23 November 1960.

11. The cantata, by R. S. Morrison, was presented 10 April 1949.

12. The cantata, by E. L. Ashford, was presented 9 April 1950.

13. Diary of the Fry's Valley Moravian Congregation, 13 July 1952, Fry's Valley, Ohio.

14. Ibid., 25 July 1952.

15. Diary of the Fry's Valley Moravian Congregation, 13 July 1952, Fry's Valley, Ohio.

18

IMPORTANT MUSICIANS

HERBERT L. GRAY

Born in Gnadenhutten in 1901, Herbert L. Gray was the son of Otto and Amelia (Simmers) Gray. He and his family were originally members of the Gnadenhutten Methodist Church, but Gray joined the Moravian church in 1944.

Gray demonstrated musical talent early. A cornetist, he attended the Dana Conservatory of Music in Warren, Ohio, and after graduation, performed as a professional musician for a number of years. Upon his return to Tuscarawas County he joined the Dover Concert Band and, from 1935 to 1965, served as Gnadenhutten's postmaster.

After joining the Moravian congregation he played in the trombone choir and directed the Sunday School orchestra until his death in 1970.

FLORENCE GRAY

Florence Kinsey Gray has been associated with Dover First for over fifty years. Her initial appearance in church records is as a member of the trombone choir that performed on 15 May 1921. She became active in the church after this date, serving as choir director by 1934. From this point on she served the church as director of the junior and senior choir, vocal soloist and member of various musical organizations.

She held the choir director post on two different occasions. The first was 1934 to 1945, while her second tour of duty lasted from 1946 to 1952. Thus, she served the church as choir director a total of seventeen years.

Her second term of service coincided with the pastorate of Roy Grams. Consequently, she was closely involved with Ruth Grams's introduction of Moravian music to Ohio. After attending the 1955 and 1957 Moravian Music Festivals, Miss Gray assisted Mrs. Grams in presentations dealing with Moravian music. One of these was held 10 October 1957 as part of the 500th anniversary observances. It was given at Dover First and opened with

historical comments by Pastor Grams. The program presented music performed by a vocal quartet that included Margaret Jean Pfeiffer Gotschall
(soprano), Florence Gray (alto), Richard Jones (tenor), and Tom Adams
(bass). Accompanied by Ruth Grams this group sang many pieces from the
Moravian heritage.[1]

Miss Gray's efforts were capped by her labors for the Ohio Moravian Music
Festival. She was one of the Dover representatives to the committee that
prepared this festival and served as Chairperson for the Transportation
Committee.

MRS. RUTH PETER PFEIFFER

Ruth Peter was born in Newark, Ohio, 11 April 1904. She was the
daughter of Maurice and Minnie Secrist Peter and, as such, a direct relative
of David Peter. The family returned to the father's home town of
Gnadenhutten in 1914 and settled into the musical life of the Moravian
church.

Mrs. Pfeiffer began piano lessons in the third grade, studying first with
Leona Miksch Parks[2] and, later, with Carrie Seiss. By 1922 she was Sunday
School organist and, in 1925, became the accompanist of Pastor Nitzschke's
newly formed junior choir. Her name appears often during the 1920s as organ
soloist at church services. She also performed in duets with Nitzschke, trios
with Nitzschke and Wilbur Demuth, and quartets with Nitzschke, Demuth,
and Olin Pfeiffer.

An interesting story from this period concerns the church organist, Mary
Demuth Van Vleck Wohlwend. Mrs. Wohlwend performed all aspects of the
church service well except anthem accompaniment. Since she did not read
choral scores well, this job was turned over to Ruth Peter. Thus, Mrs.
Wohlwend played the service, while Miss Peter accompanied the anthem.[3]

Ruth Peter married Carl Pfeiffer in 1926 and they moved to Dover in 1928
where they joined Dover First. Since the organist position at Dover First was
set, with Regina Lenz succeeding Georgia Hill Cunning, Mrs. Pfeiffer
became the assistant organist, serving for forty-three years, and a member of
the choir. During the Grams pastorate she was also accompanist for the junior
and chapel choirs.

MARGARET JEAN PFEIFFER GOTSCHALL

Born 25 December 1928, Margaret Jean Pfeiffer came from a musical
family. Her father, Carl Pfeiffer, rarely performed in public, but two of his
relatives, Olin and Mary Pfeiffer, were important performers at Gnadenhut-

ten.[4] Through her mother, the former Ruth Peter, she inherited an enviable heritage that reaches back to her great-great-great-granduncles, Simon and John Frederick Peter.[5]

The earliest musical comment we have concerning Margaret Jean is a 1938 Dover First diary entry. On this date she and her mother sang a duet for a mother-daughter Banquet.[6] After this she became very active as a soloist and choir member.

In 1946 she entered Muskingum College at New Concord, Ohio. Four years later she graduated with a music education degree. As she and her voice teacher, John Bloom, began the process of selecting pieces for her senior recital many different currents came together to create a unique situation of vast importance to Ohio Moravian music.

John Kendall, Head of the String Department at Muskingum, was of Quaker background and knew the Moravian heritage. He was also aware of the new publications of Moravian music then being published. He suggested that, with her Moravian background, Margaret Jean might want to include some pieces from *Ten Sacred Songs for Soprano, Strings and Organ* on her recital.[7] This set, which included sacred songs by Jeremiah Dencke, Johann Frederick Peter, Simon Peter, Johannes Herbst, Georg Gottfried Müller, and John Antes, had been published in 1947, and was edited by Hans T. David.

Following Kendell's suggestion Margaret Jean and her voice teacher selected a group of six songs from the set. Of these four were by Dencke, *Ich will Singen von einem Könige, Freuet euch, ihr Tochter seines Volks, Gehet in der Geruch seines Bräutigams-Namens* and *Meine Seele erhebet den Herrn*, and two by her famous Peter relative, *Der Herr ist in Seinen heiligen Temple* and *Leite mich in Deiner Wahrheit*. These were done with string accompaniment and, as the titles suggest, were sung in German.[8]

Margaret Jean began teaching in Washington County, Ohio, and on 11 June 1951 married Dale Gotschall. By 1955 she was very active in the Dover First music program, and, when the Gramses left Ohio, she was a member of the committee that took charge of the church's music program. Eventually, she and her family moved to Cambridge, Ohio where she now resides.

MARGIE CRAFT

Mrs. Margie Craft has served as choir director at Uhrichsville since 1960. Her participation in the church's musical life, however, reaches back to the 1940s. Under her maiden name, Margaret Elizabeth Schneider, she is listed as a choir member as early as 1948.

A pianist, she often performed in piano-organ duets with Mrs. Alma Arthurs. Eventually, Mrs. Craft became the assistant Sunday School pianist and assistant church organist.

In 1953 Anne Riske began her second term as choir director. Concerned with the care of a new infant, she felt the need for an assistant and Mrs. Craft served in that capacity. Not only did Mrs. Craft assist Mrs. Riske, she also assisted during the directorship of Mrs. Gooding (1958–60). By 1960 she had become the choir director.

PHYLLIS RONALD

Phyllis Sherer was born in 1934 and married Richard Ronald in 1953. Prior to her marriage she had been active in Sharon musical circles for ten years. Her name is first mentioned in church records 28 April 1943 when she and Eugene Haupert sang a duet at a new member reception.[9]

Young musicians at Sharon during the 1940s and 1950s had many performance opportunities. One particularly excellent arena was the "Home Talent Program" held on New Year's Eve before Watchnight services. These programs mostly consisted of musical performances, and Phyllis appeared on them often as a piano soloist and in all-girl trumpet quartets.

By 1949 she and Jeanne Cribbs, daughter of the church organist, were performing piano-organ duets. She assumed the position of assistant organist in 1951. She is also an accomplished pianist, and has performed recitals of works by Bach, Beethoven, Schubert, and Chopin.

In 1953 she became Sharon's organist, replacing Mrs. Esther Cribbs; two years later, she became the choir director, a position she still holds. Through her positions of organist and choir director Mrs. Ronald has fostered the growth of talented musicians at Sharon. During her tenure as organist many young pianists performed piano-organ duets in church services. One of these, Joyce Rolli Sainato, eventually succeeded her as church organist.

MONA LOU AND EUGENE HAUPERT

Mona Lou and Eugene Haupert were the children of Frederick and Florence (Schumaker) Haupert. They attended Sunday School at Sharon after their parents transferred to the church in 1938, and became important vocalists within Sharon's musical life over the next two decades.

Being the older, Eugene's appearance came first. In 1943 he performed both as a vocal and piano soloist. As might be expected, many of his early appearances were at the New Year's Eve Home Talent Programs.

It was at the 1945 Home Talent Program that Mona Lou Haupert made her first appearance in the Sharon diaries.[10] Over the years this was followed by numerous performances as a vocal soloist and as a member of several vocal ensembles.

The Hauperts sang in the senior choir in the late 1940s and early 1950s. In addition, they frequently performed duets together. Their accompanist was often Kathryn Stull, who eventually attended Baldwin-Wallace College in Berea, Ohio as a music major.

Mona became Mrs. Robert Wilson in 1950, and by 1956 was serving as Sharon's junior choir director. When the Ohio Moravian Music Festival was held in Tuscarawas County she sang soprano in the chorus.

IMOGENE BATTERSHELL EMIG AND DOROTHY SICKINGER

Imogene Battershell was born in New Philadelphia in 1900. The daughter of Francis and Isabella (Demuth) Battershell, she was confirmed in the Methodist Church, but eventually attended Sharon where she was choir director from 1947 to 1949. She was a frequent soloist and a member of the Banks Trio, a local vocal group that performed at various functions.

When the future Schoenbrunn congregation was established in 1947, many of its charter members transferred from Sharon. One of these was Imogene Battershell. She tried to maintain a dual role as choir director at both churches. The two positions created certain strains, but they also provided unique opportunities and Miss Battershell was resourceful enough to emphasize the positive. On 12 December 1948 the Sharon and Schoenbrunn choirs combined to present Christmas music at a Sharon service.[11] The strain finally became too much, however, and Miss Battershell resigned the Sharon position in April 1949. She married Elmer Emig in 1957 and they transferred to First Methodist in 1965.

Next to Imogene Battershell, Dorothy Sickinger was the most important choral musician in the early life of the Schoenbrunn Church. She also was one of the many charter members who originally attended Sharon. An early member of Schoenbrunn's choir, she was elected president in 1948.

After Schoenbrunn's junior choir was established Miss Sickinger served as its accompanist and, in 1958, became its director. Under her guidance the choir grew to over thirty children. The large size eventually required a reorganization, which was effected in November 1960. The ensemble was divided into two groups, a cherub choir (ages 5–10) and a junior choir (11–up). Miss Sickinger was director of both ensembles and maintained those positions into the 1960s.

JANICE KENNEDY AND CAROL HYER

As mentioned earlier Dover South's membership is primarily of Welsh extraction. Since the Welsh, like the Moravians, have a strong love of music, it was natural for the church to desire the best music program it could obtain. Eventually this desire led to the creation of a choral program.

By the early 1950s there were enough children to form a youth choir. Two young ladies, Janice Kennedy and Carol Hyer, took matters in hand and in 1952 established a junior choir. Janice was sixteen at the time and served as director, while Carol, only fourteen, was the pianist.

The choir's first appearance was 20 October 1952 when it performed an operetta entitled "Molly Be Jolly." Through the efforts of Janice, Carol, and several mothers, the choir grew in numbers and acquired robes. By 1953 it numbered twenty-two members and was considered a vital part of Dover South's musical life.

Eventually, Janice would become active at Dover First, transferring to the north side in 1957. She moved to Easton, Pennsylvania in 1960 and joined First Moravian Church in that city.

It appears that Carol Hyer took charge of the junior choir in 1954. In addition, she served the church as downstairs assisstant pianist in the Sunday School program and in 1955 as president of the Youth Fellowship.

NOTES

1. Church Diary [of the Dover Moravian congregations], 10 October 1957, Dover, Ohio.
2. A cousin of her father and a choir director at the Gnadenhutten Church.
3. Interview with Ruth Peter Pfeiffer, Dover, Ohio, 2 July 1985.
4. Olin Pfeiffer has been mentioned many times in this book. Mary Pfeiffer, his sister, came to prominence as a keyboard performer in the late 1920s. She became Gnadenhutten's church organist in 1938 and seems to have served in that capacity until a move to Canton, Ohio took place in 1944.
5. See "David Peter," in chap. 6.
6. Diary of the Dover Congregations, 22 June 1938, Dover, Ohio.
7. Hans T. David, ed., *Ten Sacred Songs for Soprano, Strings and Organ*, (New York: New York Public Library, 1947).
8. The full significance of this recital will be discussed in chap. 21.
9. Diary of the Sharon Moravian Congregation, 28 April 1943, Tuscarawas, Ohio.
10. Diary of the Sharon Moravian Congregation, 31 December 1945, Tuscarawas, Ohio.
11. Diary of the Sharon Moravian Congregation, 12 December 1948, Tuscarawas, Ohio.

PART SEVEN

*Moravian Music
and Ohio*

19

THE CHURCH ORGANIST

One of the unique characteristics of twentieth-century Moravian life in Ohio is longevity of service for organists. During the period 1930 to 1961 we find that each church was blessed with organists of good to excellent ability who maintained their positions over a long period of time. The shortest span was nine years, served by Mrs. Isabel Everett Bregenzer at Fry's Valley; while the longest tenure was forty-three years, given to Dover First by Miss Regina Lenz. In between these we find tenures of fifteen, sixteen, twenty-four, twenty-five, and thirty-six years.

The stability provided by such extended terms helped each church maintain a consistent music program. Therefore, it seems appropriate to devote a chapter to these organists, their instruments, and their contributions.

ISABELLE EVERETT

Isabelle Everett was born in 1919. She was in the group of young people Reuben Gross organized into a singing school at Fry's Valley in 1934.[1] It was this group of thirteen people that he trained as a choir and it provided Isabelle with her earliest recorded church music experiences. During the next two years she also began singing duets (with Mrs. Gross, Martha Rank, and Mrs. Harold Everett) and trios that included Isabelle Horsfall and Martha Rank.

The first recorded evidence of her playing piano in church comes from December 1934, when she performed in a piano duet with Annabelle Everett. By January 1937 she was the assistant Christian Education pianist and four years later, in 1941, she succeeded Anne Montague as church organist.

The senior youth program at Fry's Valley was quite active at this time and its members decided to raise money for a new church organ. The campaign was launched in May 1943 and came to fruition in 1945 with the installation of a Hammond electric organ. The dedication service was held 28 January 1945, by which time the youth had collected enough money to pay for the instrument. Isabelle Everett gave a recital on the new instrument in June

1945 in which she played works by Handel, Dvorak, Sibelius, Hawthorne, Johnson and Wagner.[2]

While a student at Moravian Seminary Karl Bregenzer served the Fry's Valley–Port Washington congregations as student pastor during the summers of 1946, 1947, and 1948. After assuming the full-time pastorate, he married Isabelle Everett at Fry's Valley 25 June 1948. Two years later Bregenzer accepted a call to the Moravian Church in Berea, Minnesota and he and Isabelle left Ohio for several years. They have since returned and are active in the church.

LUCY MCCONNELL MILLER

Lucy McConnell Miller was the daughter of Anna M. Eggenberg and William McConnell. Through her maternal grandmother, Louisa Peter Eggenberg, she represents yet another musical descendent of David Peter.[3]

Born at Gnadenhutten in 1899, she was seventeen when her name first appears as a musician. At a 1916 reception held in the parsonage musical entertainment was provided by the choir and four girls. The girls, Leona and Ruth Miksch, Carrie Seiss, and Lucy McConnell would all become musicians within the church program. Leona Miksch would become Mrs. Henry Parks and, at different times during the 1930s and 1940s, would serve as choir director at Gnadenhutten. Carrie Seiss became a well-known pianist and piano teacher, while Lucy McConnell would become a mainstay in the Gnadenhutten music program during the 1940s and early 1950s.

She married Edwin Miller in 1922 and settled into serving as Sunday School pianist through the 1930s. She became the church organist in 1944 and continued in that position for fifteen years. If one counts her years spent as Sunday School pianist the total number is in excess of forty years.

Mrs. Miller was particularly kind to young organists in the church, permitting them many performance opportunities. Often this would mean a single number during the service or, for those who were more advanced, the entire service. In this way she helped prepare for the future of the organist position.

Several programs of recitals given by Mrs. Miller can be found in the diaries and, of course, the church bulletins list the type of music she played for services. Typical is a recital given in 1944 which included Bizet's *Intermezzo*, a *Pastorale* by MaHei, and a *Postlude in G* by Stultz.[4]

The organ on which Mrs. Miller played is still in use today. It was given in memory of Elizabeth Heck by her son, D. V. Heck, and was dedicated 19 June 1927. The instrument is a two-manual, electro-pneumatic organ with pedal and chimes built by the Moller Company of Hagerstown, Maryland. It has about 750 pipes and is typical of Moller instruments of that period.

ALMA ARTHURS

Mrs. Alma Arthurs was born in Newcomerstown, Ohio in 1907. Her family attended St. Paul's Lutheran Church and it was there that she started her music career. Her first instrument was St. Paul's old Sunday School pump organ. By the time she reached her teenage years she was demonstrating considerable talent and her mother began saving money for a college education at Wittenberg.[5] Unfortunately, Alma's mother died and her stepmother was far less sympathetic toward the young girl's talent. Not only did Alma not attend college, she found it impossible to complete high school.

When she was an eighth-grader at St. Paul's, the Sunday School performed a pagaent at the State Theater. Alma Arthurs's playing so impressed the theater owners that they offered her the position of theater pianist. Thus, she earned money playing for the silent movies for some time afterward.

She married William Arthurs in 1924, moved to Uhrichsville, joined the Methodist Church and raised a family. Their daughter Susan developed close friendships with several girls who attended the Uhrichsville Moravian Church. Three of these, Dorothy Smith, Dorothy Aeshlimann, and Margie Schneider[6] sang in the choir, and soon Susan joined the ensemble.

Mrs. Beatrice Medley Romig, the church organist, became pregnant in 1943 and resigned her position. Elder Henry Spring contacted Mrs. Arthurs concerning the job. She accepted and immediately found herself struggling with Passion Week services.

Mrs. Arthurs served from 1943 to 1946 and then from 1948 to 1970, a total of twenty-two years. She so liked the church that she and Susan joined in 1950. Mrs. Arthurs often performed piano-organ duets with many younger pianists. This ensemble was popular with Ohio Moravians, and among those who performed with Mrs. Arthurs were Margaret Schneider Craft, Mary Lois Ginther, Frances Edwards, and Mrs. Edith Gooding.

The organ at Uhrichsville was built by the Hinners Organ Company of Pekin, Illinois. The dedication services took place 21 November 1909 with several local Moravian organists participating. Among these were Theodore Van Vleck and Edith Fidler. The instrument was a two-manual, tracker-action organ with pedal; it was located in the front of the church.

Mrs. Arthurs had an amusing remembrance concerning the organ in its last years. At different times she would pull a drawbar to change registration and, instead of stopping as it was supposed to, the drawbar continued out of its socket. Undaunted, Mrs. Arthurs would place the drawbar on the top of the organ case and continue to play. The choir, of course, would try to maintain its composure, not always successfully.[7]

When Mrs. Arthurs died in 1985 she left her entire collection of organ music to the Uhrichsville Moravian Church. The collection is important in that it demonstrates the type of organ music performed at the church during her tenure. Although it has yet to be catalogued, a quick perusal indicates some interesting items, among which can be found all of the then published Moravian organ music.[8]

LEONA ARTH

The Port Washington organist with the longest period of service was Leona Arth. Born at Port Washington in 1907 as Leona Glazer, she married John Eldridge Stocker in 1925. Her husband was the brother of Dr. F. P. Stocker who, for many years, served the church as president of the Northern Province Eastern District Board and the Provincial Elder's Conference. Two years after her husband's death in 1958 Mrs. Stocker married Homer Arth.

The earliest musical record that mentions Mrs. Arth comes from 8 September 1918 when she was part of a choir of eight school girls, "who sang very sweetly," according to Pastor Roland Bahnson.[9] After this Mrs. Arth became quite active in the musical life of the church.

Port Washington never seemed to lack organists and she worked her way up through the ranks as Sunday School organist, assistant church organist and, finally, church organist. Beginning in 1938 she would hold the latter position for thirty-six years, until the Port Washington congregation was disbanded in the early 1970s. Since the organist at Port Washington was also the choir director, Mrs. Arth worked with both the senior and junior choirs.

The Port Washington organ on which Mrs. Arth played had been in the church since 1905. It received major repair work in the mid-1940s and again in 1960, thus, it was in good operating condition when the congregation was dissolved. Consequently, John Morman made arrangements to have the instrument packed and shipped to Pennsylvania where it is now used as a practice organ at Linden Hall, the Moravian girls school located in Lititz.

BLANCHE McCLEAN

Mrs. Blanche McClean served Schoenbrunn Community Church as organist from its beginnings in 1947 into the 1960s. She was born in Uhrichsville as Blanche Miller in 1910 and married Frank Crites McClean in 1929. Methodists for many years, they transferred their membership to Schoenbrunn in 1950.

During the first years of the Schoenbrunn congregation services were held in Trinity Episcopal Church in New Philadelphia. Thus, that church's organ was employed. At this time there were two organists, Mrs. McClean and Mrs. Clarence Myer. Mrs. Myer was the former Carrie Oerter, daughter of

M. F. and Bertha Tietze Oerter, and sister of Sharon's organist, Mrs. Esther Cribbs.

Apparently, the church organist-assistant organist positions had not been clearly defined when the new congregation was begun and some difficulty arose early in 1948. The congregation's pastor, Bishop Moses, was able to solve the problem and from 7 March 1948 Mrs. McClean served as the church organist and Mrs. Myer as assistant.

When Schoenbrunn's church building was dedicated between 24 April and 8 May 1955 the McCleans were very much involved. Frank McClean was president of the board of trustees and treasurer of the building committee, and his wife, of course, helped plan and organize the extensive musical presentations.

The organ in the new church was a gift of Mr. Robert D. Saurer, an elder and member of the building committee. It is a Baldwin electronic organ installed by Hahn and Company of Canton, and is still in use today.

REGINA LENZ

Regina Lenz served Dover First from 1932 to 1975, forty-three years. That in itself is quite a record, but it is only part of the story. From 1920 to 1932 she was the assistant organist, serving under Georgia Hill Cunning. When these two terms are added together Miss Lenz is found to have served the church for fifty-five years!

Born in 1900 she was the daughter of Isaac and Callie Lenz. A graduate of Miami University at Oxford, Ohio, she attended courses at Ohio Wesleyan University and served Tuscarawas County as an elementary school teacher.

Among Regina's earliest musical experiences were her years in the junior choir under the directorship of Mrs. F. W. Stengel (1911–15).[10] She studied organ under Georgia Hill Cunning during the years she served as assistant organist.

The major remodeling program Dover First underwent in 1947 included a new church organ. The old Moller pipe organ had served the church since 1915 and was very much in need of replacement. The Reuter Organ Company contracted to build a new organ that incorporated as many pipes from the Moller as was feasible.

On 18 July 1948 the old organ was finally retired at a service in which Miss Lenz reviewed the history of organs at Dover First.[11] Her research uncovered two hymns that had been used at the 1915 dedication of the Moller instrument. These, "God Reveals His Presence" and "Rock of Ages," were performed as the instrument's last offerings to the church.

By 9 December 1949 the first ranks of the new organ had been completed, making it possible to play the instrument. Roy Grams's diary provides us with a beautiful description of the emotions created by the first sounds of the new instrument:

> In the evening, following a hurried decision late last night, about forty-five individuals, members of the original planning committee, the finance committee, the building committee and the trustees, with wives and friends, met in the shavings, g——— and tools and scaffolding of the church to hear the first ranks of pipes on the organ. Regina Lenz played "Now Thank We all our God." It was emotionally a very high experience.[12]

The new organ, which is still in use, consists of three manuals, pedal, echo organ, and chimes. It has 1,188 pipes (766 were retained from the Moller organ) and twenty-six stops.

Regina Lenz was heavily involved with the activities of the Ohio Moravian Music Festival. Serving on the housing committee and as rehearsal pianist, she also sang alto in the festival chorus. She figured prominently in the news releases connected with the Festival. An article in a local newspaper contains a picture of her with the famous "crackerbox".[13] The crackerbox collection was entrusted to Miss Lenz when the Grams family left Dover. She took care of the collection until it was given to Dr. Donald McCorkle, Director of the Moravian Music Foundation, in 1958.

FRANCES KORNS

Dover South never owned an organ during the period covered by this study. Consequently, the position was actually that of church pianist. Also, the demands of a Moravian church pianist were more than any one person at the church could accept. For this reason the position was rarely held by one individual. Even so, Mrs. James Korns seems to have served with a great deal of consistency through the period 1938 to 1958.

Frances Manley was born at Dover in 1913 and married James Korns at Wheeling, West Virginia in 1931. From September 1938 to November 1939 she appears to have been the full-time church pianist. Finding she could not handle the entire load she submitted her resignation. This precipitated a co-pianist solution with Mrs. Janet Aebersold assisting.

The solution did help, but eventually both ladies withdrew. Mrs. John Daniels and Mrs. Fred Mason were co-pianists from 1944 to 1948 when a new arrangement established a team consisting of Mrs. Korns, Mrs. Aebersold, and Mary Jane Souers.

Mrs. Aebersold was the former Janet Williams. She had married Robert Klein in 1927. He died in 1934, and Mrs. Klein married George Aebersold in 1939. She served as one-third of the piano team until ill health forced her to retire in 1957.

Mary Jane Souers was born in 1931. The daughter of Louis and Clara

Souers, she had spent her entire life at Dover South and was sixteen when she became one-third of the church pianist team. She also served as pianist in the Sunday School program and frequently played in the trombone choirs that performed at Schoenbrunn Indian Village at Easter. In 1954 she married Paul Aeschliman of Uhrichsville and, ultimately, served on the Dover South board of trustees.

By 1957 both Mary Jane Aeschliman and Mrs. Aebersold had ceased to be church pianists and Mrs. Korns took the position on a full-time basis. One year later she resigned and seems never to have served in that capacity again.

ESTHER CRIBBS

Mrs. Esther Cribbs served the Sharon church as organist for many years. Born at Graceham, Maryland she was a daughter of the Reverend Maurice F. and Bessie Teitze Oerter. She came to Sharon with her family in 1910 when her father assumed the church's pastorate. Six years later she entered Linden Hall, becoming one of the few Ohio Moravians to receive an education at the Lititz institution.[14]

She married Elmer Cribbs in 1929 and they had two daughters, Jeanne (b. 1931) and Janice (b. 1933), who became active in Sharon's musical life. Apparently, Mrs. Cribbs became Sharon church organist in the late 1920s. If that is so this would make her tenure from about 1929 to 1953, or approximately twenty-four years.

Like Mrs. Arthurs at Uhrichsville, Mrs. Cribbs enjoyed performing piano-organ duets. Over the years at Sharon she performed these with her daughter Jeanne, choir director Mrs. Robert Ervin, and her successor Phyllis Sherer (the future Mrs. Richard Ronald).

Mrs. Cribbs accompanied Sharon's musical ministers when they sang away from the church. Her work of this type was heard over the Dover air waves in 1950 when Pastor and Mrs. Michel sang duets during the Sharon portion of WJER's religious radio show.

Although Mrs. Cribbs retired in 1953 she did not leave the organ bench. She served as a substitute organist at Sharon and at the Schoenbrunn Community Moravian Church during the period 1954–56.

The affection held for her can be gleaned from a statement in the last church bulletin to list her as Sharon's full-time organist. "Our Deepest Gratitude goes to Sister Elmer Cribbs for her faithful and valuable service to the congregation as organist, through quite a number of years."[15]

The same could be said for all of the organists discussed in this chapter.

NOTES

1. Diary [of the] Fry's Valley Moravian Congregation, no. 5, 24 August 1934, Fry's Valley, Ohio.

2. Diary of the Fry's Valley Moravian Congregation, no. 7, 10 June 1945, Fry's Valley, Ohio.

3. See chap. 10.

4. Sunday Bulletin, 10 December 1944, John Heckewelder Memorial Moravian Church, Gnadenhutten, Ohio.

5. Interview with Alma Arthurs, Uhrichsville, Ohio, 22 September 1983.

6. Margie Schneider would become Mrs. Margie Craft, the current Uhrichsville choir director. See chap. 18.

7. Interview with Alma Arthurs, Uhrichsville, Ohio, 22 September 1983.

8. Harvey Gaul, *Moravian Morning Star*, (New York: H. W. Gray Co., 1942). *Easter Procession of the Moravian Brethren*, (New York: H. W. Gray Co., 1945). *Moravian Evening Hymn*, (New York: H. W. Gray Co., 1947). Robert Elmore, *Three Meditative Moments Based on Moravian Hymns*, (New York: Harold Flammer, 1958).

9. Diary 1907–22, Port Washington, 8 September 1918, Port Washington, Ohio.

10. Interview with Regina Lenz and Florence Gray, Dover, Ohio, 19 February 1983.

11. Diary of the Dover Moravian Congregation, 18 July 1948, Dover, Ohio.

12. Ibid., 10 December 1949.

13. "Dover Church's 'Crackerbox' Held Moravian Music Wealth," *Daily Times*, 24 June 1961, Uhrichsville, Ohio.

14. *A Century and Three-Quarters of Life and Service, Linden Hall Seminary; Lititz, Pennsylvania, 1746–1921* (Lititz, Pa., 1921), p. 68.

15. Church Bulletin, Sharon Moravian Church, 23 August 1953.

20

OHIO MORAVIAN COMPOSERS

The need for large quantities of music led many Moravian ministers to musical composition. Christian Gregor seems to have composed the earliest examples of Moravian concerted church music during the early 1750s.[1] Following Gregor's lead a large number of Moravian ministers began to write such music for their churches.

Jeremiah Dencke brought the Moravian school of composition to America when he composed this country's earliest examples of concerted church music.[2] By following Dencke's example Moravian composers from 1750 to 1850 produced the finest examples of concerted church music ever created for the regular worship life of an American church.

One of the more dramatic discoveries resulting from the present study is that, to some extent, eight Moravians engaged in musical composition during their tenure in Ohio. Thus, we can refer to them as Ohio Moravian composers. Of these eight people three, Georg Gottfried Müller, Henry J. Van Vleck and Ruth Grams, have been mentioned previously. Thus, their basic biographical sketches are to be found in earlier chapters of this book.

Five of these composers, Peter Wolle, Robert Hill, Emmet Earl Blind, Elizabeth Ervin, and George Stucky, have not been previously discussed. Therefore, brief biographical sketches for them will be given in this chapter.

GEORGE GOTTFRIED MÜLLER

Müller has the distinction of being the first Moravian composer to work in Ohio. It is possible that he was the first Ohio composer, yet that honor probably belongs to Harmon Blennerhassett of Marietta, Ohio.[3] In any event, it is certainly safe to say that Müller was Ohio's first composer of concerted sacred music.

The earliest catalog of Müller's compositions to be published is found in Hans T. David's *Catalogue* of 1938.[4] Eight compositions are listed there, covering a period from 1787 to 1814. Subsequent discoveries have added three more works to this list.

Among the newly discovered works is the most historically important composition in the crackerbox collection, "Lamb of God, Thou Shalt Remain Forever." The title page of this work contains the notation "Beersheba, Ohio State, April 1, 1814," making it the earliest datable composition written in Ohio by a Moravian composer.

"Lamb of God" does not appear in the David *Catalogue* because it was in Ohio at the time he conducted his survey. Although two copies existed in Salem collections these were apparently unknown in 1938.[5]

The anthem, which was originally written for SATB Chorus, Flutes I, II, Violin I, II, Viola, Violoncello, and Organ, was arranged and edited by Ewald V. Nolte, and was published in 1961.[6]

Because of the orchestral parts it is unwise to believe this work was intended for Ohio. Müller was completing his Ohio pastorate when this piece was written. Thus, it is highly likely that it was intended for his new church (First Moravian in Philadelphia, Pennsylvania) or for another eastern congregation. In any event, the manuscript found its way into the Bethlehem congregation collection and from there back to Ohio.

Among the eight Müller compositions listed in the David *Catalogue* we find only one with an English text, "O Sing All Ye Redeem'd from Adam's Fall." David states that this piece is the only composition Müller ever wrote to an English text. Since David did not have access to "Lamb of God" he obviously felt justified in making that statement. All extant copies of "Lamb of God," however, use an English text. Since there is no indication on the scores that the text is a translation, one must assume that Müller composed at least two English language anthems.

The English text, and the date 1814, which appears on the title page, strongly imply that "O Sing" was written at the same time as "Lamb of God." This would mean that the former composition was most probably written in Ohio. If so, it represents a second Ohio composition by Müller. Without realizing it, Hans T. David suggests one more possible Ohio composition.

David states that Müller's *Sey gegrüsst, erblasstes leben* was probably written between 1800 and 1810.[7] On several occasions we have mentioned the arrival of the Blickensderfer family group in 1812 and its importance to Ohio Moravian music. Although they actually arrived in May, the lovefeast given in their honor was not held until July. Consequently, Müller had forty-four days to prepare or compose any compositions he wished to use at the lovefeast. *Sey gegrüsst*, a short arietta with choral and instrumental parts, gives the appearance of originally being a solo. As a solo with keyboard accompaniment it could easily have been performed at the 1812 lovefeast.

PETER WOLLE

Like Müller, Peter Wolle was a well-known composer long before he came to Ohio. Again, like Müller, only one Wolle composition can be documented as definitely being written in Ohio. Unlike Müller, however, there is no evidence that other works might have been written in the state. Thus, any claim that Wolle was an Ohio composer is most tenuous. He is included here simply for completeness.

Aside from his compositions,[8] Bishop Peter Wolle's significance as a Moravian musician comes from his *Hymn Tunes, Used in the Church of the United Brethren*.[9] This text became invaluable as a companion to Moravian hymnals, which at that time were text books. In fact, Wolle's text provided the four-part settings intended to be used with the first American Moravian *Hymnal*, which was published in 1851.[10]

After retiring from the active ministry, Wolle traveled as a sort of ambassador for the Northern Province of the Church. While on such a visit to Ohio the pastorate at Dover First became vacant and, at the request of the PEC, Wolle served as interim pastor from 1853 to 1855. Similarly, he served as pastor *pro tem* at Sharon from 1861 to 1862.

While at Dover, Bishop Wolle diligently applied himself to the musical activities of the church. All accounts tend to support the belief that the good Bishop served as the church's choir director. During his tenure one finds that the Dover choir is constantly singled out in the diaries of the other churches as being particularly fine.

On 2 April 1854 the Gnadenhutten church was the scene of the ordination of a Brother Myers. This occasion provided the opportunity for Bishop Wolle to exercise his compositional powers. Following the actual consecration by the Bishop, the Moravian service of ordination calls for the singing of a Doxology on the text "Glory be to Thy most meritorious ministry, O Thou Servant of the true tabernacle, who didst not come to be ministered unto, but to minister, Amen, Hallelujah!"

Wolle set this text SATB and trained the Dover choir in its performance. According to the Gnadenhutten diary,

> At 2 o'clock the ordination of Br. Myers as a Deacon of the U. B Church took place, Bishop Wolle officiating. Our meeting house was filled with attentive hearers. The choir from Dover was present and added to the solemnity of the meeting with good singing.[11]

Wolle's copy of this Doxology, the title page of which reads "composed by P. W. at Canal Dover, March 1854," was eventually placed in the Bethlehem collection where it now resides.

HENRY J. VAN VLECK

In the diary of the Uhrichsville church there is a small newspaper clipping of a local concert. The clipping was cut in such a way that no date appears, although evidence strongly suggests 19 March 1896 as the probable concert date. The clipping states that the Bishop played a *March* and *Voluntary* of his own composing. "This aged performer [Bishop Henry J. Van Vleck], much to the surprise, yet to the pleasure of the audience, artfully touched from the piano keyboard two well arranged pieces, one a voluntary and the other a march of his own composition."[12] Lamentably, no copies of this music have been found.

The *Moravian Music Journal* noted that the contents of a music collection held by Mabel Holyer of Minnesota contained music by one HJVV.[13] These were described as "gospel-style" hymns. Since Henry J. Van Vleck often signed items with his initials, and since, as a retired Bishop, he did spend some time in Minnesota (Winter 1892), it seems safe to consider these hymns as his compositions.

Mabel Holyer died before the writer was able to contact her for copies of these hymns and it is currently impossible to procure the hymns for study.

ROBERT HILL

Robert Hill was born in Port Washington 15 September 1870. He was the son of George and Sarah (Nelson) Hill. Mrs. Hill was one of the charter members of the Port Washington Moravian Church when it was established in 1882. From that time forward mother and children were quite active members. Robert and his sister Edna were particularly involved in the Sunday School and music programs. Edna was Sunday School organist, while Robert served as treasurer.

By 1899 Hill and his wife (Lydia Kinsey) moved to the Pittsburgh, Pennsylvania area, where he secured a position as an accountant with Carnegie Steel. He served Carnegie for thirty-eight years, retiring to Porterville, Pennsylvania in 1937. Although he lived in Pennsylvania, he and his wife maintained their Sharon church membership which they had acquired in 1908.

Hill's ties to the Ohio Moravians were quite strong, so much so that at his death, his body was returned to Ohio and buried in the Sharon Cemetery.[14]

The Port Washington diary states that on 26 January 1890, "An anthem entitled 'Praise ye the Lord,' composed by our young Robert Hill, was rendered by the choir."[15] The anthem shows a good understanding of compositional craft and text setting, and was published by the John Church Company of Cinncinati, Ohio in 1889.

Hill was nineteen at the time of publication. We do not know how he procured his music education except to assume that much of it was at the hands of local church musicians. One hypothesis would be that Port Washington's choir director, Mr. Cronebach, provided such instruction. Cronebach was a school teacher and would have had the necessary knowledge to teach elementary composition.

A second piece, the Easter anthem "He Is Risen" was written in 1890, but apparently never published. In fact, it does not seem to have been performed until the Sharon choir did so Easter 1954. The choir sang from manuscript copies which are still located in their choir files. The penmanship is excellent, showing the use of draftsmen's tools.

Both of Hill's compositions look like the early work of someone in the process of learning his craft. It is hoped that more pieces exist, and that they will be found for further study.

EMMET EARL BLIND

Emmet Earl Blind was born in Gnadenhutten 10 February 1903. He was confirmed in 1917 and graduated from Gnadenhutten High School in 1919.

Blind received college degrees from Ohio University (1926) and the University of Cincinnati (1936). Following his college work he served in various teaching posts, with his final position being vocal and instrumental music director at Elkton High School in Maryland.[16]

Retiring from active teaching in 1951, he relocated in Gnadenhutten. Being a pianist he opened a piano studio and, at least once, appeared as soloist with the Tuscarawas Philharmonic in the Grieg Piano Concerto.[17]

Blind became choir director at the Gnadenhutten Moravian church about 1954 and served until 1957. Eventually, he transferred to Schoenbrunn Community Moravian Church in 1959.

As a composer Blind has written more than one hundred songs, several piano pieces, two anthems and two operettas. Most of the songs, piano pieces, and the operettas were written when he was teaching. Although Blind did some composing when he returned to Ohio, none of it seems to have been for the church. In this respect Blind is a rarity within the Moravian Church, whose composers tend to emphasize sacred, over secular composition.

ELIZABETH ERVIN

Elizabeth Kytle Ervin was born in Tuscarawas, Ohio 22 April 1920. Prior to her marriage to Robert C. Ervin in 1943, she served the Sharon Church as junior choir director. She continued in this capacity for several years and often performed the piano in piano-organ duets with church organist, Mrs. Esther Oerter Cribbs. By 1949 Mrs. Ervin had become the senior choir director.

As a composer Mrs. Ervin wrote a junior choir anthem entitled, "Oh, Lord, We Thank You," which was sung at the Sharon Harvest Home Service 23 November 1952. The words were by fellow Sharon member and hymn writer, Mrs. Bessie Van Lehn. Mrs. Van Lehn penned many hymn texts during her life, but this is the only instance of her writing a text for an anthem.

RUTH PFOHL GRAMS

Ruth Grams, the composer, wrote at least two compositions while living in Ohio. The first of these was an anthem entitled "The People Had a Mind to Work." This was written for the dedication of the new Reuter pipe organ in 1950. The anthem incorporated all three Dover choirs (junior, chapel, and senior), and was sung 19 February 1950.

The second piece that can be identified is a choral benediction which was performed 10 September 1951. This piece was performed at a vespers service held by the Music Study Club, of which Mrs. Grams was a member.

GEORGE STUCKY

George Stucky was born in Dover in 1921. He and his sister Eleanore Stucky Engler were the children of Wilford and Margaret Stucky. George was a clarinetist, while Eleonore was a violinist and vocalist. In these capacities they became an integral part of the Dover First music program.

George assisted Ruth Grams in the direction of the brass choir for the 115th Anniversary of the first Easter celebrated at Schoenbrunn Indian Village.[18] Eventually, he would assume the directorship when the Grams's left for Downey, California in 1958.

The loss of this family was a major blow to the church in general, and the music program in particular. To soften the problems and provide for a smooth transition, a committee was established to take charge of the music program. The membership of this committee consisted of Regina Lenz (organist), Florence Gray (former choir director), Mrs. Margaret Pfeiffer Gotschall, and George Stucky. As part of the efforts of this committee, Stucky became the choir director, and would serve in this position until 1976.

Stucky has composed several compositions for various combinations, both vocal and instrumental. Both sacred and secular pieces can be found in his portfolio. Particularly interesting for Moravian music is his "Dover Anniversary Hymn."[19]

NOTES

1. Hans T. David, "Musical Life in the Pennsylvania Settlements of the Unitas Fratrum," *Moravian Music Foundation Publication, No. 6* (Winston-Salem, N.C.; Moravian Music Foundation, 1959), p. 10.

2. Karl Kroeger, "The Moravian Tradition in Song," *Moravian Music Foundation Bulletin* 20 (Fall–Winter 1975): 9.

3. Blennerhassett moved to Ohio in 1797 and built a sizable estate on an island in the Ohio River several miles to the west of Marietta. He was a musical amateur who composed light secular music. There is presently no evidence that he wrote music while living in Ohio, however, it seems safe to assume that he did. For further information see, E. O. Randall, "Blennerhassett," *Ohio Archealogocal and Historical Society Publication* 1 (1887): 127–63.

4. Rau and David, *Music by American Moravians*, pp. 58–60.

5. Cumnock, *Catalog of the Salem Congregation*, 257 [.1] and SS 133.

6. G. G. Müller, "Lamb of God Thou Shalt Remain Forever," ed. Nolte, SATB, organ, (Brodt Music Co., 1968).

7. Rau and David, *Music by American Moravians*, p. 60.

8. Ibid., pp. 112ff.

9. Peter Wolle, *Hymn Tunes, Used in the Church of the United Brethren, Arranged for Four Voices and the Organ or Piano-forte* (Boston: Shepley & Wright, 1836).

10. *Liturgy and Hymns for the Use of the Protestant Church of the United Brethren or Unitas Fratrum* (Bethlehem, Pa.: Julius W. Held, 1851).

11. Diary of the Gnadenhutten Congregation for the Year 1854, 2 April 1854, John Heckewelder Memorial Moravian Church, Gnadenhutten, Ohio.

12. "Musical Entertainment," 1896 (?) (Unidentified newsclipping found in the Uhrichsville Church Diary.)

13. "Notes and Queries," *Moravian Music Journal* 29 (Summer 1984): 46.

14. Hill died in the Sewickly Valley Hospital near Pittsburgh, Pa., 2 January 1960.

15. Diary of the First Moravian Congregation, 26 January 1890, Port Washington, Ohio.

16. During his many years as a teacher Blind published several articles in such periodicals as *Etude, Music Magazine,* and *Music Supervisor's Journal.*

17. "Devotes Entire Time to Composing," Dover, Ohio, *Daily Reporter,* 10 October 1951.

18. Diary of the Dover Moravian Congregations, 4 April 1947, Dover, Ohio.

19. Copies of this hymn are pasted to the back of many hymnals at Dover First.

21

THE MORAVIAN CHURCH, MORAVIAN MUSIC, AND OHIO

Until the General Synod of 1857 American Moravians were very strongly tied to the church in Germany. Actions taken at that Synod, however, gave Americans considerable self-rule, and was the first step in the eventual separation of the American church from Herrnhut control. Together with the relaxing of German direction one can also detect a certain Americanization of the Moravian church.

The late nineteenth and early twentieth centuries saw Moravians succumbing to the homogenization that was then running rampant throughout the United States. As a result of camp meetings, religious revivals, temperance activities, and ecumenical programs, many uniquely Moravian qualities were being reduced in importance, if not actually discarded.

Internal divisions also contributed to this Americanization. The most important of these was the discarding of the Moravian economies. By this process Moravian settlements ceased to be closed societies and began to permit non-Moravian immigration, thereby exposing Moravians to intense pressure to conform to the American lifestyle.

Like their eastern brethren and sisters, Ohio's Moravians faced tension from outside influences. Pastor Georg Gottfried Müller often complains, in his diary, that Methodists were recruiting among his flock. Much of this activity resulted from the work of a young Methodist circuit rider, James Finley. His route included Methodists who had settled on Moravian land. Previous circuit riders had attended only to their charges and were not concerned with the Moravians. Finley, however, saw no conflict in attempting to convert Moravians who seemed to enjoy his emotional approach to religion. Unfortunately for Pastor Müller, Finley was particularly successful among Beersheba Moravians.

The Americanization process also effected changes in Moravian music. The church's love of music was not reduced, although the type of music preferred underwent considerable change. The introduction of inexpensive, printed anthems of the type composed by Dudley Buck and Harry Rowe

138

Shelly began to flood the church market. As printed anthems became readily available the need for manuscript music diminished. Thus, the congregational collections were boxed and deposited in attics, cellars, closets, and empty rooms where they would be forgotten for many years. The effective result of this move was that anthems performed in Moravian churches were the same as those performed in other denominations.

The same was true in Ohio. When church diaries mention the titles of anthems and solos performed at the turn of the century, and through the first half of the twentieth century, they are typical of all American churches and there is nothing of a uniquely Moravian cast.

Gospel hymns began to compete with traditional Moravian chorales, causing a sense of divided loyalty within congregations. While the eastern congregations were less prone to the effects of this music than the western congregations, their acceptance in the East can be observed in two ways: first, by the presence of some gospel hymns in the current *Hymnal* (1969);[1] and, second, by the use of the gospel style by Moravian composers such as Massah Warner.[2]

The particularly strong influence of gospel hymns in Ohio may be gleaned from the Uhrichsville diary. When the church's first pastor, the future Bishop J. Mortimer Levering, arrived in 1875 he found that many of his people were quite fond of these hymns. Levering attempted to solve the problem in the following manner, "Rec'd . . . fifty copies of 'The Gospel Songs' from John Church & Co., Cincinnati, O. for use in SS and Prayer meetings. In the latter we intersperse the singing of chorales [Moravian hymns] with these Gospel Songs."[3]

Because of the encroachment of American popular religion many Moravian congregations developed attitudes toward Moravian traditions that ran from disregard to strong dislike. This was just as true in Ohio as it was elsewhere. The reintroduction of things Moravian required loving care and strong faith on the part of ministers determined to stand up for those things that made the Moravian Church the Moravian Church.

One such Ohio pastor was M. F. Oerter of Sharon. When he arrived he found that lovefeasts had not been celebrated at Sharon for some time. These were restored along with other characteristic practices. Although quite successful, Oerter would have to wait until the pastorate of his successor, Edwin Kortz, to see all of his desires accepted by the congregation.

A major musical reawakening within the Moravian Church occurred at Central Moravian Church in Bethlehem during the late nineteenth century. In an effort to redirect the type of choral literature performed there, the organist-choirmaster, Dr. J. Fred Wolle, began to introduce music by Johann Sebastian Bach. This took place at a time when America knew little of Bach's music. The Central Moravian choir, as would have been the case with any American church choir at the time, found the music to be unfamiliar and demanding. However, through Wolle's determined efforts, coupled with the choir's musical background, success was achieved. In fact, that very success led to the establishment of America's first Bach Festival in 1900.[4]

The Bach Festival established by J. Fred Wolle did not directly affect the Moravians living in Tuscarawas County. It did, however, affect the greater Cleveland area. Dr. Albert Riemenschneider and his wife Selma had been attending the Bethlehem festivals for some time. Riemenschneider, a noted Bach scholar whose edition of the *Orgelbüchlein* is still considered an important contribution to Bach organ study,[5] had established the Conservatory of Music at Baldwin-Wallace College in Berea, Ohio.

He would eventually establish the Riemenschneider Bach Institute which has become a major research center for the study of Bach and his music in particular, and eighteenth-century music in general. Dr. Wolle's influence on Riemenschneider can be best understood through the following statement made by Mrs. Riemenschneider:

> As my husband and I returned in our automobile from one of our annual spring visits to the Bethlehem Bach Festival (1932), my husband feelingly expressed the thought that it was such a loss for a community like Cleveland to be so entirely without opportunity to hear and know the choral works of Bach. I suggested that we attempt something similar on our own campus, and the outcome was that we resolved to plan a Bach Festival for the next spring of 1933.[6]

Wolle was succeeded as organist at Central Church by Dr. Albert G. Rau. This move led to the next step in the reawakening process. Rau discovered the old Bethlehem congregation collection in the attic at Central Moravian Church. According to Dr. Hans T. David, Rau was the first person to realize the value of the Central collection and Moravian music.[7]

Rau was able to arouse the interest of the eminent musicologist, Dr. Hans T. David who, through a grant from the American Philosophical Society, undertook the task of cataloging the collection. Rau and David's work was published in a groundbreaking text entitled *A Catalogue of Music by American Moravians, 1742–1842*. Published in 1938 the book's value to the study of American music is such that it was reprinted by AMS Press in 1970.[8]

Rau and David's work touched Ohio soon after it was completed. Aware of the Peter connection in Ohio, Dr. Rau informed the *Columbus* [Ohio] *Dispatch* religious editor of the J. F. Peter pieces uncovered during the cataloging process. The editor would have been most interested in the information as she was Miss Alice Peter, formerly of Gnadenhutten.

Miss Peter wrote an article about her relative's compositions that appeared in the 23 August 1938 issue of the *Dispatch*.[9] This article, which mentioned Peter's sacred songs, "The Lord is in His Holy Temple" and "Our Lord Jesus Christ Died for Us," seems to have been the first indication of Moravian music's importance printed in a modern Ohio newspaper.

Once scholarly study proved the value of Moravian music, the next step in the reawakening process was publication of the music. This was undertaken by Hans T. David, who edited a set of sacred songs with orchestral accompaniment, which was published in 1947.[10]

In addition to David's work Clarence Dickenson began to edit many Moravian anthems. Working primarily between the years 1954 and 1956, Dickenson edited more than twenty pieces, which were published by H. W. Gray Music Publishers.[11]

The editions that were produced in the 1940s directly affected the reintroduction of Moravian music in Ohio. During the week of celebrations at Dover First that marked the completion of their remodeling program, Edward W. Leinbach's *Hosanna* was performed. This piece had been published in 1943 in an edition by James Christian Pfohl.[12] Pfohl was the brother of Ruth Pfohl Grams and the Dover First presentation represents the first documented modern performance of a Moravian anthem in Ohio.

The next significant performance occurred at the senior recital of Margaret Jean Pfeiffer Gotschall held at Muskingum College 17 March 1950. As mentioned in chapter eighteen, this recital marks the earliest modern performance of Moravian sacred songs in Ohio.[13]

As the interest in Moravian music grew the noted conductor, Dr. Thor Johnson, with the help of many fellow Moravians, established the first Early American Moravian Music Festival and Seminar.[14] The festival was held at Bethlehem from 26 June to 2 July 1950 with Johnson acting as music director. He would serve as music director for the festivals until his death in 1975.

Ohio's connection with the festivals was immediate. Pastor Richard Michel took a group of Sharonites to the 1950 event.[15] Virtually every festival held since that date has been attended by many Ohioans, most of whom have sung in the festival choirs.[16] Having heard and sung the music of their church it was only natural that a desire to perform it at home developed among these people.

That their desires did not create on immediate revolution is attested to by Pastor Kenneth Robinson, who remembers no Moravian music being performed during his pastorate in the County (1951–54). Even so the seeds had been sown. Only one month after Robinson took charge of his new duties at Home Church in Winston-Salem, North Carolina, James Gross could write in the Gnadenhutten bulletin, "This morning's choir anthem is distinctly Moravian. Written originally by F. F. Hagen, edited and arranged by James Christian Pfohl, son of Bishop J. K. Pfohl and brother of Mrs. Ruth Grams of Dover."[17]

Throughout international Moravianism the 500th anniversary of the Ancient Unitas Fratrum provided a strong reminder of things Moravian. As mentioned in chapter sixteen part of the festivities surrounding this event involved the combined choirs of Fry's Valley, Port Washington and Gnadenhutten. At the anniversary service, held at Gnadenhutten on 25 February 1957, this union choir sang Jeremiah Dencke's "Lord, Our God" and John C. Bechler's "O the Blessedness is Great."[18] These are the first documented modern performances of eighteenth-century Moravian anthems in Ohio.

Through the efforts of Thor Johnson, Dr. Dale Gramly (Dean and President of Salem College at the time), and with the financial support of Charles Babcock, Jr., the Moravian Music Foundation was established in 1956.[19] Located in Winston-Salem, the foundation exists to advance musical research and publication, and to further the appreciation of Moravian music. It is also the agent for the music archives of the Moravian church in America and Great Britain.

From the very beginning of the Moravian Music Foundation Miss Lily Peter has been an active supporter. Although Miss Lily lives in Arkansas, her Ohio connections are strong. A descendant of David Peter, she took her schooling at Gnadenhutten High School. Through her kind generosity the Peter Library of the foundation has become an excellent research center for the study of American and Moravian music.[20]

In 1958 Dr. Donald McCorkle, first Director of the Moravian Music Foundation, visited the Ohio churches. On 13 July 1958 he spoke at Dover First during the morning service, and conducted an information session on Moravian Music in the afternoon. Dr. McCorkle's visit rightly takes us to the last chapter in our history of Ohio Moravian Music, the Ohio Moravian Music Festival of 1961.

NOTES

1. "Amazing Grace," "There is a Fountain Filled with Blood," and "I Need Thee Every Hour."

2. "Softly the Night is Sleeping" is particularly affected by the use of the gospel-style refrain.

3. Diary of the First Moravian Church of Uhrichsville, Ohio, 1 May 1875, Uhrichsville, Ohio.

4. Elmer L. Mack, *The Bach Choir of Bethlehem, 1898-1973* (Bethlehem, Pa.: Privately printed, 1973), p. 8.

5. J. S. Bach, *Orgelbüchlein*, ed. Albert Riemenschneider, (Bryn Mawr, Pa.: Oliver Ditson, 1933).

6. Selma Marting Riemenschneider, "Bach Festival—1933–1964," in *50 Years of Bach in Berea: A History of the Baldwin-Wallace College Bach Festival* (Berea, Ohio: Typescript, n.d.), pp. 3–4.

7. Rau and David, *Music by American Moravians*, Introduction.

8. Rau and David, *Music by American Moravians*, passim.

9. "Old Compositions Found in Pennsylvania Church Loft," Columbus, Ohio, *Columbus Dispatch*, 23 August 1938.

10. David, *Ten Sacred Songs for Soprano, Strings and Organ*, (New York: New York Public Library, 1947).

11. Among these were the first editions of works by Bechler, Dencke, Gregor, Hagen, Herbst, J. F. and S. Peter, and P. Wolle.

12. Leinbach was a North Carolina Moravian who lived from 1823 to 1901. Two Pfohl editions of the anthem are available, one for double chorus and keyboard, and one for band, orchestra and chorus. Both arrangements are published by Brodt Music Co.

13. A facsimile of Mrs. Gotschall's recital program is given in appendix F.

14. Louis Nicholas, *Thor Johnson: American Conductor* (Wisconsin: The Music Festival Committee of the Peninsula Arts Association, 1982).

15. Diary of the Sharon Moravian Church, 25 June 1950, Tuscarawas, Ohio.

16. The single, largest Ohio contingent seems to have been the Gnadenhutten group of twelve people who attended the 1957 Festival with Pastor and Mrs. James Gross.

17. Church Bulletin, John Heckewelder Memorial Moravian Church, Gnadenhutten, Ohio, 23 May 1954.

18. Both of these anthems are Clarence Dickenson arrangements that were published in 1954.

19. Interview with Dr. Dale Gramley, Winston-Salem, N.C., 26 August 1985.

20. "Foundation Gets Library Grant," Moravian Music Foundation Bulletin 5 (Spring–Summer 1961: 1 and 6.

22

THE OHIO MORAVIAN MUSIC FESTIVAL

Dr. Donald McCorkle visited Ohio in May 1958 and again in July. During the second visit he raised the possibility of an Ohio Moravian music festival. Apparently, the reaction was favorable for in November Dr. F. P. Stocker, president of the Northern Province PEC, came to Ohio to pursue the issue.

Dr. Stocker was originally from Port Washington and, therefore, knew the people with whom he was dealing and their potential for supporting such a festival. Always one to proceed methodically, Dr. Stocker held meetings with Mr. Gilbert Roehm, conductor of the Tuscarawas Philharmonic,[1] and a select committee consisting of representatives from each Moravian church. At the latter meeting, held at Dover First, several objections were raised: (1) there was no adequate location for the meetings and public concerts; (2) no pipe organ was available in the public high school; (3) housing was lacking; (4) there was a general lack of interest in good music in the area, especially American Moravian music.

The first two objections can be understood in light of previous festivals. These had been held on college campuses. Thus, auditorium and classroom facilities were available in a central location, something that was not possible in the county at that time. The lack of an organ was solved by not programming music that required the instrument. The third point was absolutely true. The pre-festival planning, however, was quite good and all who came to the festival were able to find accommodations.

The fourth point is an old argument that is sometimes voiced even today. While it is true that Tuscarawas County is not in a cultural center, this does not indicate lack of interest in good music. Also, interest in Moravian music was growing in the county and the festival can be seen as a culmination of that interest.

Eventually, the matter was placed before the church boards for further consideration and they decided to accept the challenge. Consequently, a festival committee was established with Thomas R. Scheffer, President of Reeves Bank of Dover and the Reverend Richard Michel of Sharon as co-chairmen, and Mr. William Drumm of Gnadenhutten as secretary to the committee.[2]

144

Working throughout 1959, 1960, and 1961 the festival committee handled all matters concerning the event. The major thrust began with an August 1960 meeting between the committee and Dr. Thor Johnson, festival conductor. At this meeting, held in Uhrichsville's Buckeye Hotel, plans were finalized concerning the concerts and compositions to be performed.

As the time of the festival neared the pace of life in the county increased dramatically. By May 1961 the festival committee, which had been meeting once a month, began to meet once a week. In addition, all of the other committees associated with the Festival Committee, namely, finance, housing, publicity, properties, pageant, transportation, hospitality, and tours, were meeting once or twice a week.

While the instrumental musicians were mostly professionals from outside the county, the chorus consisted primarily of amateur musicians from Moravian churches throughout the country. Sixty of these were from the local area and they were the first group to rehearse with Thor Johnson 12 June 1961.

There were approximately 250 pre-festival registrants. Most of these were members of the 200-voice chorus and they began to arrive on 21 June. A dinner was held that evening at the Union Country Club, at which host T. R. Scheffer commented that he hoped the visitors "could come to know [the] scenery and Moravian heritage of the county as its residents loved it."[3] There was plenty of opportunity for the visitors to do just that as a pageant, "The Cross at Welhik Tuppeck," was presented at Schoenbrunn Indian village. To this was added many tours of the local area.

The first rehearsal of the complete festival chorus took place at Dover High School at 7 P.M. 21 June. Dr. Johnson and his orchestral personnel arrived at 8:15 P.M. and the practice continued until 10 P.M.

Thursday proved to be an even busier day with choir rehearsals at New Philadelphia High School from 9 to 11 A.M. This was followed by an orchestra rehearsal from 11:15 to 1:00 P.M., and from 3:30 to 5:00 P.M. at Dover High School. A few anxious moments attended the first orchestral rehearsal. Piano soloist Mayne Miller was late. He had given a concert in Baltimore, Maryland the previous evening and his bus had broken down. Through the efforts of several people he arrived at 12:30 P.M. and was able to participate, to the relief of all concerned.

The first concert was held at Dover High School and was completely instrumental in its program.[4] All but the Haydn *Scherzandi* had been heard at previous festivals. More than one thousand people attended this concert which received very fine reviews. Mayne Miller's efforts were particularly well liked; reviewers called them "stellar performances," and noted that "[he] was called back after each appearance by the enthusiastic audience."[5]

The second concert was held at Sharon Moravian Church. Its audience was restricted by the size of the church auditorium, but about five hundred people attended. The Moravian band from Winston-Salem played chorales on the church lawn before the concert. The band, under the direction of Austin E. Burke, Jr., had not performed at the earlier concert. This concert included instrumental compositions, sacred songs with Miss Ilona Kombrink as soloist, and a brief commentary on the concert's music by Dr. McCorkle.

The John Heckewelder Memorial Moravian Church was the site of the third concert. In format it was like the Sharon concert, except that a Quartet by Pleyel replaced the Antes Trio and Johann C. Bach's Concertante, Op. 7, No. 2 replaced the Wranitzky Trio.

The final concert was to have been held at Schoenbrunn Indian village. Because of inclement weather this was not possible and the Dover High School auditorium was used instead. This concert was the most Ohio oriented of the four. Also, three of the eleven items on the program had never been performed at previous festivals. These were the Müller anthem, "Lamb of God, Thou Shalt Remain Forever," which received its first modern performance; the Hovhaness "Prayer of Saint Gregory"; and "How Beautiful Upon the Mountains," by John Antes.

The Antes sacred song "Loveliest Immanuel" was also performed. Its use at the festival was appropriate for at the time it was believed that the copy of this aria found in the Crackerbox was a holograph. Subsequent research, however, strongly suggests that the copyist was a single sister living in Bethlehem and not Antes.

One other aspect of the concert is of interest for Ohio. Two Tuscarawas vocalists appeared as soloists. The professional soloist, Ilona Kombrink, was assisted in J. F. Peter's *It is A Precious Thing* by baritone Robert Lane. Lane was the vocal music instructor in the Gnadenhutten public schools and the choir director of the Gnadenhutten Moravian congregation.

Miss Kombrink was assisted by tenor Richard Jones and bass Robert Lowe in the Leinbach *Hosanna*. Jones is a member of Dover First. He had been blessed with a fine voice from childhood and had become well-known as a boy soprano. Eventually, his tenor voice was heard throughout the county as he appeared as soloist in virtually every Moravian church. Local Moravian wind performers were also able to participate in the final concert, since the Winston-Salem Band was augmented with Tuscarawas musicians and performed chorales before and after the concert.

Despite the various problems connected with such an endeavor, the Ohio festival was highly successful. The Reverend John Morman kept track of the audience size and his totals indicate that the festival drew approximately 4,650 people. An important benefit of the concert was the fact that many of the festival musicians gave their talents for Sunday church services. The majority of these, including Johnson, Kombrink, and McCorkle attended services at Gnadenhutten. Other instrumentalists performed at Dover First, Uhrichsville, and Sharon.

Through the festival Tuscarawas Moravians began to realize their part in the growing awareness of the importance of American Moravian music. Non-Ohio Moravians became aware of the significance of Ohio Moravianism. But most important Moravians and non-Moravians had an opportunity to sample the contribution of Moravian musicians to American music. As a message from the festival committee found in the Schoenbrunn Community Moravian Church Bulletin for 2 July 1961 so appropriately states, "Each of us who attended the Festival can rejoice at the spiritual blessing we received through the fine music we heard."[6]

NOTES

1. The meeting was held to discuss the availability of local instrumental musicians.

2. A picture of these gentlemen with Thor Johnson appears over the article, "1961 Moravian Music Festival Planned Here," New Philadelphia, Ohio, *Daily Times*, 30 August 1960.

3. "Over 200 Participants Attend Moravian Music Festival Dinner," New Philadelphia, Ohio, *Daily Times*, 23 June 1961.

4. Programs for all of the concerts are found in appendix G.

5. "Pianist Gives Stellar Performance," New Philadelphia, Ohio, *Daily Times*, 23 June 1961.

6. Church Bulletin, Schoenbrunn Community Moravian Church, New Philadelphia, Ohio, 2 July 1961.

Appendixes

APPENDIX A
CHURCH MINISTERS

GNADENHUTTEN

Dates of Service	Name of Minister
1800–1805	Ludwig Huebner
1805–1814	Georg Gottfried Müller
1814–1826	Jacob Rauschenberger
1826–1827	George F. Troeger
1827–1835	Samuel Huebner
1836–1837	George F. Troeger
1837–1841	Herman J. Tietze
1841–1849	Sylvester Wolle
1849–1850	Charles Bleck
1850–1852	Lewis Kampmann
1852–1859	Henry C. Bochman
1859–1865	Clement L. Reinke
1865–1873	James Haman
1873–1874	Louis Huebner
1874–1882	Henry J. Van Vleck
1882–1888	Henry T. Bachman
1889–1893	Edmund Oerter
1893–1987	William Oerter
1897–1909	William H. Rice
1909–1913	William Strohmeir
1913–1919	Joseph E. Weinland
1919–1922	Charles Sperling
1922–1931	Frederick R. Nitzschke
1931–1941	Robert Brennecke
1941–1944	Chester Quear
1944–1958	James Gross
1958–1966	John Morman

BEERSHEBA

Dates of Service	*Name of Minister*
1805–1814	George Gottfried Müller
1814–1823	Jacob Rauschenberger

SHARON

Dates of Service	*Name of Minister*
1815–1827	Jacob Rauschenberger
1827–1835	Samuel Huebner
1835–1837	George F. Troeger
1837–1841	Herman J. Tietze
1841–1849	Sylvester Wolle
1849–1850	Charles Bleck
1850–1851	Lewis Kampmann
	F. W. Damus
1851–1853?	Theophilus Wunderling
1853–1858	Francis R. Holland
1858–1861	Eugene Leibert
1861–1862	Peter Wolle
1862–1867	Henry T. Bachman
1867–1870	David Zeisberger Smith
1870–1875	Edmund Oerter
1875–1890	Joseph J. Ricksecker
1890–1898	Paul M. Greider
1898–1903	George M. Schulz
1903–1910	Joseph E. Weinland
1910–1936	Maurice F. Oerter
1936–1941	Edwin W. Kortz
1942–1948	Ernest Drebert
1948–1962	Richard E. Michel

DOVER FIRST

Dates of Service	*Name of Minister*
1840–1841	Herman J. Tietze
1841–1842	Sylvester Wolle
1842–1850	Lewis Kampman
1850–1853	Francis R. Holland
1853–1855	Peter Wolle

1855–1860	Henry G. Clauder
1860–1862	no regular pastor
1862–1866	Albert L. Oerter
1866–1871	S. Morgan Smith
1871–1874	Charles B. Shultz
1874–1880	Charles C. Lanius
1880	Walter Jordan
1881–1888	Edmund Oerter
1888–1896	Manuel Kemper
1896–1908	Christian Weber
1908–1911	Thomas Shields
1911–1915	F. William Stengel
1915–1919	Robert Brennecke
1919–1930	Joseph E. Weinland
1930–1936	Vernon Couillard
1937–1944	Robert Giering
1944–1958	Roy Grams
1958–1966	Gordon Stoltz

FRY'S VALLEY

Dates of Service	*Name of Minister*
1852–1859	Henry T. Bachman
1859–1865	Clement L. Reinke
1865–1873	James Haman
1873–1874	Louis R. Huebner
1874–1891	Henry J. Van Vleck
1891–1896	Calvin Kinsey
1896–1901	H. J. Hartman
1901–1907	Samuel C. Albright
1908–1910	George Miksch
1910–1914	C. J. R. Meinert
1914–1919	Albert Harke
1919–1920	Calvin Kinsey
1920–1925	Theodore Reinke
1926–1934	Robert E. Clewell
1935–1938	Reuben Gross
1938–1946	Paul Zeller
1948–1951	Karl Bregenzer
1951–1954	Kenneth Robinson
1956–1961	Dean Sauerwine

UHRICHSVILLE

Dates of Service	Name of Minister
1874–1879	J. M. Levering
1879–1884	John H. Clewell
1884–1885	William Oerter
1885–1896	William Romig
1896–1899	William Fluck
1899–1900	J. F. Kaiser
1900–1904	J. R. Dalling
May–Aug 1904	Clement L. Reinke
1904–1907	R. L. Williams
1908–1909	W. Vivian Moses
Sept.–Nov. 1909	Edmund Oerter
1909–1916	Robert E. Clewell
1916–1919	C. E. Heaveshardt
1919–1924	H. A. Kuehl
1924–1926	Samuel Wedman
1926–1931	G. F. Weinland
1932	John R. Weinlick
1933–1940	R. D. Bollman
1940–1945	Edward Fischer
1945–1948	John Morman
1948–1954	C. L. Riske
1955–1959	Otto Dreydoppel
1959–1962	W. W. Harke

PORT WASHINGTON

Dates of Service	Name of Minister
1881–1884	John H. Clewell
1884–1890	William Oerter
1890–1891	R. S. Weinland
1892–1894	Henry J. Van Vleck
1895	Christian Weber
1896–1902	Calvin Kinsey
1902–1906	O. Eugene Moore
1906–1909	William Fluck
1909–1911	Calvin Kinsey
1913–1915	C. J. R. Meinert
1915–1916	Allen Zimmerman
	Calvin Kinsey
1916–1918	Roland Bahnsen
1918–1922	Victor Flinn

1920	Howard Nelson
	(sabbatical replacement)
1922–1927	F. G. Fulmer
1927–1934	Howard Nelson
1934–1936	Samuel Wedman
1936	Charles Sperling
1936–1938	Reuben Gross
1938	Maurice Oerter
1938–1946	Paul Zeller
1946–1950	Karl Bregenzer
1950–1951	James Gross
1951–1954	Kenneth Robinson
1954	James Gross
1954–1961	Dean Sauerwine

DOVER SOUTH

Dates of Service	*Name of Minister*
1925–1930	Joseph E. Weinland
1930–1936	Vernon Couillard
1937–1944	Robert Giering
1944–1958	Roy Grams
1958	Gordon Stoltz
1958–1960	Donald Kirts
1960–1964	Gwyned Williams

SCHOENBRUNN COMMUNITY

Dates of Service	Name of Minister
1947–1950	W. Vivian Moses
1950–1951	John H. Johansen
1952–1957	William Weinland
1957–1960	Donald Kirts
1960–1964	Gwyned Williams

APPENDIX B
CHURCH ORGANISTS

GNADENHUTTEN

Dates of Service	*Name of Organist*
Prior to 1874?	Sarah Louisa McConnell
1874–1876	Fred Van Vleck
1876–1889?	Sarah Louisa McConnell
By 1889–1919	Theodore Van Vleck
1919–1928	Mary Van Vleck Wohlwend
1928–1936?	Elizabeth Ebenhack
1936–1941	Helen Demuth
1941–1943?	Ruth Blackburn
1943?–1944	Mary Pfeiffer
1944–1957	Lucy McConnell Miller
1957–1961	Barbara Williams Daniels

SHARON

Dates of Service	*Name of Organist*
1828–1837	Jacob Blickensderfer?
1837–1841	Susan Stotz Tietze?
1841–1849	Caroline Wolle?
1849–1875	?
1875–1890	Joseph John Ricksecker
1890–?	?
?–1953	Esther Oerter Cribbs
1953–1961	Phyllis Ronald

DOVER FIRST

Dates of Service	*Name of Organist*
1842–1855	Jacob Blickensderfer

ca. 1858	Israel and Lizette
	Ricksecker (asst.)
?–1880	Helen Sheeler
1880– ?	Addie Harger
1892–1908	Emma Harger
1908– ?	Adelania Sindefield
1910–1932	Georgia Hill Cunning
1920–1932	Regina Lenz (asst.)
1932–1975	Regina Lenz
	1932–1975
	Ruth Pfeiffer (asst.)

FRY'S VALLEY

Dates of Service	*Name of Organist*
1896–1901	Miss Hartman?
	Omie Kaiser
	Myra Rank
	Nellie Fox
ca. 1912	Nellie Kinsey
?–1933	Florence Everett
1933–1941	Anne Montague
1941–1950	Isabel Bregenzer
1950?–1957?	Joan Horsfall
1957– ?	Mrs. Jack Garabrandt

UHRICHSVILLE

Dates of Service	*Name of Organist*
1878–1879	Carrie Everett
ca. 1887	Mrs. Hart
ca. 1889	Katz? Peter
ca. 1900	Dollie Robinett
1905?–1906?	Zoe Peter
19? –1910	Wayne Crossland
1911–1931	Zoe Peter
? –?	Bill Rennecker
? –1942	Beatrice Romig
1943–1946	Alma Arthurs
1946–1948	Marie Morman
1948–1971	Alma Arthurs

PORT WASHINGTON

Dates of Service	Name of Organist
? –1884	Miss Hammersly
1884– ?	Nannie Kilgore
ca. 1888	Edna Hill
ca. 1895	Lida Nelson?
1905–1912	Edith Fidler
1912–1915	?
1915– ?	Clara George
1918– ?	Lois Hand
? –1936	Sadie Cappel
1936–1970s	Leona Stocker Arth

DOVER SOUTH

Dates of Service	Name of Organist
ca. 1930	Greta Gerber
1938–1939	Frances Korns
1938– ?	Janet Klein (asst.)
1944–1948	Mrs. John Daniels
	Martha Mason
1948–1957	Frances Korns
	Janet Aebersold
	Mary Jane Souers
1957– ?	Frances Korns
? –1958	Linda McGonigal
1958–1961	Linda Springer
1961– ?	Karen Aebersold
	Linda Springer

SCHOENBRUNN COMMUNITY

Dates of Service	Name of Organist
1947– ?	Blanche McClean
	Carrie Myer

APPENDIX C
CHURCH CHOIR DIRECTORS

GNADENHUTTEN

Dates of Service	Name of Director
1841–1842	Herman Julius Tietze
ca. 1848	Solomon Hoover
1874–1876	Fred Van Vleck
ca. 1888–1938	Frank Winsch
1938–?	Leona Miksch Parks
ca. 1941	Chester Quear
ca. 1944	Mrs. Chester Quear (?)
1945–1954	Leona Miksch Parks
1954–1957	Emmett Blind
1957–1959	Mabel Gallagher
1959–?	Mina Williamson
?–?	Robert A Lane

SHARON

Dates of Service	Name of Director
1841–1842	Herman Julius Tietze
1875–1890	J. J. Ricksecker
ca. 1914	A. T. Myer
1936–1942	Margaret Kortz
1947–1949	Imogene Battershell Emig
1949–1955	Elizabeth Ervin
1955–present	Phyllis Ronald

DOVER FIRST

Dates of Service	Name of Director
1853–1855	Peter Wolle
1874–?	B. B. Brashear

159

1895–1915?	Mary Wassman
1923–1932	Ben Cunning
1932–1934	Jayne Urban
1934–1945	Florence Gray
1945	Aline Damerest
1945–1946	James Eddy
1946–1952	Florence Gray
1952–1958	Ruth Pfohl Grams
1958–1976	George Stucky

FRY'S VALLEY

Dates of Service	*Name of Director*
Prior to 1900	Henry J. Van Vleck
1926–1934	Robert E. Clewell
1934–1941	Anne Montague (?)
1941–1950	Isabel Everett Bregenzer (?)

UHRICHSVILLE

Dates of Service	*Name of Director*
Prior to 1900	John H. Clewell (?)
ca. 1909	Horace Eggenberg
1911–1931	Zoe Peter
?–1940 ?	Theo Schug
?–1945 ?	Beatrice Romig
1946–1947	Bill Rennecker
1948	Marie Morman
1948–1951	Anne Riske
1951	Mary Lois Ginther
1951–1953	Charles A. Selbee
1953–1955	Anne Riske
	Margie Craft
1955–1956	Leroy Jaffe
1956–1958	Dorothy Miller
1958–1960	Lillian Gooding
1960–present	Margie Craft

PORT WASHINGTON

Dates of Service	Name of Director
ca. 1888–1902?	Prof. Cronebach
ca. 1902	Mrs. O. Eugene Moore
ca. 1906	Benjamin Fidler
ca. 1909	Curtis Maud
ca. 1919	Margaret Lawer
1936–1958	Leona Stocker Arth

DOVER SOUTH

Dates of Service	Name of Director
1952–1953	Janice Kennedy
1954–?	Carol Ann Hyer

SCHOENBRUNN COMMUNITY

Dates of Service	Name of Director
1947–?	Imogene Batthershell Emig
(1951)	Mrs. J. Davis Williams (substitute)

APPENDIX D
YOUTH CHOIR DIRECTORS

GNADENHUTTEN

Dates of Service	*Name of Director*
	Junior Choir
1925–1931	F. R. Nitzschke
ca. 1935	Leona Parks
ca. 1960	Grace Day
	Ruth Baker
	Girls Choir
ca. 1950	Leona Parks
ca. 1954	Emma Gross
ca. 1960	Marie Morman
	Primary Choir
ca. 1960	Marie Morman
	Sextet and Jr-Hi Girls Choir
ca. 1960	Jeanette Garrett

SHARON

Dates of Service	*Name of Director*
	Chapel Choir
ca. 1961	Mrs. J. Daniel Garver
	Cherub Choir
1959–1961	Virginia Crites
	Junior Choir
ca. 1941	Margaret Kortz?
1941–1956?	Elizabeth Kytle Ervin
1956–?	Mona Haupert Wilson

162

DOVER FIRST

Dates of Service	*Name of Director*
	Junior Choir
1911–1915	Mrs. F. W. Stengel
?–1946	Florence Gray
1946–?	Eleanor Stucky
ca. 1950	Ruth Pfohl Grams
1959–1973	Ruth Peter Pfeiffer
	Girls Choir
?	Lawrence H. Oerter
?	Georgia Hill Cunning
	Chapel Choir
1947–1958	Ruth Pfohl Grams
1959–1973	Ruth Peter Pfeiffer
	Intermediate Choir
1946–1958	Ruth Pfohl Grams

UHRICHSVILLE

Dates of Service	*Name of Director*
	Junior Choir
1953–1955	Margie Craft
1955–?	Dorothy Smith
ca. 1960	Adelia Spring
	Cherub Choir
ca. 1955	Mrs. J. Hammersley

PORT WASHINGTON

Dates of Service	*Name of Director*
	Children's Choir
ca. 1919	Margaret Lawer

DOVER SOUTH

Dates of Service	*Name of Director*
	Junior Choir
1952–1953	Janice Kennedy
1954–?	Carol Ann Hyer

SCHOENBRUNN COMMUNITY

Dates of Service	*Name of Director*
	Junior Choir
1950–1953	Mrs. Jess Born
1958–1961	Dorothy Sickinger
	Cherub Choir
1960–1961	Dorothy Sickinger

APPENDIX E
INSTRUMENTAL MUSIC DIRECTORS

GNADENHUTTEN

Dates of Service	*Name of Director*
	Trombone Choir
?–1934	Frank Winsch
1934–?	Wilbur O. Demuth
ca. 1950s	Richard Shamel
	Church Orchestra
1922–1925	F. R. Nitzschke
ca. 1944	William Padgett
ca. 1956	Herbert L. Gray

SHARON

Dates of Service	*Name of Director*
	Trombone Choir
1957–1958	Vera Schupp
ca. 1961	Shirly Schaar

DOVER FIRST

Dates of Service	*Name of Director*
	Trombone Choir
1923–1945	Eugene Lightell
1945–1957	Ruth Pfohl Grams
1958–?	George Stucky
	Church Orchestra
1879	Mr. Mckeeven ?
1921–1945	Eugene Lightell
1945–1950?	Ruth Pfohl Grams

165

UHRICHSVILLE

Dates of Service	*Name of Director*
	Trombone Choir
1945–1946	Charles W. Ginther

APPENDIX F
MARGARET PFEIFFER SENIOR RECITAL PROGRAM

Muskingum College Conservatory of Music

Presents

in

Senior Recital

Margaret Pfeiffer, *Soprano*

Dorothy Milligan
at the piano

Marilyn R. Taylor, *Violinist*

Barbara Swartz
at the piano

Assisted by

College String Group

JOHN D. KENDALL, First Violin
JANIS ASHDOWN, First Violin
MARILYN R. TAYLOR, Second Violin
DOROTHY MILLIGAN, Second Violin
BILL GARNER, Viola
MARTHA BORTON, Cello
PATRICIA BOWER, String Bass

BROWN CHAPEL

Tuesday, March 21, 1950   8:15 p. m.

167

Program

Das Fischermädchen .... Franz Schubert

Allerseelen .. .. Richard Strauss

Zueignung .... Richard Strauss

Sonata in A Major for Violin and Piano .... Mozart
    Allegro di Molto
    Tema con Variazioni—Andante

The Way That Lovers Use .... Bainbridge Crist

Hedgerow .. .. Arthur Benjamin

Two Shakespeare Songs .... Roger Quilter
    O Mistress Mine
    Blow, Blow, Thou Winter Wind

Early Morning .... Cecil Burleigh

Fairy Sailing .... Cecil Burleigh

Dew .... Cecil Burleigh

Yuletide .... Cecil Burleigh

Ich will singen von einem Könige .... Jeremiah Dencke
(I Speak of the Things)

Freuet euch, ihr Tochter Seines Volks .... Jeremiah Dencke
(O, Be Glad, Ye Daughters of His People)

Der Herr ist in Seinem heiligen Temple .... Johann Friedrich Peter
(The Lord is in His Holy Temple)

Leite mich in Deiner Wahrheit .... Johann Friedrich Peter
(Lead Me in Thy Truth)

Gebet in der Geruch Seines Brautigams-Namens .... Jeremiah Dencke
(Go Ye Forth in His Name)

Meine Seele erhebet den Herrn .... Jeremiah Dencke
(My Soul Doth Magnify the Lord)

Concerto in E minor .... Nardini
    Andante
    Allegro

APPENDIX G
OHIO MORAVIAN MUSIC FESTIVAL
PROGRAM

SEASON 1961

TUSCARAWAS
COUNTY

OHIO

THOR JOHNSON, Music Director

Festival Program

First Program

Thursday, June 22, 1961   8:00 P.M.

HIGH SCHOOL, DOVER, OHIO

Quintet No. 5 in B flat major . . . John Frederik Peter (1746-1813)

I. Allegro moderato   II. Adagio   III. Allegro
CHARLES TREGER, Violin   RALPH JACKNO, Viola
ANN RYLANDS, Violin   ENDEL KALAM, Viola
GORDON EPPERSON, Violoncello

Symphony in D major . . . . Josef Riepel (1709-1782)

I. Allegro molto   II. Allegretto   III. Allegro
THE FESTIVAL ORCHESTRA

Sonata in B flat major for Piano, Opus 3, No. 3
Christian I. Latrobe (1758-1836)

I. Adagio molto   II. Andante pastorale   III. Allegro
MAYNE MILLER, Piano

Scherzando No. 5 in E major . . Franz Joseph Haydn (1732-1809)

I. Allegro   II. Menuett/Trio   III. Adagio   IV. Presto
(First modern U. S. Performance)

Scherzando No. 2 in C major . . Franz Joseph Haydn (1732-1809)

I. Allegro   II. Menuett/Trio   III. Adagio   IV. Presto
(First modern U. S. Performance)

Intermission

Concerto in F major for Piano and Orchestra, K. 413
Wolfgang Amade Mozart (1756-1791)

I. Allegro   II. Larghetto   III. Menuetto
MAYNE MILLER, Piano

Symphony in C major, Opus 3, No. 1
Johann Gabriel Meder (c. 1730-c. 1800)

I. Allegro con brio   II. Adagio   III. Rondo Allegretto
CHARLES TREGER, Violin   ENDEL KALAM, Viola
WALTER SMOLENSKI, Violin   RALPH JACKNO, Viola

Page five

Second Program

Friday, June 23, 1961   8:00 P.M.

THE SHARON MORAVIAN CHURCH, (near) TUSCARAWAS, OHIO

Prelude of Chorales on the Church Lawn (7:30 P.M.)
> THE MORAVIAN BAND (Winston-Salem, North Carolina),
> AUSTIN E. BURKE, Jr., Director

Trio in C major, Opus 3, No. 3 . . . . John Antes (1740-1811)
> I. Larghetto   II. Grave sostenuto; Allegro
> RALPH WINKLER, Violin   MARY CANBERG, Violin
> HAROLD CRUTHIRDS, Violoncello

Three Songs for Soprano and Strings
> I. "I Speak of the Things" .... Jeremiah Dencke (1725-1795)
> II. "My Saviour Lies in Anguish" .... George Godfrey Mueller (1762-1821)
> III. "I Love to Dwell in Spirit" .... David Moritz Michael (1751-1827)
> ILONA KOMBRINK, Soprano

Trio in G major, Opus 53, No. 2 . . . Paul Wranitzky (1756-1808)
> I. Allegro   II. Adagio   III. Allegro
> JOHN MEACHAM, Flute   CHARLES TREGER, Violin
> GORDON EPPERSON, Violoncello

COMMENTARY ON THIS EVENING'S MUSIC: Donald M. McCorkle

Anthems of the Moravian Church
> I. "O the Blessedness Is Great" ...... John Christian Bechler (1781-1857)
> II. "Hearken! Stay Close to Jesus Christ" David M. Michael (1751-1827)
> III. "O Sacred Head, Now Wounded" .... arr. Johannes Herbst (1735-1812)
> IV. "Sing, O Ye Heavens" .... John Frederik Peter (1746-1813)
> THE FESTIVAL CHORUS and ORCHESTRA

Page six

Third Program

Saturday, June 24, 1961   8:00 P.M.

HECKEWELDER MEMORIAL MORAVIAN CHURCH, GNADENHUTTEN, O.

Prelude of Chorales on the Church Lawn (7:30 P.M.)
THE MORAVIAN BAND (Winston-Salem, North Carolina),
AUSTIN E. BURKE, JR., Director

Quartet No. 1 in G major for Flute and Strings
Ignace Pleyel (1757-1831)
(arr. Francois Devienne)

I. Moderato   II. Adagio consordini   III. Rondo

JOHN MEACHAM, Flute   ENDEL KALAM, Viola
CHARLES TREGER, Violin   HAROLD CRUTHIRDS, Violoncello

Three Songs for Soprano and Strings

I. "I Speak of the Things" .... Jeremiah Dencke (1725-1795)
II. "My Saviour Lies in Anguish" .... George Godfrey Mueller (1762-1821)
III. "I Love to Dwell in Spirit" .... David Moritz Michael (1751-1827)

ILONA KOMBRINK, Soprano

Sinfonia Concertante in E flat major, Opus 7, No. 2
Johann C. Bach (1735-1782)

I. Allegro   II. Andante   III. Tempo di Menuetto

CHARLES TREGER and RALPH WINKLER, Solo Violins,
WARREN SUTHERLAND, Solo Oboe

COMMENTARY ON THIS EVENING'S MUSIC: Donald M. McCorkle

Anthems of the Moravian Church

I. "O the Blessedness Is Great" .... Johann Christian Bechler (1784-1857)
II. "Hearken! Stay Close to Jesus Christ" David M. Michael (1751-1827)
III. "O Sacred Head, Now Wounded" .... arr. Johannes Herbst (1735-1812)
IV. "Sing, O Ye Heavens" .... John Frederik Peter (1746-1813)

THE FESTIVAL CHORUS and ORCHESTRA

Page seven

Fourth Program

Sunday, June 25, 1961   4:00 P.M.

SCHOENBRUNN STATE PARK, SCHOENBRUNN, OHIO

Prelude of Chorales by Augmented Band, (3:30 p.m.)
AUSTIN E. BURKE, JR., Director

Hymn: "Now Thank We All Our God"
CONGREGATION

Invocation: . . . . Bishop Kenneth G. Hamilton
President, Provincial Elders Conference, North

Interlude: "Prayer of Saint Gregory"
for Trumpet and String Orchestra Alan Hovhaness (1908-   )
WILLIAM BRIAN, Trumpet   GILBERT ROEHM, Conducting

Chorale, Aria and Anthems of the Moravian Church
John Antes (1740-1811)

Chorale: "In Joyful Hymns of Praise"
Anthem: "How Beautiful Upon The Mountains"
(First Modern Performance)
Aria: "Loveliest Immanuel"
ILONA KOMBRINK, Soprano
Anthem: "Shout Ye Heavens"
THE FESTIVAL CHORUS

Hymn: "Jesus Makes My Heart Rejoice"
Grimm's Choralbuch (1755)
CONGREGATION

Interlude: "The Lark Ascending,"
A Romance for Violin and Orchestra
Ralph Vaughan Williams (1872-1958)
CHARLES TREGER, Violin

Anthems of the Moravian Church
I. "Lamb of God, Thou Shalt Remain Forever" G. G. Mueller (1762-1813)
(First Modern Performance)
II. "It Is A Precious Thing" . . . . John Frederik Peter (1746-1813)
ILONA KOMBRINK, Soprano   ROBERT LANE, Baritone
III. "Hosanna" . . . . Edward W. Leinbach (1823-1901)
ILONA KOMBRINK, Soprano   RICHARD JONES, Tenor   ROBERT LOWE, Bass
THE FESTIVAL CHORUS

Hymn: "Sing Hallelujah, Praise the Lord"
John C. Bechler (1784-1857)
CONGREGATION

Benediction: . . . . Bishop Kenneth G. Hamilton

Postlude of Chorales by Augmented Band
Austin E. Burke, Jr., Director

Page eight

BIBLIOGRAPHY

MANUSCRIPT SOURCES

Bethlehem, Pennsylvania. Moravian Archives. Diaries and other official records of the individual Indian missions of the American Moravian Church especially those of the Northern Province.

Bethlehem, Pennsylvania.Moravian Archives. Port Washington Moravian Church. Diaries and other official records.

Columbus, Ohio. Ohio Historical Society. August C. Mahr Papers.

Dover, Ohio. Dover First Moravian Church. Diaries and other official records. (The church diaries are now located at the Moravian Archives in Bethlehem, Pennsylvania. Microfilm copies of these are held by the local congregation.)

Dover, Ohio. Dover First Moravian Church. Lenz, Regina. "A History of the Moravian Church of Dover, Ohio." Dover, Ohio, n.d.

Dover, Ohio. Dover South Moravian Church. Diaries and other official records. (Until 1958 the diaries of this congregation were kept in the Dover First diaries. From 1958 to 1966 the diaries were kept with those of Schoenbrunn Community. The first separate Dover South diary to be kept at the church begins with the date 2 January 1966.)

Fry's Valley, Ohio. Fry's Valley Moravian Church. Diaries and other official records.

Gnadenhutten, Ohio. John Heckewelder Memorial Moravian Church. Diaries and other official records of the Beersheba and Gnadenhutten churches.

New Philadelphia, Ohio. Schoenbrunn Community Moravian Church. Diaries and other official records.

Tuscarawas, Ohio, Sharon Moravian Church. Diaries and other official records.

Uhrichsville, Ohio. First Moravian Church. Diaries and other official records.

Winston-Salem, North Carolina. Moravian Archives Diaries and other official records of the Salem Congregation, Salem Boys School and Salem Academy and College for Girls and Young Women.

INTERVIEWS

Arth, Leona. Port Washington, Ohio. Interview with author, 2 July 1985.

Arthurs, Alma. Uhrichsville, Ohio. Interview with author, 22 September 1985.

Demuth, Roy and Helen. Gnadenhutten, Ohio. Interview with author, 3 February 1983.

Gottschall, Margaret Pfeiffer. Cambridge, Ohio. Interview with author, 2 July 1985.

Gramley, Dale. Winston-Salem, North Carolina. Interview with author, 26 August 1985.

Lenz, Regina, and Florence Gray. Dover, Ohio. Interview with author, 14 February 1983.

Michel, Richard and Winifred. Tuscarawas, Ohio. Interview with author, 17 March 1985.

Pfeiffer, Ruth Peter. Dover, Ohio. Interview with author, 2 July 1985.

Reed, Dr., and Mrs. H. E. Dover, Ohio. Interview with author 12 March 1985.

Robinson, Kenneth. Winston-Salem, North Carolina. Interview with author, 6 December 1984.

Steelman, Robert. Bethlehem, Pennsylvania. Interview with author, 22 August 1982.

Stocker, Dr. F. P. Bethlehem, Pennsylvania. Interview with author, 19 April 1985.

Zollar, Margaret Ricksecker. Dover, Ohio. Interview with author, 6 February 1983.

NEWSPAPERS

The Columbus Dispatch. Columbus, Ohio, 23 August 1938.

The Daily Iron Valley Report. Dover, Ohio, 1 June 1872–1 January 1910.

The Daily Times. New Philadelphia, Ohio, 2 January 1936–31 December 1936; and 1 January 1942–7 July 1961.

The Dover Daily Reporter. Dover, Ohio, 1 January 1940–7 July 1961.

The Ohio Democrat. New Philadelphia, Ohio, 22 December 1865–1 January 1900.

PERIODICALS

Baer, Elizabeth. "Music: An Integral Part of Life in Ohio, 1800–1860." *Bulletin of the Historical Society of Ohio* 65 (July 1956): 197–210.

Betterman, Wilhelm. "Wie das Posaunen-blasen in der Brüdergemeine aufkam." *Jahrbuch der Brüdergemeine* 33 (Winter 1937–38).

Blickensderfer, Jesse. "Establishment of the Moravian Congregations in Ohio." *Transactions of the Moravian Historical Society* 1 (1857–58): 154–76.

Boeringer, James. "Francis Florentine Hagen." *Journal of Church Music* (October 1982): 12–13.

———. "A Guide to the Moravian Lovefeast." *Moravian Music Journal* 26 (Winter 1981): 86–87.

———. "Johann Christian Bechler." *Journal of Church Music* 25 (June 1983): 7 and 13.

———. "Musical Instruments: Lititz Congregation Musical Instruments." *Moravian Music Journal* 26 (Winter 1981): 88–89.

Brickenstein, H. A. "Sketch of the Early History of Lititz, 1742–75." *Transactions of the Moravian Historical Society* 1 (1873): 343–74.

Clare, Israel Smith. "Historic Lititz." *The Pennsylvania-German* 10 (May 1909): 210–20.

Clark, David Sanders. "Moravian Mission of Pilgerruh." *Transactions of the Moravian Historical Society* 12 (1913): 53–80.

Claypool, Richard D. "Archival Collections of the Moravian Music Foundation and Some Notes on the Philharmonic Society of Bethlehem." *Fontes Artis Musicae* 23 (1976): 177–90.

———. "Johann Friedrich Frueauff." *Moravian Music Journal* 26 (Winter 1981): 76–81.

———. "Mr. John Antes: Instrumentmaker." *Bulletin of the Moravian Music Foundation* 23 (Fall–Winter 1978): 10–13.

Claypool, Richard D., and Robert Steelman. "The Music Collections in the Moravian Archives." *Transactions of the Moravian Historical Society* 23 (1979): 13–49.

Crawford, Richard. "The Moravians and Eighteenth-Century American Musical Mainstreams." *Bulletin of the Moravian Music Foundation* 21 (Fall–Winter 1976): 2–7.

Cumnock, Frances. "The Salem Congregation Collection: 1790–1808." *Bulletin of the Moravian Music Foundation* 17 (Spring–Summer 1972): 1–4.

David, Hans T. "Background for Bethlehem (i.e., the Bach Festival): Moravian Music in Pennsylvania." *Magazine of Art*, 1938, pp. 222–35, and 254.

———. "Music of the early Moravians in America." *Musical America*, 1938, pp. 5 and 33.

Dickinson, C. E. "The First Church Organization in the Oldest Settlement in the Northwest Territory." *Ohio Archaeological and Historical Publication* 2 (1888): 289–308.

Ellis, Frank R. "Music in Cincinnati." *Proceedings of the MTNA* Series 8 (1913): 7–15.

Falconer, Joan O. "The Second Berlin Song School in America." *The Musical Quarterly* 59 (July 1973): 411–40.

Farrar, William M. "The Moravian Massacre." *Ohio Archaeological and Historical Society Publication* 3 (1984): 276–300.

Finney, Theodore M. "The Collegium Musicium at Lititz, Pennsylvania, during the Eighteenth Century." *Papers read by members of the American Musicological Society at the Annual Meeting held in Pittsburgh*, [Pa.] (1937): 45–55.

Giesler, John H. "Bicentennial of Gregor's Hymnal 1778." *Bulletin of the Moravian Music Foundation* 23 (Fall–Winter 1978): 15–16.

Greenfield, John. "David Zeisberger." *Ohio Archaeological and Historical Society Publication* 18 (1909): 189–98.

Hall, Harry H. "Early Sounds of Moravian Brass Music in America: A Cultural Note From Colonial Georgia." *Brass Quarterly* 7 (Spring 1964): 115–23.

———. "The Moravian Trombone Choir: A Conspectus of Its Early History and the Traditional Death Announcement." *Moravian Music Journal* 26 (Spring 1981): 5–8.

Haller, Mabel. "Moravian Influence on Higher Education in Colonial America." *Pennsylvania History* 25 (July 1958): 205–22.

Hamil, Frederick Coyne. "Fairfield on the River Thames." *Ohio Archaeological and Historical Society Publication* 68 (1939): 1–19.

———. "The Establishment of the Second Moravian Mission on the Pettquotting." *Ohio Archaeological and Historical Quarterly.* 58 (1949): 207–13.

Hamilton, J. T., trans. "Autobiography of Bernhard Adam Grube." *Transactions of the Moravian Historical Society* 11 (1936): 199–207.

Hamilton, Kenneth G. "Cultural Contributions of Moravian Missions among the Indians." *Pennsylvania History* 18 (January 1957): 1–15.

Hamm, Charles. "Patent Notes in Cincinnati." *Bulletin of the Historical and Philosophical Society of Ohio* 16 (October 1958): 293–310.

Hark, J. Max. "Meniolagomeka-Annals of a Moravian Indian Village 130 Years Ago." *Transactions of the Moravian Historical Society* 2 (1886): 129–44.

Hartzell, Lawrence W. "Musical Moravian Missionaries: Part I: Johann Christopher Pyrlaeus." *Moravian Music Journal* 28 (Winter 1984): 91–92.

———. "Musical Moravian Missionaries: Part II: Bernhard Adam Grube." *Moravian Music Journal* 30 (Spring 1985): 18–19.

———. "Musical Moravian Missionaries: Part III: Johann Jacob Schmick." *Moravian Music Journal* 30 (Fall 1985): 36–37.

———. "Trombones in Ohio." *Moravian Music Journal* 28 (Winter 1983): 72–74.

Hellyer, Roger. "The Harmoniemusik of the Moravian Communities in America." *Fontes Artis Musicae* 27 (April–June 1980): 95–108.

Hood, Marilyn G. "Schoenbrunn Easter Rites Mark 200 Years." *The Ohio Historical Society Echoes* 12 (April 1973): 1.

Huebener, Mary Augusta. "Bicentennial History of the Lititz Moravian Congregation." *Transactions of the Moravian Historical Society* 15 (1949): 199–271.

Hulbert, Archer Butler. "The Moravian Records." *Ohio Archaeological and Historical Society Publication* 18 (1909): 199–226.

Hulbert, Archer Butler, and William Nathaniel Schwarze. "David Zeisberger's History of North American Indians." *Ohio Archaeological and Historical Society Publication* 19 (1910): 1–173.

———. "The Moravian Records, Vol. II. The Diaries of Zeisberger Relating to the First Missions in the Ohio Basin." *Ohio Archaeological and Historical Society Publication* 21 (1912): 1–125.

Huntington, Pelatiah Webster. "Old-Time Music of Columbus, Ohio." *Old Northwest Genealogical Quarterly* 8 (1905): 136–40.

Ingram, Jeannine. "Music in American Moravian Communities: Transplanted Traditions in Indigenous Practices." *Communal Societies* 2 (Autumn 1982): 39–51.

———. "Repertory and Resources of the Salem Collegium Musicum, 1780–1790." *Fontes Artis Musicae* 26 (October–December 1979): 267–81.

Jordan, John W. "Biographical Sketch of Rev. Bernhard Adam Grube." *The Pennsylvania Magazine of History and Biography* 25 (1901): 14–19.

———. "Notes of Travel of William Henry, John Heckewelder, John Rothrock, and Christian Clewell, to Gnadenhutten on the Muskingum, in the Early Summer of 1797." *The Pennsylvania Magazine of History and Biography* 5 (1886): 125–57.

Kohnova, Marie J. "The Moravians and Their Missionaries, a Problem of Americanization." *Mississippi Valley Historical Review* 19 (1932): 348–61.

Kortz, Edwin W. "The Liturgical Development of the American Moravian Church." *Transactions of the Moravian Historical Society* 18 (1962): 267–382.

Kroeger, Karl. "A Singing Church: America's Legacy in Moravian Music." Moravian Music Foundation reprint of an article that originally appeared in *Journal of Church Music* (March 1976).

———. "Moravian Music in Nineteenth-Century American Tunebooks." *Bulletin of the Moravian Music Foundation* 18 (Spring–Summer 1973): 1–3.

———. "On the Early Performance of Moravian Chorales." *Bulletin of the Moravian Music Foundation* 24 (Fall–Winter 1979): 2–8.

———. "The Moravian Tradition in Song." *Bulletin of the Moravian Music Foundation* 20 (Fall–Winter 1975): 8–10.

Mahr, August C., ed. and trans. "A Canoe Journey from the Big Beaver to the Tuscarawas in 1773: A Travel Diary of John Heckewelder." *Ohio State Archaeological and Historical Quarterly* 61 (July 1952): 283–98.

———. "Diary of a Moravian Indian Mission Migration across Pennsylvania in 1772." *Ohio State Archaeological and Historical Quarterly* 62 (July 1953): 247–70.

Mathews, William Smythe Babcock. "Art Music in the Middle West: 1 The Large Cities. Cleveland, Milwaukee, Cincinnati, etc." *The Etude* 23 (1905): 95–97.

———. "Art Music in the Middle West: 2 In the Smaller Towns and Cities." *The Etude* 23 (1905): 139–41 and 170.

Maurer, Joseph A. "America's Heritage of Moravian Music: Contributions of Early Pennsylvania Composers." *The Historical Review of Berks County* 18 (April–June 1953): 66–70 and 87–91.

———. "The Moravian Trombone Choir, Bicentennial of Bethlehem's Historic Music Ensemble." *The Historical Review of Berks County* 20 (October–December 1954): 2–8.

McCorkle, Donald M. "Church Attics and Crackerboxes." *Bulletin of the Moravian Music Foundation* 5 (Spring–Summer 1961): 2.

———. "Early American Moravian Music." *Music Journal* 13 (November 1955): 11 and 45–47.

———. "Foundation Gets Library Grant." *Bulletin of the Moravian Music Foundation* 5 (Spring–Summer 1961): 1 and 6.

———. "Prelude to a History of American Moravian Organs." *American Guild of Organists Quarterly* 3 (October 1958): 142–48.

Mueller, Paul E., trans. "David Zeisberger's Official Diary, Fairfield, 1791–1795." *Transactions of the Moravian Historical Society* 19 (1963): Entire issue.

Nitzschke, F. R. "Obituary." *The Moravian*, 28 February 1944.

Randall, E. O. "Blennerhassett." *Ohio Archaeological and Historical Society Publication* 1 (1887): 127–63.

———. "David Zeisberger Centennial." *Ohio Archaeological and Historical Society Publication* 18 (1909): 157–81.

———. "Heckewelder's Narrative." *Ohio Archaeological and Historical Society Publication* 18 (1909): 258–61.

Rau, Albert G. "John Frederick Peter." *The Musical Quarterly* 23 (1937): 306–13.

Rau, Robert. "Sketch of the History of the Moravian Congregation at Gnadenhutten on the Mahoning." *Transactions of the Moravian Historical Society* 2 (1886): 399–414.

Reichel, W. C. "Wyalusing and the Moravian Mission at Friedenshuetten." *Transactions of the Moravian Historical Society* 1 (1871): 179–224.

Rice, William. "The Rev. John Heckewelder." *Ohio Archaeological and Historical Society Publication* 7 (1898): 314–48.

Rosenberry, M. Claude. "The Pennsylvania German in Music. The Moravians." *Pennsylvania German Society* 61 (1930): 39–43.

Schwarze, William N. "Characteristics and Achievements of David Zeisberger." *Ohio Archaeological and Historical Society Publication* 18 (1909): 182–88.

Steelman, Robert. "The First Trombone Choir of Lititz." *Moravian Music Journal* 27 (Spring 1982): 4–6.

Stevens, Harry R. "Adventures in Refinement: Early Concert Life in Cincinnati, 1810–1826." *Bulletin of the Historical and Philosophical Society of Ohio* 5 (September 1947): 8–22.

———. "Folk Music in the Midwestern Frontier, 1788–1825." *Ohio State Archaeological and Historical Quarterly* 57 (April 1948): 126–46.

———. "The Haydn Society of Cincinnati, 1819–1824." *Ohio State Archaeological and Historical Quarterly* 52 (1943): 95–119.

———. "New Foundations: Cincinnati Concert Life." *Bulletin of the Historical and Philosophical Society of Ohio* 10 (January 1952): 26–38.

Stocker, Harry Emilius, trans. "The Biography of Brother Abraham Luckenbach." *Transactions of the Moravian Historical Society* 10 (1917): 361–408.

———. "A History of the Moravian Mission among the Indians on the White River in Indiana." *Transactions of the Moravian Historical Society* 10 (1917): 231–358.

Stolba, K. Marie. "Evidence for Quartets by John Antes, American-Born Moravian Composer." *Journal of the American Musicological Society* 33 (Fall 1980): 565–74.

Strauss, Barbara. "The Concert Life of the Collegium Musicum, Nazareth 1796–1845." *Bulletin of the Moravian Music Foundation* 21 (Spring–Summer 1976): 2–7.

Wallace, Paul A. W. "The John Heckewelder Papers." *Pennsylvania History* 27 (July 1960): 249–62.

Wilkin, Robert M. "Joseph E. Weinland, Rebuilder of Schoenbrunn." *Ohio Archaeological and Historical Society Publication* 62 (1933): 116–23.

Williams, Henry L. "The Development of the Moravian Hymnal." *Transactions of the Moravian Historical Society* 18 (1962): 239–66.

Zorb, Elizabeth. "Reflections on Moravian Pietism." *Pennsylvania History* 25 (April 1958): 115–21.

GENERAL BACKGROUND TEXTS

Arnold, Samuel Greene. *History of the State of Rhode Island and Providence Plantations.* New York: D. Appleton & Co., 1874. 2 vols. For Moravian work only volume 2 is helpful.

Battershell, C. F. *The Demuth Family and the Moravian Church.* Privately printed, 1938.

Blankenberg, Walter. "Die Musik der Brüdergemeine in Europa." In *Unitas Fratrum*, edited by van Buijtenen et al. Utrecht: Rijksarclief, 1975.

Chase, Gilbert. *America's Music*. 2d ed. New York: McGraw-Hill, 1966.

Church Music and Musical Life in Pennsylvania History. Vol. 2, "The Moravian Contribution to Pennsylvania Music." Prepared by the Committee on Historical Research of the Colonial Dames of America. Philadelphia: 1926–1947. Reprint. AMS, 1972.

Drummond, Robert R. *Early German Music in Philadelphia*. New York: 1910. Reprint. New York: Da Capo Press, 1970.

Ellinwood, Leonard. *The History of American Church Music*. Rev. ed. New York: Morehouse-Gorham Co., 1953. Reprint. New York: Da Capo Press, 1970.

Gerson, Robert A. *Music in Philadelphia*. Philadelphia: Theodore Presser Co., 1940.

Grout, Donald J. *A History of Western Music*. New York: W. W. Norton & Co., 1960.

Lang, Paul Henry, ed. *One Hundred Years of Music in America*. New York: G. Schirmer, 1961.

The New Grove Dictionary of Music and Musicians. Edited by Stanley Sadie. 20 vols. London: MacMillan, 1980.

Stevenson, Robert. *Protestant Church Music in America*. New York: W. W. Norton & Co., 1966.

GENERAL MORAVIAN HISTORY TEXTS

Blankenburg, Walter. "The Music of the Bohemian Brethren." Translated by Hans Heinsheimer. In *Protestant Church Music, A History* by Friedrich Blume. New York: W. W. Norton & Co., 1974.

Bricker, Alice Haverstick. "An Examination of the Records of the Aufseher Collegium of the Community at Lititz, Pennsylvania, from 1802 to 1844." Bachelor's thesis, Cornell University, 1898.

A Century and Three-Quarters of Life and Service. Linden Hall Seminary. Lititz, Pennsylvania, 1746–1921. Lititz, Pa., n.d.

Clewell, John Henry. *Historical Outline of the Moravian Seminary and College for Women from 1742 to the Present*. Bethlehem, Pa.: Moravian Publications Office, 1911.

de Schweinitz, Edmund. *The History of the Church Known as The Unitas Fratrum of the Unity of the Brethren*. Bethlehem, Pa.: Moravian Publications Office, 1885.

―――. *Some of the Fathers of the American Moravian Church*. Bethlehem, Pa., 1881.

―――. *The Moravian Manual*. Philadelphia: Lindsey & Blakiston, 1859.

Erbe, Helmuth. *Bethlehem, Pennsylvania: Eine Herrnhuter-Kolonie des 18. Jahrhunderts*. Herrnhut, Germany: Gustav Winter, 1929.

Fliegel, Rev. Carl John, comp. *Index to the Records of the Moravian Mission among the Indians of North America.* New Haven, Conn.: Research Publications, Inc. 1970.

Fries, Adelaide L. *Funeral Chorales of the Unitas Fratrum or Moravian Church.* Winston-Salem, N.C.: 1905.

———. *The Moravians in Georgia, 1735–1740.* Raleigh, N.C.: 1905.

Gollin, Gillian Lindt. *Moravians in Two Worlds.* New York & London: Columbia University Press, 1967.

Hacker, H. H. *Nazareth Hall.* Bethlehem, Pa.: 1910.

Haller, Mable. "Early Moravian Education in Pennsylvania." Ph.D. diss., University of Pennsylvania, 1953.

Hamilton, John Taylor. *A History of the Missions of the Moravian Church, during the Eighteenth and Nineteenth Centuries.* Bethlehem, Pa.: Times Publishing Co., 1901.

Hamilton, John Taylor, and Kenneth G. Hamilton. *History of the Moravian Church: The Renewed Unitas Fratrum 1722–1957.* Bethlehem, Pa. and Winston-Salem, N.C.: Interprovincial Board of Christian Education Moravian Church in America, 1967.

Hamilton, Kenneth Gardiner. *John Ettwein and the Moravian Church during the Revolutionary Period.* Bethlehem, Pa.: Times Publishing Co., 1940.

———, ed. and trans. *The Bethlehem Diary,* vol. I, 1742–1744. Bethlehem, Pa.: Archives of the Moravian Church, 1971.

Heckewelder, John. *History, Manners, and Customs of the Indian Nations.* Philadelphia: Historical Society of Pennsylvania, 1876.

———. *Narrative of the Mission of the United Brethren among the Delaware and Mohegan Indians.* Philadelphia: McCarty & Davis, 1820.

Henry, James. *Sketches of Moravian Life and Character.* Philadelphia: J. B. Lippincott, 1859.

Hutton, Joseph E. *A History of the Moravian Missions.* London: Moravian Publications Office, 1923.

Levering, Joseph Mortimer. *A History of Bethlehem, Pennsylvania.* Bethlehem, Pa.: Times Publishing Co., 1903.

Loskiel, George. *History of the Mission of the United Brethren among the Indians in North America.* Translated by I. C. LaTrobe. London: The Brethren's Society for the Furtherance of the Gospel, 1794.

Neisser, Georg. *A History of the Beginnings of the Moravian Work in America.* Translated by William N. Schwarze and Samuel H. Gapp. Bethlehem, Pa.: Archives of the Moravian Church, 1955.

Records of the Moravians in North Carolina. 11 vols. Raleigh, N.C.: State Department of Archives, 1922–1969.

Reichel, Levin T. *A History of Nazareth Hall from 1755–1855.* Philadelphia: 1855.

Reichel, William C. and Bigler, William H. *A History of the Moravian Seminary for Young Ladies at Bethlehem, Pennsylvania.* Bethlehem, Pa.: 1901.

Ritter, Abraham. *History of the Moravian Church in Philadelphia.* Philadelphia: 1857.

Schwarze, Edmund. *History of the Moravian Missions among Southern Indian Tribes.* Bethlehem, Pa.: Times Publishing Co., 1923.

Schwarze, William N. *History of the Moravian College and Theological Seminary, Founded at Nazareth, Pennsylvania.* Bethlehem, Pa.: Times Publishing Co., 1909.

Stocker, Harry Emilius. *A History of the Moravian Missions among the Indians on the White River in Indiana.* Bethlehem, Pa.: Times Publishing Co., 1917.

Towlson, Clifford W. *Moravian and Methodist: Relationships and Influences in the Eighteenth Century.* London: 1957.

Two Centuries of Nazareth, 1740–1940. Nazareth, Pa.: Nazareth, Pennsylvania Bi-Centennial, 1940.

Wallace, Paul A., ed. *Thirty Thousand Miles with John Heckewelder.* Pittsburgh, Pa.: University of Pittsburgh Press, 1958.

Weinlick, John R. *Count Zinzendorf.* New York-Nashville: Abingdon Press, 1956.

MORAVIAN MUSIC TEXTS

Adams, Charles B. *Our Moravian Hymn Heritage.* Bethlehem, Pa.: Department of Publications, Moravian Church in America, 1984.

Armstrong, William H. *Organs for America: The Life and Work of David Tannenberg.* Philadelphia: University of Pennsylvania Press, 1967.

Asti, Martha Secrest. "The Moravian Music of Christian Gregor (1723–1801): His Anthems, Arias, Duets, and Chorales." Ph.D. diss., University of Miami, 1982.

Bahr, Marian Hughes. "A Study of the Published Editions of Early American Moravian Sacred Arias for Soprano." Master's thesis, Kent State University, 1969.

Ballinger, Larry Desmond. "The Music of The Moravians." Master's thesis, Fresno State College, 1967.

Cumnock, Frances, ed. *Catalog of the Salem Congregation Collection.* Chapel Hill, N.C.: University of North Carolina Press, 1980.

David, Hans T. "Musical Life in the Pennsylvania Settlements of the Unitas Fratrum." *Moravian Music Foundation Publication, No. 6.* Winston-Salem, N.C.: Moravian Music Foundation, 1959. Reprinted from *Transactions of the Moravian Historical Society,* 1942.

———. *Ten Sacred Songs.* New York: C. F. Peters, 1954.

Falconer, John Ormsby. "Bishop Johannes Herbst (1735–1812), an American-Moravian Musician, Collector and Composer." Ph.D. diss., Columbia University, 1969.

Gregor, Christian. *Choral-Buch*. Leipzig: 1784. Reprint ed. James Boeringer. Winston-Salem, N.C.: Moravian Music Foundation Press, 1984.

Gombosi, Marilyn. *A Day of Solemn Thanksgiving*. Chapel Hill, N.C.: University of North Carolina Press, 1977.

————, ed. *Catalog of the Johannes Herbst Collection*. Chapel Hill, N.C.: University of North Carolina Press, 1970.

Grider, Rufus A. "Historical Notes on Music in Bethlehem, Pennyslvania [from 1741 to 1871]." *Moravian Music Foundation Publication, No. 4*. Winston-Salem, N.C.: Moravian Music Foundation, 1957. Reprint of the original edition of 1873.

Giesler, John H. "Twelve Moravian Hymns and Chorales." *Moravian Music Foundation Publication, No. 8*. Winston-Salem, N.C.: Moravian Music Foundation, Inc., 1978.

Hahn, Katherine Ann. "The Wind Ensemble Music of David Moritz Michael." Master's thesis, University of Missouri–Columbia, 1979.

Hall, Harry Hobart. "The Moravian Wind Ensemble: Distinctive Chapter in America's Music." Ph.D. diss., George Peabody College, 1967.

Hertel, Marilyn. "The Development of the Moravian Sacred Music as Typified in the Sunday Musical Services of the Early American Moravian Congregations." Master's thesis, Bob Jones University, 1968.

Hoople, Donald Graham. "Moravian Music Education and the American Moravian Music Tradition." Ed.D. diss., Columbia University Teachers College, 1976.

Hymnal and Liturgies of the Moravian Church (Unitas Fratrum). Bethlehem, Pa.: Provincial Synod, 1920.

Hymnal and Liturgies of the Moravian Church. Chicago: Rayner Lithographing Co., 1969.

Johansen, John. "Moravian Hymnody." *Moravian Music Foundation Publication, No. 9*. Winston-Salem, N.C.: Moravian Music Foundation, 1980. Reprint from vol. 30 of *The Hymn*.

Keehn, David P. "The Trombone Choir of the Moravian Church in North America." Master's thesis, West Chester State College, 1978

McCorkle, Donald M. "The Collegium Musicum Salem: Its Music, Musicians, and Importance." *Moravian Music Foundation Publication, no. 3*. Winston-Salem, N.C.: Moravian Music Foundation, 1956. Reprint of *The North Carolina Historical Review*, October 1956.

————. "John Antes, 'American Dilettante.'" *Moravian Music Foundation Publication, no. 2*. Winston-Salem, N.C.: Moravian Music Foundation, 1956. Reprint from *The Musical Quarterly*, October 1956.

————. "The Moravian Contribution to American Music." *Moravian Music*

Foundation Publication, no. 1. (Winston-Salem, N.C.: Moravian Music Foundation, 1956. Reprinted from Music Library Association, September 1956.

———. "Moravian Music in Salem: A German-American Heritage." Ph.D. diss., Indiana University, 1958.

Mack, Elmer L. *The Bach Choir of Bethlehem, 1898–1973.* Bethlehem, Pa.: Privately printed, 1973.

Muller, J. T. "Bohemian Brethren's Hymnody." In *A Dictionary of Hymnology,* edited by John Julian. London, 1908.

Nicholas, Louis. *Thor Johnson: American Conductor.* Wisconsin: Music Festival Committee of the Peninsula Arts Association, 1982.

Poole, Franklin Parker. "The Moravian Music Heritage: Johann Christian Geisler's Music in America." Ph.D. diss., George Peabody College for Teachers, 1971.

Pruett, James Worrell. "Francis Florentine Hagen: American Moravian Musician." Master's thesis, University of North Carolina, 1957.

Rau, Albert G., and Hans T. David. comps. *A Catalogue of Music by American Moravians, 1742–1842.* Bethlehem, Pa.: Moravian Seminary and College for Women, 1938. Reprint. New York: AMS Press Inc., 1970.

Reed, Tracy L. "Johann Christian Bechler, Moravian Minister and Composer: The American Years, 1806–1836." Master's thesis, Indiana University of Pennsylvania, 1973.

Rierson, Jr., Charles Frederick. "The Collegium Musicum Salem: The Development of a Catalogue of Its Library and the Editing of Selected Works." Ed.D. diss., University of Georgia, 1973.

Roberts, Dale Alexander. "The Sacred Vocal Music of David Moritz Michael: An American Moravian Composer." D.M.A. diss., University of Kentucky, 1978.

Runner, David Clark. "Music in the Moravian Community of Lititz." D.M.A. diss., Eastman School of Music, 1976.

Schnell, William Emmett. "The Choral Music of Johann Friedrich Peter, 1746–1813." D.M.A. diss., University of Illinois, 1973.

Scott, Ruth H. "Music among the Moravians, Bethlehem, Pa., 1741–1876." Master's thesis, Eastman School of Music, 1938.

Steelman, Robert, ed. *Catalog of the Lititz Congregation Collection.* Chapel Hill, N.C.: University of North Carolina Press, 1981.

Steelman, Robert. *The Tietze Music Collection.* Bethlehem, Pa.: Moravian Archives. Unpub. shelf list prepared 1978–79.

Strauss, Barbara Jo. "A Register of Music Performed in Concert, Nazareth, Pennsylvania from 1796 to 1845: An Annotated Edition of an American Moravian Document." Master's thesis, University of Arizona. 1976.

Wolle, Peter. *Hymn Tunes, Used in the Church of the United Brethren, Arranged for Four Voices and the Organ or Piano-forte.* Boston: Shepley and Wright, 1836.

Zeisberger, David. *A Collection of Hymns for the Use of the Christian Indians of the Missions of the United Brethren in North America*. Philadelphia: Henry Sweitzer, 1803.

OHIO INFORMATION TEXTS

Blickensderfer, Jacob. *History of the Blickensderfer Family in America*. Privately printed, n.d.

Bliss, Eugene F., trans. *Diary of David Zeisberger*. 2 vols. Cincinnati, Ohio: Robert Clarke & Co., 1885. (Covers the period 1781–98.)

Brunner, Edmund de Schweinitz. *Survey of Fry's Valley, Ohio*. Easton, Pa.: Moravian Country Church Commission, Pamphlet no. 13 [1914].

Combination Atlas Map of Tuscarawas County, Ohio. Philadelphia: L. H. Everts & Co., 1875.

de Schweinitz, Edmund. *The Life and Times of David Zeisberger*. Philadelphia, Pa.: J. B. Lippincott & Co., 1870. Reprint. New York: Arno Press, 1971.

Finley, James Bradley. *Autobiography of Rev. James B. Finley; or, Pioneer Life in the West*. Ed. W. P. Strickland. Cincinnati, Ohio: Printed at the Methodist Book Concern, for the author, 1856.

Frank, Leonie C. *Musical Life in Early Cincinnati and the Origin of the May Festival*. Cincinnati, Ohio: Privately printed by the Rufer Press, 1932.

Freedman, Frederick, comp. *Music in Ohio. (A Preliminary Bibliography)*. Cleveland, Ohio: An unpaged set of mimeographed sheets. n.d.

Gray, Leslie R., ed. *From Fairfield to Schönbrunn, 1798*. London, Ont., Canada: By the Author. n.d.

Grossman, F. Karl. *A History of Music in Cleveland*. Cleveland, Ohio: Case Western Reserve University, 1972.

Hagloch, Henry L. *The History of Tuscarawas County*. Dover, Ohio: Dover Historical Society, 1956.

Harmount, S., et al. *Reminiscences of Dover*. Canal Dover, Ohio: Iron Valley Reporter, 1849.

The History of Tuscarawas County, Ohio. Chicago: Warner, Beers & Co., 1884.

Howe, Henry. *Historical Collections in Ohio*. 3 vols. Columbus, Ohio: Henry Howe, 1889.

Huebner, Francis Christian. *The Moravian Missions in Ohio*. Washington, D.C.: Simms & Lewis, 1898.

Kaiser, D. H. *The Moravians on the Cuyahoga*. Cleveland, Ohio: Mount and Co., 1894.

Lentz, Andrea D., ed. *A Guide to Manuscripts at the Ohio Historical Society*. Columbus, Ohio: The Ohio Historical Society, 1972.

Lewis, John, Jr. *An Historical Study of the Origin and Development of the Cincinnati Conservatory of Music*. Ed.D. diss., University of Cincinnati, 1943.

Lohrman, H. P., and Ralph H. Romig. *Valley of the Tuscarawas*. Dover, Ohio: Ohio Hills Publishers, 1975.

Mitchener, L. H., ed. *Ohio Annals . . . Historic Events in the Tuscarawas and Muskingum Valleys. . . .* Dayton, Ohio: Thomas W. Odell, [ca. 1875].

Oerter, Rev. Maurice Frederick. *A Brief Historical Sketch of the Moravian Congregation at Sharon. Tuscarawas, Ohio*. Canal Dover, Ohio: Seibert Printing Co., n.d.

———. *The Story of the Sharon Moravian Church*. Tuscarawas, Ohio: Privately printed, n.d.

Porter, III, Daniel R. *Schoenbrunn Story: Excerpts from the Diary of The Reverend David Zeisberger 1772–1777 at Schoenbrunn in the Ohio Country*. Trans. August C. Mahr. Columbus, Ohio: Ohio Historical Society, 1972.

Portrait and Biographical Record of Tuscarawas County, Ohio. Chicago: C. O. Owen & Co., 1895.

Randall, Emilius O., and Daniel J. Ryan. *History of Ohio*. 2 vols. New York: Century History Company, 1912.

Rhodes, Edwin S. *The First Centennial History and Atlas of Tuscarawas County, Ohio*. New Philadelphia, Ohio: Edwin S. Rhodes, 1908.

Riemenschneider, Selma Marting, and Elinore Barber. *50 Years of Bach in Berea: A History of the Baldwin-Wallace College Bach Festival*. Berea, Ohio: MS., n.d.

Robertson, R. "Musical History of Cincinnati." Master's thesis, University of Cincinnati, 1941.

The Sixth Early American Moravian Music Festival. Thor Johnson, Music Director. Festival Program. Tuscarawas County, Ohio: 22–25 June 1961.

A Sketch of the Moravians in Ohio. Dover, Ohio: Provincial Synod, 1951.

Smucker, Isaac. *History of Our Moravian Missions in Ohio and Memorial Sketches of Our Missionaries*. Pamphlet in Moravian Archives, Bethlehem, Pa.

Speary, Nellie Best. *Sketches of Music and Life in Marietta, Ohio*. Marietta, Ohio: MacDonald Printing Co., 1939.

Thwaites, R. G., and L. P. Kellog. *The Revolution on the Upper Ohio, 1775–1777*. (1908). Reprint. Port Washington, New York: Kennikat Press, 1970.

Virtue, Ross M. *A History of Gnadenhutten 1772–1976*. Gnadenhutten, Ohio: Ross M. Virtue, 1976.

Weinland, Joseph. *The Romantic Story of Schoenbrunn*. Tuscarawas County, Ohio: Privately printed, n.d.

INDEX